From Ch

Jacqueline Jenkins

From Church To Church…:
Copyright © 2009 by Jacqueline Jenkins

Library of Congress Cataloging-in Publication Data
Jenkins, Jacqueline
From Church To Church…: a novel/Jacqueline Jenkins
p. cm.
Includes index
ISBN:
ISBN
LCCN:

First Asta Publications, LLC trade paperback edition _____
2009.

1. Religion-Fiction. 2. Self-realization-Fiction. 3. Christian-Fiction.
I. Title

Unless otherwise indicated, all scripture quotations are taken from the *New King James Version* ®. Copyright © 1982 by Thomas Nelson, Inc. Used by permission. All rights reserved. Scripture quotations marked AMP are taken from *THE AMPLIFIED BIBLE*, Copyright ©1954, 1958, 1962,1964,1965,1987 by The Lockman Foundation. All rights reserved. Used by permission. (www.Lockman.org)

All songs were written and produced by Jacqueline Jenkins, *I Stand Here Worshipping You* © 2009 and *Out Of Shiloh Comes Bits of Praise* © 1997.

All rights reserved. No part of this publication may be reproduced, stored in a retrieval system, or transmitted in any form or by any means without the prior permission of the publisher or author, except for brief quotations in reviews or articles.

Printed in the United States of America.

DEDICATION

I dedicate this book to my mother-in-law, Julia Jenkins, and my last two surviving aunts: Inez Marshall and Ruby Lee Griffin. I love you all. May God continue to shine upon you.

A huge THANKS to my family and friends who worked so diligently with me on the book and upcoming CD project. Words cannot express my gratitude. Family, you really came through for me. May God continue to bless you all!

Yvonne Marshall and Danielle McCurry, thanks again for your eyes. To my main reader and sister, Janet Willis, thanks for all the time you spent reading and rereading the manuscript. I love you and appreciate you so much!

Father God, I give You all the glory, honor, and praise. Thank You for the dream! Amen.

INTRODUCTION

While nestled up in my warm, cozy bed, I had an amazing dream. I dreamt of a young woman searching for the "perfect" church. In the dream, she began strategizing how she would accomplish this task. In the multiple, picturesque scenes depicted, I observed the various churches visited, ranging from storefronts to mega-churches.

Upon awakening, I queried God as to what it all meant. You see, I was confident there was a message, or some spiritual interpretation concealed in it, and there was. Secreted in its multiple layers was a definite interpretation, which led to the writing of this book.

The churches that the young woman, Mayah Johnson, the main character of this book, visits are the seven churches in the Book of Revelation; however, in today's vernacular. As you read each chapter, please note the traits of that specific church and determine if you can locate it in the Book of Revelation, chapters two and three.

Little did I know as I began penning this book that God would cause me to literally take this journey along with Mayah and Kyle in my own personal church life.

CHAPTER 1

"Nan! Nan!" Mayah Johnson screamed. Catching her breath, she abruptly awakened from a hellish nightmare. Mayah was mortified and attempted to compose herself. She took deep breaths, inhaling and exhaling in an attempt to retard her heart rate.

"Man, I feel like my heart is about to leap out of my chest."

She squinted to see the time on the clock, and realized she'd only been asleep for approximately an hour. After calming down, Mayah reclined in bed. She tossed and turned the remainder of the night, as she couldn't get that dream out of her head.

As the sun beamed through her bedroom window the next morning, she turned over in bed. What kind of dream was that? *Nan, what are you trying to tell me? I know you're trying to convey something, but I'm missing it. I can't seem to figure it out.*

Mayah lumbered out of bed and cleaned her three-bedroom luxury apartment. After completing that two-hour chore, she ran a warm tub of water and gently slithered into the bubble-filled bathtub. While relaxing, she refocused on the dream again. Before she knew it, she realized she'd been in the tub for almost one hour. As she added more hot water to the tub, she had an epiphany.

"Oh my!" she gasped. "I think I got it! I think I understand the meaning of the dream."

Mayah leapt out of the tub, threw on her bathrobe, and with water dripping all over the wood flooring, ran to telephone Kyle, her only sibling.

"Hello," he said.

"Hi, Kyle. Do you have a few minutes? I had a dream last night and Nan was in it. I need to tell you what I believe the dream meant."

"Yeah, I have a few minutes. Tell me the dream."

"Okay, in the dream Nan was sitting in a rocking chair, just rocking away. However, as I focused on her face and the tears—oh, the tears—they were running down her face. As I looked closer, I could tell she'd been crying for such a prolonged time that her blouse was stained from the salty tears dripping off her chin.

"You would've had to see it to believe it. I mean, Nan's blouse was soaking wet. I looked into her eyes, and there was such sadness, a sadness I'd never seen before. I asked her what was wrong, but she only stared at me.

"Kyle, in all the years that Nan visited us, played with us, babysat, and took us to church, I never saw such an agonizing expression like what she displayed in the dream. When I awakened this morning, I pondered on the dream and its possible meaning. While I was in the bathtub, the interpretation unfolded right before my eyes. Remember when we were kids and Mama didn't want to take us to church and Nan took us?"

"Yes, I do."

"After Nan died," she continued, hardly missing a beat. "You and I stopped going because Mama wouldn't go with us. We'd ask why she wouldn't take us to church, and her response was, 'My mother had me in church every Sunday for years and I hated it; therefore, I'm not going, nor am I going to take you guys.'

"For most of our childhood, Nan had us in church with her and Pops. Even when Pops died, Nan still took us to church the next three years before she died. However, when she passed we just stopped going. Everything else became more important than going to church. Although Mama wouldn't take us, as we matured we began to use our Sundays as rest days and even socializing days.

"Kyle, I believe Nan was crying in my dream because we've gotten away from the Christian foundation she had laid for us. I believe what her appearance meant in the dream was this," Mayah paused a moment, taking a deep breath to bolster her confidence. "It's time—it's time for me to get back in church. I think she was

From Church to Church

distraught by the fact that I had stopped going, and possibly you too. I know we were still young when Nan died, but we're older now, and we still don't go. We don't even have to rely on anyone taking us. All we have to do is take ourselves." As usual whenever she had these one-way conversations with her brother, he remained quiet to let her get everything out that was on her mind.

"I have a huge favor to ask of you," she said. "I'll understand if you say no. I need to find a church to go to. Will you go with me?"

"Oh, Mayah…" Kyle inhaled as if attempting to reach a decision. "Hmm. Yeah, I'll go with you so *you* can find a church. But don't think because I'm going on this mission with you that I want to be back in church, okay?"

"Alright, let me figure out how I want to accomplish this and I'll call you back."

"That's fine. Just don't call me back today with this. I think I've heard enough for the day," he said, chuckling.

"Alright, I'll call you tomorrow."

Mayah hung up the telephone and gently shut her eyes as she tried to envision how she would go about finding a church. It's been quite some time since attending a church service. She thought about going online to *Google* it. However, she picked up the telephone book, turned to the yellow pages, and searched under the heading "churches." She jotted down the names of seven nearby churches.

She decided they'd go to these churches and see if she liked one of them. If she did, then she'd start going to it. But she might have a problem with Kyle when she told him how she wanted to accomplish this. She'd sleep on it tonight and give him a call tomorrow so as not to overwhelm him today.

The following day the phone rang just as Mayah put on her favorite, old jeans. She quickly answered it.

"Hello."

"Hi, Mayah." The voice of Tia, her best friend, broke the silence in her apartment. "Just want you to know that we had a great time last night. However, we truly missed you. What did you do last night?"

"Well, I simply went to bed and had a rather unusual dream. My grandmother was in it, and she was rocking in a rocking chair, crying. But that's not why you called me. What's up?"

"I felt awful last night because you didn't come to the club with us. You're my closest friend and I really wanted you to be there."

"Don't worry about it. I'm okay. I think I was supposed to be at home dreaming my dream."

"Well, your twenty-first birthday is coming up soon and we're going to celebrate, right?"

"I'm not sure about that." Mayah paused for a moment. "I'm on a mission right now trying to find a church."

"A *what*?" Tia shouted.

"A church. I need to get back in church. So I'm not sure what I'll be doing on my birthday. Let's just put all birthday plans on hold. I need to focus on this church thing for now."

"Girl, have you bumped your head? Put your birthday plans on hold? Last night you were more than a little disappointed that you couldn't go with us. What's up with all of this church stuff?"

"Nothing. I just feel a need to reprioritize my life right now. I think my grandmother's appearance in my dream last night really jarred me into thinking about God and church again."

"Alright, girl. I don't understand what's happening in your life, but give me a call later."

"Okay. I'll holler at you later. Bye."

Mayah quickly hung up the phone and plopped down onto the sofa. All her friends had turned twenty-one, and she was the last one to have a birthday. She thought they would've waited a few weeks so Tia and she could've celebrated their twenty-first birthdays' together, but that's okay. She'd be twenty-one soon and it would be her turn. She could hardly wait. Her new birthday outfit hung in the closet, just waiting for her to slide into it at the appropriate time.

Then she thought about the way Tia suddenly ended their call just now and wondered if her unexpected announcement about church had put her off. She couldn't stand to lose her best friend, yet she could no longer neglect the spiritual heritage Nan had passed down to her either. *Oh God, I pray that I won't lose Tia as a friend while I'm searching for a church. I hope she understands what I need to do at this juncture in my life. I can party anytime.* Although Mayah hadn't attended church for quite some time, she yet held on to a tradition that Nan instilled in her as a child. She still managed to pray.

* * * *

That following morning, Mayah called Kyle.
"Hello."
"Hi, Kyle. Well, I have a plan."
"Girl, you sound a little down. What's up?"
"I feel somewhat dejected. Tia called and wanted me to go out with her and some of the girls as they celebrate her twenty-first birthday last night. I'm a little down because I won't be twenty-one for several weeks. I personally felt they could've waited so we could've celebrated our birthdays together. But that's okay. I'll be alright."
"Girl, don't be upset. Listen to your brother. You ain't missing a thing."
"Yeah, right. You're twenty-five years old and you've been legal for four years. You don't understand how I feel."
"Listen, when your birthday comes, I'll take you out, and we'll celebrate it big time. Your celebration will put hers to shame," he laughed. "Now tell me your plan. I hope I'm not going to be sorry for agreeing to do this thing with you."
"Well, okay, just listen. Don't say a word until after I've finished telling you my entire plan. Okay?"
"Alright, sis."

"This is what I've done. I searched the phonebook and found seven churches that we—"

"Seven churches!"

"Hold on. I asked you to wait until I finished telling you my entire plan."

"Alright, go ahead. But I really don't like the sound of this."

"Like I was saying, I found seven churches in the phonebook. What I'd like to do is visit all of them, and then make a decision about which one I think is viable for me. There's so much happening in churches these days; I just want to identify the perfect church for me."

"Mayah, so—"

"That's not all of it. I want to visit each church for at least two weeks so I can see what it's really like. Sometimes people can be phony when they know you're just visiting them. I want to spend some quality time in each church. You'd only have to go with me on Sundays, but I'd go to their Bible class and maybe a church meeting to get a feel for the church. Now tell me what you think?"

"Whew! You're asking me to take nearly *four months* out of my life to go to some churches with you? I wash my car and do laundry on Sundays. You want me to give up approximately fourteen Sundays out of my life so you can find a church that you think is perfect for you? Girl, you got to be playing. This has *got* to be a joke."

"No, I'm serious. If you don't want to go with me, then I guess I'll have to go all alone. That's fine. I can go by myself. I do many things by myself already, but I thought you'd want to be a part of this. I'm just trying to do the right thing for my life and also what I believe Nan would want me to do."

After a lengthy pause, Kyle let out a long, loud sigh. "Whew. Girl, I don't know how you do it. You always have a knack of getting your way or making me feel guilty if I don't go along with something you want to do."

"Kyle, you're all that I have. I don't have anyone else but you. Who else would commit to doing this with me?"

"Okay, I'll go with you, but I'm only going to church on Sundays. Oh, and when football season begins, we just might have to renegotiate this agreement. Additionally," he said as he laughed, "you're going to owe me *big* time."

"Thanks, brother. I knew I could count on you. I'll figure out the order in which we'll visit these churches. Maybe we'll go to the ones that are the closest first. We'll talk. I'll call you each week to remind you of our agreement." She laughed. "I'm not trying to stop you from going out or anything like that. Think about it; how many dates do you have on Sunday mornings? Also, you'll only have to be in church for about two to three hours max per Sunday, and you can have the remainder of your day for fun."

"Yeah, yeah, yeah. Call me on Friday to tell me which church and what time I need to be ready. Don't call me about it before then. My understanding is that we'll be at that church for two weeks. Girl, you had better start praying for me *now*, and pray that I don't get bored with those preachers. And by the way, for your information, I do date on Sundays; sometimes at breakfast, lunch, and dinner time," he stated adamantly.

Mayah laughed to herself. "Okay Kyle. I won't call you until Friday afternoon. Guess what? We can spend some quality time talking on our ride to and from church on Sundays. Thanks, Kyle."

"Yeah, right. I'll talk to you later. I don't know *what* I've gotten myself into." Kyle hung up the phone.

* * * *

In keeping with their agreement, Mayah telephoned Kyle the following Friday.

"What's up?" he asked.

"Hey. Just calling to let you know that the first church we'll be attending is The Church of Love. It's on Trinity Avenue. Church starts at ten o'clock."

"Alright. Girl, I thought you would've changed your mind," he sighed. "What time do you want me to be ready?"

"You're not driving?" Mayah asked, puzzled.

Kyle laughed heartily. "No. This is your adventure; therefore, you can finance the trips."

"You're right. I'll be at your house at nine-thirty. Make sure you're ready. See you then."

She hung up the phone as a tingle crawled up her spine. She wasn't sure if she was excited or terrified, but she'd soon find out.

CHAPTER 2

The sound of the alarm clock pierced Mayah's eardrums. She quickly reached over and shut it off. After stretching and giving herself a moment to shake off her sleepiness, she pulled herself out of bed and stumbled into the shower. As the warm water pattered on her face and stimulated life back into her, she mumbled to herself.

"Nan, you have to know that I love you. No way would I be doing this had you not shown up in my dream. Oh, how I miss you. I even miss you taking Kyle and me to church. I hope I can find a church that doesn't have a lot of *stuff* going on. I just want to find that perfect church. I've seen and heard a lot of negative things on the news and from people on my job about churches today, but, I'm up and my quest begins today."

Mayah rummaged through her closet and finally located something appropriate to wear to church. She put on a royal blue, silk dress, and adorned it with a necklace. This wasn't just some ordinary string of beads; this was Nan's old, pearl necklace. After getting completely dressed, she grabbed her cosmetic robe and carefully draped it over her shoulders. She had to be extra careful so as not to stain her delicate dress. After her makeup was intact, she removed the rollers from her lengthy, dark brown hair and her hair fell into place as it caressed her shoulders. Yes, this was a good hair day for Mayah.

She repeatedly looked at herself in the mirror. "Okay, I think I look alright. Let me get out of here before I'm late. I can't believe that I'm actually doing this."

Mayah hastened to get into the car. She kept looking at her watch because she didn't want to be late picking up Kyle; after all, this was their first time attending church since Nan's funeral twelve years ago.

She drove up in front of Kyle's apartment and honked the horn three times. Kyle practically flew outside to meet her.

"Mayah, what are you doing; are you crazy? Don't you know some people are still asleep? You just can't roll up in front of someone's apartment honking the horn this early in the morning."

"Sorry. I wasn't thinking. Hey, I wonder if your neighbors get perturbed during the week when someone pulls up and honks for them to come out to go to work."

"I don't know, but in the future, just call me on my phone and I'll come down. I don't want anyone hating me."

"Alright. Are you ready for this?"

"Not really sis, but I'm doing this for you, especially since you had that crazy dream."

Mayah continued driving for about fifteen additional minutes, when they finally arrived at The Church of Love.

"They have a lot of cars in the parking lot, huh?" she asked as she looked for a spot for her car.

"Yep, but that don't necessarily mean a thing. It could be one person in each car."

Mayah finally parked, and as she approached the beautiful brick-front church, her legs trembled. She stopped, took multiple deep breaths, and stared at Kyle.

"Mayah, what's up with you? What's the matter? Are you okay?"

"I'm just a little nervous about going inside. It's been so long since I've been inside a church."

"Sis, quit trippin' and let's get this over with," Kyle said in an impatient tone of voice. She knew that tone well, as he'd used it on her a lot down through the years.

Mayah ascended the church stairs, and with each step, she took another deep breath. They finally reached the main church entrance.

"Listen, Kyle, you can hear them singing." She turned an ear toward the beautiful music wafting out to them from the sanctuary.

"Make a joyful shout to God all the earth. Sing out the praises of His name. Make His praise glorious. Make His praise glorious. Make His praise glorious. Make His praise glorious."

"Yeah, I hear them. They're jamming, huh? Girl, we could stay out here and listen to everything, if you're still nervous about going in."

"No. I didn't come this far to turn around."

The singing continued, and it tugged at Mayah's heart.

"All the earth shall worship You. Sing praises to You. Sing praises to Your holy name. They'll shout for joy and sing, praises to Your name, and make Your praise glorious. Make Your praise glorious."

As they entered the foyer, an usher greeted them.

"Can I help you find a seat?"

"No, ma'am, we'll just sit in the back," Mayah said.

They entered the five-hundred-seat sanctuary as quietly as they could. The small platform barely had enough room for the choir, musicians, and pastor. Some of the musicians were on the main floor with their instruments. The sanctuary was decorated in muted hues of browns and tans, with a hint of burgundy, nothing really elaborate or expensive. They took their seats on the wooden pew in the rear of the auditorium just as the choir finished their song.

"Wasn't that song a blessing up in here this morning?" the preacher shouted.

The church responded with, "Hallelujah, Praise the Lord."

Mayah nervously scooted closer to Kyle; in fact, she was so close that she was almost in his lap. He gave her a strange look and gestured for her to move over.

It was offering time and the preacher called the ushers forth. "You know, everyone in here needs to be paying their tithes and offerings. There's no way we can make it by selling chicken dinners and other things. We all need to do our part. Now, we shouldn't have to take up two and three offerings every Sunday just to get enough money to pay the bills. God has blessed every one of you and you need to act like it."

The preacher came around the side of the ornate pulpit and leaned one arm against it. "Dig deep into your wallets and purses and get out some *real* money. Now, we don't want to hear the sound of coins falling in the offering basket—we want a silent offering drop into the basket today—that means cash and no coins." He chuckled as if he'd told a good joke. "If you need an envelope, please raise your hand and the ushers will bring one to you. Okay, does everyone have an envelope?" He looked around to make certain no one raised his or her hand. "Now, follow the leading of the ushers and bring God's money up front."

After hearing the instructions of the preacher, Mayah and Kyle looked at each other. He looked every bit as baffled as she felt. An envelope? What was the purpose of an envelope? She vaguely remembered placing coins in an offering basket when attending church with Nan, but they no longer accept coins.

The usher gestured for them to get out of their seats and walk up front with their offering. Mayah followed along behind the previous row and dropped some cash in the basket, as did Kyle, and they made their way back to their seats.

Following the offering, a middle-aged, thin-faced man walked up to the pulpit and nodded to the musicians. They began to play, and he soon joined them with a wonderful tenor voice.

> "Father, I thirst for You. Let Your living water flow through me. Nothing can satisfy my thirst. Holy Spirit flow through me."

The gentleman sang so sincerely, Mayah thought the precious look on his face meant he really felt it. As he continued singing, his

From Church to Church

voice full of emotion, Mayah's eyes began to well up. She fought back the tears, as she wasn't certain why she felt like crying.

The man continued.

> "Spirit of God fill this vessel. Power of God flow through me. No more contentment in the shallow things of this world. Holy Spirit consume me. I thirst, I thirst for You. I thirst, I thirst for You."

Glancing up at the overhead screen, she began to meditate on a portion of the words. *No more contentment in the shallow things of this world.* Was that what she'd been doing—focusing on the shallow things of this world?

The singer took his seat and the rather young pastor quickly arose to preach. While he spoke, Mayah's concentration remained fixed on the words of the song. Still puzzled by a few of the phrases, she pondered what he meant when he said he was 'thirsty' for God.

The pastor's voice elevated to a louder decibel as if screaming at the congregation. She couldn't figure out why he had to yell so much. Was he mad at the people? Now, what was he doing? With all that screaming, moaning, and dancing, Mayah couldn't concentrate on anything he said, and she wondered if anyone else understood this man's message.

She glanced over at Kyle, who had somewhat of a smirk on his face. He made eye contact with her, shook his head, and slowly bowed it. He also closed his eyes as if to shut out the theatrical scene before them.

The pastor finally finished, in Mayah's opinion, verbally abusing the people, and he asked all visitors to stand. Mayah looked over at Kyle, and he gave her one of his *what have you gotten me into* looks. Cautiously, they stood. Their names were asked as well as if they were members of a local church.

"Sir, my name is Kyle Johnson," he said, surprising Mayah for his boldness. "And this is my sister, Mayah Johnson. She found your church in the phonebook, and we decided to come here today and maybe for a couple of weeks, sir."

"Well, we're certainly happy to have you here. You can stop by anytime, and you're welcome to come for longer than a couple of weeks," he chuckled, "if you like." The entire congregation burst out in laughter. "We're pleased to have you here. Please, come back again."

The service was dismissed, and as they left the sanctuary, the congregants dashed by them without voicing a solitary word. Additionally, as they approached their car numerous people passed them without uttering a word to them.

This bothered Mayah as she remembered how Nan made a point of personally greeting every newcomer in church.

"Kyle, did you notice that no one said a word to us? No one came up to us or anything. It was as if they just couldn't wait to get out of church, jump in their cars, and go do something else. The Church of Love, huh?"

"Yeah. I noticed that. But I also noticed how you were about to cry when that man was singing that song," he said. "What was going on in that little head of yours?"

"I was so captivated by the words. He sang about how 'thirsty' he was for God. I don't think I've ever heard anyone say anything like that before. I began to visualize how dry, dehydrated, and thirsty I get at times, and I tried to transfer those thoughts into thirsting for God. Then he said how no one could satisfy his thirst, and how he couldn't be content in the shallow things of this world. Whew, that's real commitment, huh?"

"Yes. I heard the song, but I didn't really trip on the words because I thought the brother was just singing. You know, just mouthing words with no real meaning behind them. I guess I was probably wrong, huh?"

"Yes you were. I think there was more to it. Anyway, I'm coming back to this church on Wednesday night. I want to see how they conduct Bible class."

"Okay, sis. Remember our agreement. I'm only coming on Sundays and that's it."

"I know."

Mayah dropped Kyle off at his apartment and returned home to find her telephone message light blinking. She checked her voicemail and the message was from Tia. First slipping into clothes that were more comfortable, she then telephoned her.

"Hello."

"Hi, Tia, you called?"

"Girl, where were you at so early this morning?"

"Kyle and I went to church."

"Went to church?" She mocked. "I thought you were joking."

"Yes, we went to church, and we'll be going to numerous churches for several months as I attempt to find the right one."

"What's up with you? You're not getting all *holy* on me, are you?"

"No, Tia. I had that dream, and I decided it was probably time for me to get back in church."

"Okay, girl. You go ahead and go to church. As for me, I have better things to do with my Sundays. Oh, are you still thinking about what you want to do for your birthday?"

"No, I haven't given it another thought."

"Your birthday is coming soon and it's on a Wednesday. You'd better start making plans because we're going to party from Wednesday through the weekend. This is the big one, girl!"

For some reason, Mayah felt a little perturbed by this, as her present focus wasn't on partying or even celebrating her birthday. However, she knew Tia couldn't grasp or comprehend what she was saying. Frustrated, she tried to maintain her composure, but Tia was really challenging her patience.

Jacqueline Jenkins

"Tia, I'll get back to you on that. I don't want to think about this at this moment. My mind is somewhere else and I don't want to be rude right now."

"Alright, you don't have to get all huffy. I'll give you a call later on this week. Bye," she said abruptly.

"Goodbye, Tia."

After clearing her mind from the belaboring conversation with Tia, Mayah plunged into the overstuffed sofa in her bedroom, still meditating on the lyrics of the song. She couldn't get beyond what it would be like to 'thirst' after God. This thought was so alien to her, yet it drew her in like a cold glass of water on a hot day.

* * * *

Wednesday arrived and so did the end of Mayah's workday. Gathering all her personal belongings, she promptly left work. She rushed home, grabbed a ready-made salad, and jumped back into the car so as to make it to Bible class on time.

"Oh my," she moaned when she realized she didn't have a Bible and needed to stop at the Christian Bookstore to purchase one. However, she didn't have time. She'd either purchase one on her lunch hour the following day, or contact her mother to procure Nan's, as she was certain her mother wasn't using it—not at all.

There were quite a few parked cars in the church parking lot, as well as people still parking and exiting their vehicles as she arrived at The Church of Love. She parked her car and headed toward the church. Everyone passed her again and didn't say a word.

"Hello, sir," she said to one of the men as he passed by.

"Hello," he bellowed.

Wow, I wonder what was wrong with him. All I said was hello.

Upon entering church, she scanned the sanctuary for a good seat and sat midway in the sanctuary.

She inwardly moaned when she learned the pastor was also the Bible class teacher. He summoned a woman up front to pray, who prayed for what Mayah deemed an eternity.

What was up with the 'let us love one another' stuff in her prayer? No one had any love in this church; they just arrived, departed, and spoke only to those they were familiar with. She guessed one day someone would greet her or say something—anything —to her.

The pastor started out by warning the class about false prophets and preachers. He even spoke about some ministers and members living dishonest or compromised lives. Subsequently, he commented on people not being holy. Finally, he referenced members who weren't tithing.

Was money the only thing that concerned him, she thought. There were a lot of people in this church doing a lot of things, at least that's what the pastor said, except they weren't tithing. When was this man going to talk about God and not just about what the people are or aren't doing?

About forty-five minutes later, Bible class was brought to a close, and everyone charged out of the front and side doors. Once again, no one articulated a word to Mayah. She headed to her car disenchanted and with sadness in heart about the lack of friendliness in The Church of Love.

Mayah didn't remember people being like this in church when she went with Nan. Everyone had been so friendly. After pops died, they would even invite Kyle, Nan, and her over for dinner. *I'm not expecting an invitation of any kind from these people. They'll do good just to say 'good morning' to me.*

CHAPTER 3

The week flew by and Saturday night was at hand. Mayah telephoned Kyle as a reminder of their church date on Sunday and that she would call him as she pulled up to his apartment.

Mayah had another sleepless night. She awakened Sunday morning somewhat exhausted, desiring to sleep in, but she kept flashing back on Nan. She peeled herself out of her warm, comfortable, king-sized bed and headed toward the shower. The water refreshed her. She put on the clothes that she had laid out the night before and headed out to pick up Kyle. As she pulled up in front of his apartment, she telephoned him.

"Hey, I'll be right down," he told her.

"Okay."

Within a couple minutes, Kyle slowly made his approach to the car.

"Good morning, sis. Thanks for not honking your horn. I could've stayed in bed today, but I'm going to be a man of my word."

"Thanks, Kyle. I had a hard time remaining asleep. It was hard for me to get up, but I'm here." She smiled as she sipped her coffee. "I wonder what's going to happen in this church today."

"I don't know. How did it go on Wednesday night?"

"It was okay. But no one spoke to me. It was as if I was invisible."

"Well, you won't have to worry about being invisible today because, girl, you are dressed!"

"I didn't know what to wear, so I just threw on this baby blue leather suit. You know blue is my favorite color."

From Church to Church

Mayah knew the leather suit looked tailor-made for her curvy body.

Upon their arrival at church, no one spoke to them prior to entering the building; however, when they entered the sanctuary, an usher walked up to seat them.

As on the previous Sunday, the pastor got up and enlightened the members on how they still had not raised enough money to pay all the church's monthly expenses. He made an appeal for them to go beyond their best in the offering that day.

As she reached into her wallet, she leaned toward Kyle and whispered. "How does someone go beyond their best? I thought best was the best."

Kyle shook his head and stifled a laugh.

After the offering, the preacher introduced his subject, *Loving One Another, God Style*. His text dealt with people loving one another.

During the sermon, Mayah looked around as people said 'Amen' to his comments, but they weren't able to show love to strangers in this church. Her mind quickly vacated that thought and she tried to concentrate on the message. After all, hadn't Nan always told her she wasn't responsible for others' actions, just her own?

She scanned the choir loft trying to locate the man who had sung that previous Sunday. When Mayah spotted him, she hoped he would sing again.

The pastor concluded his sermon and invited the gentleman up to sing. He also asked the deacons to come forward as he "open the doors of the church" for their new members. Three elderly deacons approached the altar with three padded chairs.

Mayah whispered to Kyle, "Open the doors of the church? What's up with that? I thought the ushers were the ones who opened the doors for us. I don't think I ever saw the preacher at the back door. Why haven't they let the new members into the building sooner than this? And what are those chairs for?"

Kyle didn't respond.

The gentleman approached the microphone, gently took it off the stand, and began singing.

> "Don't let this time, pass you by. Every concern just lay them aside. Open up your heart, and let Him in. Jesus is knocking, just let Him in."

Mayah nudged Kyle. "Look, there are people going up front and sitting in chairs. What does that mean?"

"I don't remember," he whispered back.

The singer continued.

> "Don't harden your heart, let Him in today. Cast all your cares on Him and He'll take them away. Open your heart, and let Him in. Jesus is knocking, just let Him in."

The pastor addressed the people who had come up front and were now seated in a row of softly padded metal chairs. He said they were joining the church.

"Oh, I got it," Mayah whispered. "They just became a member of this church. Duh."

"Do you want to become a member, Mayah, and stop all this foolishness?"

"No. Shhh."

The preacher had the existing members of the church come forward and greet their newest members.

"Wow! People in this church can really smile and hug each other. I guess they just won't hug us unless we join the church," she murmured.

The service concluded, and according to their usual pattern, people dashed out of the church as if they had left a pan cooking on the stove or received an urgent telephone call.

"So Mayah, what do you think about this church? This was your second Sunday here, and you only have one Wednesday night left."

"Kyle, I don't think I want to be a part of this church. They don't show the type of love that the pastor was talking about today.

From Church to Church

They're friendly with those they're acquainted with, but they don't seem to like you or me. However, I'm going to honor the commitment that I made. I'll come back on Wednesday night just to see if something different occurs."

"Alright. I'm with you on that."

* * * *

Wednesday night came quickly. Mayah still hadn't called her mother for Nan's Bible.

Since the church showed the Bible verses on the screen, she decided it would be okay not to bring one that night. However, she made a mental note to remind herself to call her mother to inquire about Nan's old Bible.

Mayah arrived at church and found their traditions had not changed. She mustered up enough courage to speak to someone. "Hello, ma'am." The woman merely nodded her head at her.

She wondered what type of church this was. She'd put quite a bit of money in their envelopes. Why hadn't they inquired as to who was the Mayah Johnson who had given such large sums of money in the offerings? Instead, they just ran in and out of the church. She had hoped this Wednesday night would prove differently. Also, she prayed the pastor's teaching would be totally different from what she'd heard previously.

The slender-framed pastor stood up, gazed around the church, and began speaking. "Well, I thought I'd take a little time out tonight to discuss the finances of the church."

At this juncture, she blotted out the message as her mind raced. *Are we all just slot machines where the preacher pulls down the handle and we dispense cash, and more cash? Okay. This is not the church for me. I've been here for two weeks and all he's done is beg for money and tell us how to love one another, and no one has shown me an ounce of love here.*

That night Mayah left The Church of Love disheartened. She came to realize that the only thing she really appreciated there was the man singing the songs. The words had touched her heart, especially the song from that past Sunday which encouraged people not to let the time pass them by and to let Jesus into their hearts.

Mayah arrived home, kicked off her shoes, and carefully placed them into her closet. After putting on her pajamas, she telephoned Kyle. He wasn't home so she left a voicemail for him to call her back. She wondered where he was.

As she slumped down in her recliner, she started meditating on one of the songs. She didn't remember how all this church stuff goes; however, she was sure God was more concerned about people going to church and hearing the preacher preach instead of him always begging for money. He had some good points. She knew it took money to run a church as it does any organization, but did God want them to talk about money every time the people came to church? And those people at that church were so cold to Kyle and her.

"I can't remember it being that way when we went to church with Nan. I just don't understand," she said aloud.

She was very grateful for that man's singing. It caused her to think about some things. The lyrics had challenged her. Maybe that was the message she was supposed to get from this church.

"The pastor said if we don't understand something," she said as she bowed her head and folded her hands, "we should ask You. Well, I'm asking You now, God. What does it mean to thirst or to be thirsty for You? What did the singer mean when he said that nothing could satisfy his thirst for You? I understand the part about not being content in shallow things of this world, but can You please explain the rest to me? I have no one that I can call. My mother wouldn't know. Could You please introduce me to someone during these fourteen weeks who can explain all this stuff to me? Thank you, God. Amen."

Just as she ended her prayer and climbed into her high, platform bed, the phone rang. She looked at the Caller ID and it was Kyle.

"Hey, Kyle."

"Hey baby girl. What's up?"

"Well, you need to be ready to go to church with me on Sunday."

"What happened?"

"I just don't think this was the right church. The people weren't friendly at all. The only one who spoke to me was the usher, and that was because she wanted to show me where to sit. I greeted a few people in the parking lot, and they acted as if it was a dirty chore just to say 'hello.' So I decided to pass on this church. Also, the pastor just wanted my money—and not just mine, but everyone else's too. I don't mind giving money, but each service he was begging. He even had people stand up and commit to giving a hundred dollars tonight. This just doesn't feel right to me. But I've been out of church for so long, maybe this is what they do now. I don't know, but one thing is certain; we need to visit another church."

"Okay. Call me this weekend and let me know what time I need to be ready. I sure hope this next church is the one. I'm not sure if I got anything out of this one. Did you?"

"Yes, I did. That man who was singing really pricked something in my heart and I prayed a little while ago—"

"You *prayed*?"

"Yes, I've always prayed. Anyway, I was talking to God about some of the words in the song. You know, the one about thirsting for God. Hey, it would do you good to pray a little bit too." Mayah laughed.

"Nah, that's your thing. Remember, I'm just going with you on Sundays only. I didn't say anything about praying either."

"You're so funny. I'll call you this weekend. Wait a minute. I can get the name of the second church and give you the information right now. Hold on. Let me get my list." She ran downstairs to retrieve the list out of her home office. "Okay, I'll be picking you up on Sunday at nine-thirty. This church starts at ten o'clock."

"Alright, baby girl. I'll see you then."

CHAPTER 4

The alarm sounded and Mayah quickly leapt out of bed and promptly got in and out of the shower. She was refreshed and mentally ready to go to the new church. For some reason, she felt very energetic. She put on a black and grey pinstriped pantsuit, along with Nan's pearls, and made a pot of coffee. She kept peeping at her watch, determined to be on time to pick up Kyle. As soon as the coffee finished brewing, she grabbed her travel mug, filled it, and headed out the door.

As she stepped into the car, she spilled a couple drops of coffee on her designer shoes. She simply wiped them with a tissue and was on her way to pick up Kyle. She was almost in front of his apartment when she remembered to telephone him.

"Hey, Kyle. I'm pulling up now."

"Okay. I'll be right down."

Within a minute or so, out walked Kyle, all six feet, one hundred and seventy-five pounds of him, looking as if he had just stepped off the cover of G.Q. Magazine. He opened the car door, and just stared at Mayah for a moment.

"Why are you so chipper this morning, girl? What did you do after I talked to you?"

"Nothing, I just watched TV for a little while, and as soon as my head made contact with my pillow, I drifted off to sleep." She paused a moment, noticing he hadn't gotten into the car yet. "What's wrong with you this morning?"

"Nothing really. I got a call this morning from a girl that I've been trying to track down. She wanted me to meet her for breakfast today. I told her I couldn't because I had obligated myself to do something this morning."

"Did you tell her that you were going to church with me?"

"You're joking, right? No, I didn't tell her where I was going."

"Why not?"

"Girl," he shook his head rather slowly. "You don't tell a woman of her caliber that you're going to *church* with your sister. What I wanted to do was telephone you and cancel out, but, like I said, I *will* fulfill my obligation." He sighed, got into the car, reclined the passenger's seat as far back as it would go, and put on his sunglasses.

Mayah pulled off and looked over at him in amazement. "Are you pouting? If you don't want to come, you don't have to. I can make a u-turn, take you back home, and go to church by myself."

"It's okay. I've already turned her down, and she's probably already called someone else to go to breakfast with her. This girl is *fine*. I know she won't have a problem finding a breakfast date or any other type of date."

"I'm sorry, Kyle. I didn't mean to interrupt or interfere with your social life."

"It's okay—one down and six to go. Where are we going today?"

"We're going to The Church of Blessings on First Street."

"Girl, just get us there. I hope this is the church for you." He then fell asleep.

Mayah drove a little further, rounded the corner, and couldn't believe what she saw.

"Kyle, wake up!"

"What's wrong?"

"Look at this church. It's nothing like the last one, huh?"

"Nah, girl, did you drive us to the hood?"

"No, we're on First Street."

"Girl, I've never been on this side of First Street." He kept rubbing his eyes as if the view would change.

"Me neither. But since we're here, let's go on in."

"Okay, sis, lead the way."

She parked the car, and they both got out at a snail's pace as they carefully examined all their surroundings.

"Kyle, this church looks real small, huh?"

"Uh hm."

"There aren't a lot of cars here either."

"Nope." He stared directly into Mayah's eyes. "And to think, I gave up a date to come here."

They approached the tiny storefront church. There were no ushers to lead them, so they just walked in and took a seat in cold metal chairs near the back of the church. About that time, a lady with a warm smile walked over and greeted them. She also asked if they would like to move up toward the front of the church.

"No, ma'am, we're just fine where we are, but thank you," Mayah said.

The lady agreed to let them remain where they were and handed them a visitor's card and asked them to fill it out.

"Alright, ma'am," Mayah said.

Mayah and Kyle took visual inventory on this rather small church. She observed cracks in the walls, with paint chips holding on for dear life to the interior structure. The décor was very modest. There were a lot of dollies on things, such as the piano and pulpit stand.

They no sooner got settled in their chairs, when the members of the small band began to play loudly. Almost immediately, many of the people jumped up and started dancing and whirling all over the sanctuary.

Mayah poked Kyle in his side, "Look. They look like they're in a trance as they're dancing."

"Girl, will you just be quiet and just see if you like this church."

The music stopped. People took turns testifying about what God had done for them. This transpired for several minutes. Mayah was all ears—listening to every word.

"I see we have a few visitors here today. I need everyone to go up to them and greet them with the love of the Lord," a woman said.

Many of the people jumped out of their seats and eagerly sought out the visitors. Mayah and Kyle shook hands with the congregants, and some of the women even embraced Mayah and kissed her on the cheek.

She turned to Kyle. "Wow, they sure are friendly in here, huh?"

"Yes, Mayah. Can you just be quiet?"

"Well, God is Good!" the lady said, and the church went crazy as they shouted in agreement. "I'd like to call up the choir to give us a selection followed by Sister Raegan blessing us with a solo."

"Amen!" some of the members blurted out.

The choir began singing.

> "Shout it from the mountaintop. Shout it from the valley low. Shout it everywhere you go, that Jesus Christ is Lord."

"Kyle, they can sing, huh?"

"Yes, they can sing."

"Are you still mad?"

"No, I'm not mad. But can you just be quiet so I can hear them sing?"

> "Jesus, awesome and mighty Jesus. Jesus, Jesus Christ is Lord."

The church now stood to their feet, praising God by raising their hands and shouting.

"Yes, Lord!"

"Amen!"

"Hallelujah, mighty Jesus!"

Mayah and Kyle didn't know what to do, so they remained seated.

After the choir finished, Sister Raegan, an exquisite looking nineteen-year-old, mounted the pulpit and blurted out, "He's Lord, isn't He? Is He Lord of your life? Have you turned your life over to

Him? Is He your Savior? We ain't ashamed to shout out His name, are we, church?"

The church sent up a tremendous shout. Resounding in the atmosphere all one could hear was, "No, we ain't ashamed!"

" Hallelujah!"

"Glory to God!"

"You know," Sister Raegan continued. "When the pastor asked me to sing a solo this morning, I just set my mind on Jesus, and He gave me this little song. I believe it's for someone in this church this morning. Pray for me as I sing it." Her voice rang out clear and sweet.

> "Draw me closer to You. I want to be closer to You. Draw me closer, Lord, closer to You. I want to feel Your breath as You direct my steps. Draw me closer, Lord, closer to You. I want to be closer, Lord, closer to you."

This song had a rather unusual affect on the congregants. Tears fell uninhibited down people's faces, and others mumbled or quietly murmured words that apparently held deep meaning for them.

Mayah couldn't peel her eyes away from what she observed and experienced. However, there was something incredibly familiar about what she saw. She looked over at Kyle and at the same time they softly said, "Nan." She smiled at him, knowing this church brought back sweet memories of when they had gone to church with Nan.

Just as the soloist ended her song, a preacher walked up to the podium and instructed the congregants to turn their Bibles to 2 Chronicles 7:14. He requested that they all recite the verse together in unison.

Oops! Mayah still hadn't purchased a Bible, and she'd forgotten to ask her mother for Nan's. An elderly woman walked over to her, turned her Bible to the scripture, and handed it to Mayah.

"Thank you, ma'am," Mayah said, being totally caught off guard by the kind gesture.

The preacher read the scripture and all joined in with him in one voice. "If My people who are called by My name will humble themselves, and pray and seek My face, and turn from their wicked ways, then I will hear from heaven, and will forgive their sin and heal their land."

"Let us bow our heads in prayer." The preacher waited momentarily as everyone lowered their heads and most closed their eyes. Mayah followed their lead.

"Lord, you have given us a directive. You said if we humble ourselves, pray, seek Your face, and turn from our wicked ways that You would hear from heaven and forgive all—I mean *all*—of our sins and heal our land. Lord, you know our land is sick this morning. So much is going on in this nation and globally, as well as in our personal lives. Your Word lets us know that it's because we have become too prideful, too uppity. We've stopped praying except for when we need or want something. People have stop seeking Your face and have begun seeking the face of idols, seeking the face of the almighty dollar, and seeking the face of unrighteousness. God, many in this world refuse to turn from their wicked, evil ways, and that's why our nation, as well as our own personal land—that is, our temples, our bodies—are so sick, polluted, and in need of healing. God we repent to You today."

The congregation said Amen repeatedly throughout the prayer.

"We have all gone astray, and as the sister's song said this morning, we need You to draw us back to You, Lord. Please, Lord, have mercy on us today. In the name of Jesus, I pray. Amen."

Mayah sat stiff as a statue, paralyzed with fear or something. She didn't say a word to her brother, and she was certain he was grateful for that. She noticed he too barely moved.

The preacher continued. "Church, you know we're not a rich church. The other churches around us seem to want to persecute us for living holy. They have spread vicious rumors about us, but that's okay. We're rich in God and He is our protector as well as our source. Yes, we'll all be tested and tried. Our faith and our belief will be put to the test. Yes, they will. But we must be faithful to the end. Amen?" He asked, and they responded affirmatively.

He preached a little longer regarding people "turning from their wicked ways," then he wiped his brow and sat down. A woman gracefully strolled down the short aisle, walked up to the microphone, and said it was time to take up the offering.

Mayah quickly flashed back on the other church and wondered if they were going to beg also. She could hardly wait to see how they would raise their offering.

"Now you all know what you're supposed to do," the woman continued. "Bring your tithes and offerings to the Lord. If you don't have it, let us know, and we'll pray for God to bless you with a job and finances so you'll not only have something to give back to Him, but to live on as well."

Turning to Kyle, Mayah whispered, "That's a switch, huh? This is so totally different from that other church."

He nodded.

Both of them took their offering up to the front of the sanctuary, placed it in the offering basket, and returned to their seats.

The preacher returned to the podium and fixed his eyes on Kyle and Mayah and introduced himself as Pastor Jack.

"I just want to thank our visitors for coming out this morning. Don't be strangers, and come back again. Do either of you have anything to say?"

They both shook their heads.

"That's fine." He chuckled. "We hope you enjoyed yourself. You both be blessed. Okay church, show yourself friendly, and I'll see you all on Thursday night for Bible study."

As Mayah and Kyle attempted to make their way out of church, numerous people walked up to them, telling them their names and inviting them back.

"We'll be back soon," Mayah said.

They headed out of the sanctuary to the parking lot. On their way to the car, neither of them said a word. However, when Mayah drove out of the small parking lot, it was as if they were in a race to see who would speak first—Kyle won.

"So, Mayah. What did you think about this church?"

"Honestly, when I drove up, I was somewhat hesitant about going into this little church, but I'm so glad I did."

"So, are you going to stay at this church?"

"This is my first time here. I don't know. Just hold on. I know you're just trying to get your Sunday's back. But, I just don't know."

"This church reminded me of the one that Nan used to take us to."

"Me too." A warmth washed over her. "My memory was jarred today. I could see Nan just dancing all over that floor," she said as she chuckled.

He then broke out in laughter. "Yeah, me too. I could just see her kicking up her feet, grabbing hold to her dress, waving it around, and just dancing all over that place." He laughed heartily again.

"Well, they have Bible study on Thursday, so I'll be back on Thursday night. Do you want to come with me?"

"Nope. Remember Mayah—Sundays only," he quickly reminded her.

"I know, but you can't blame me for trying." She stuck her tongue out at him and they both laughed.

She dropped Kyle off at his apartment and decided to head over to her mother's house to pick up Nan's Bible. Not willing to chance whether or not her mother was home, she decided she had better call, since she was thirty minutes away.

"Hello."

"Hey, Mama. I just dropped Kyle off at his apartment, and I was wondering if you were at home."

"Yeah, sweetie, I'm here. Where else would I be?"

"Maybe church?" Mayah giggled.

From Church to Church

"That's real funny, Mayah. Don't even go there. What do you want? I know you want something, because you only come over when you want something."

"That's not true, Mama. But I do want something. Do you still have Nan's old Bible?"

"Yes I have it, why?"

"Well, Kyle and I've been going to church and I don't have a Bible. I thought I could get Nan's old Bible."

"That's fine. Come on over and get it. So the two of you are going to church again, huh?"

"Yes, ma'am. I'll see you in a few minutes. Love you."

"Okay, Mayah. I'll see you soon."

Mayah arrived at her mother's house and found her sitting on the porch, rocking in a rickety porch swing with Nan's Bible on her lap.

"Why are you outside, Mama?" she asked hoping everything was alright.

"No reason. I just thought I'd come outside for some fresh air. I was remembering how your grandmother would come out here and sit for hours." She closed her eyes for a moment. "Here's the Bible. I knew one day you'd be going back to church, but I didn't think Kyle would. I'm not going to express an opinion one way or another about church. I just want you to do what you think is right. Nan would be so proud of you. Go ahead and keep her Bible. I'm sure she would've loved for you to have it anyway."

Tears formed in Mayah's eyes and slid down her cheeks. "Thank you, Mama. I'll treasure this forever. I love you so much." She leaned down and kissed her cheek. "Maybe one day—"

"Don't start that, Mayah Johnson. Just take the Bible and go on home. I love you too. However, I'm not ready to go back to church. When the time comes, I'll call you," she said comically. "I'm sorry I haven't cooked anything yet; otherwise, I would've offered you something to eat. Do you want some sweet tea or soda?"

"No, Mama. I'm fine. I'll talk to you later this week."

Mayah kissed her mother again and slowly walked to her car, glancing back every few seconds to look at her, as if this would be the final time she'd see her. She hoped her mother would return to church. Maybe one day soon they'd be walking hand in hand into church. Mayah entered her car and waved goodbye as she slowly drove off.

Upon her arrival home, she attempted to remember the scripture the preacher recited. Excited about finding the verse, she didn't even take off her shoes or change clothing as had become her custom each Sunday. She shuffled through loose pieces of paper in her purse trying to find the scrap that she wrote it on. What was that Scripture? Where was the paper? Then she found it at the bottom of her purse and her heartbeat sped up a little bit. She'd really enjoyed the sermon and wanted to read it from Nan's Bible.

Flipping through its pages, Mayah finally located the verse. She was amazed. Nan had that same scripture highlighted in her Bible, and she brushed a finger over the page in awe, knowing that many years ago, her Nan sat in a chair and read this very passage. She came to an abrupt decision to see what else Nan had highlighted. As she flipped through the pages, Mayah noticed many tinted verses. She decided to start at the beginning of Nan's Bible and read all the verses that were previously marked in color. With that thought in mind, Mayah determined she'd better get comfortable because this might take some time.

She started her search in the book of Genesis and found numerous scriptures with bright yellow ink. But something she read triggered her memory of the song she heard that morning. *That young lady said she wanted to be so close to God that she could feel His breath as He... what did she say?* Mayah thought for several seconds. "Oh yeah, directed her steps," she said to herself. "Man, that's real close to Him." Now that made two songs that have caused her to focus on the lyrics, and now two things that she desperately

From Church to Church

wanted to know. "What's it like to be so close to God that I can feel His breath, and what does it mean to thirst or be thirsty for God?"

She read Nan's Bible for hours until she fell asleep with the book lying across her chest. She awakened early in the wee hours of the morning, and discovered the Bible had remained on her chest. She placed it on her dresser, put on her pajamas, and climbed into bed.

She woke the next morning with the scripture and those two songs still marinating in her spirit. Her phone rang.

"Hello."

"Hey, Mayah."

"Hi, Tia."

"Well, have you thought of what you want to do for your birthday?"

"You know, I don't think I want to do anything, Tia." She hoped that would put an end to her friend calling her about her birthday.

"What? You've been waiting for this birthday all of your life, and now you don't want to do anything? Are you angry because we celebrated my birthday without you?"

"Girl, no. My head is in a different place right now. I'm trying to, as a preacher said, 'Humble myself, seek God's face, pray, and turn from my wicked ways.'"

"Mayah, what are you talking about?"

"I'm on a quest right now, and partying is *not* a part of my life, at least not for right now. Can you understand that? I don't think I can make it any clearer than that." Tia's continuous lack of understanding of her wishes vexed her.

"Not really, but I'll honor what you're attempting to do. Call me when you come to your senses, girl."

"Alright Tia. I'll talk to you sometime later. Bye."

"Don't stay away too long, Mayah. Bye."

CHAPTER 5

Thursday rolled in like an evening tide, and Mayah was ready to go to church to hear the Bible study teacher. She arrived a couple minutes early and many of the members greeted her warmly.

"Hi, where's the guy who was with you?" one of the women asked.

"You mean my brother, Kyle?"

"Girl, that's your brother? He sure is handsome. Is he married?"

"No, he's not married."

"Does he have a girlfriend or any children?"

"No, he doesn't have any children, and he's not in a serious relationship right now."

"Really? Maybe you can introduce him to me. Is he coming here tonight?"

"No, but he'll be back on Sunday."

"Okay, will you introduce him to me on Sunday?"

"Yes, I can do that," she stated, wondering what Kyle was going to think of this. Maybe she'd be better off not telling him.

"Great!"

Mayah stared at the woman as she realized she didn't even know her name. "What's your name?"

"Betty."

"It's nice to meet you, Betty. I'm Mayah."

"It's a pleasure meeting you too, Mayah."

Bible study was about to commence. Mayah inched up toward the front of the church and sat next to Betty.

The teacher energetically got out of her seat and started teaching on the "Fruit of the Spirit." In fact, she said she would be teaching on this topic for a month.

From Church to Church

Mayah thought it was nice to see some structure in the teaching. However, as the instructor was teaching, Betty kept distracting her with questions about Kyle. She wanted Betty to shut up so she could hear the teacher. Betty's interruptions had distracted Mayah from hearing most of the lesson, which was now ending. Mayah tried to quickly leave church so she wouldn't have to do any more talking about Kyle. But someone caught her arm.

"Hey, Mayah, you want to exchange phone numbers?" Betty asked.

Mayah cringed. "I don't have time right now. Perhaps we can do it another time."

"Alright. Tell your brother hello."

"I sure will, Betty." As if he would even know who she is.

Mayah hurried out to the parking lot to get away from Betty. However, a couple other ladies stopped her to inquire about Kyle also.

My goodness, are these women hard up or what, she thought.

Mayah finally broke away from them, jumped in her car, and started her drive home. While on her way home, she called Kyle.

"Hello."

"Hey Kyle. I think you need to know that you're the talk of the new church. There were many women inquiring about you tonight. I couldn't even hear the entire lesson because one of them kept questioning me about you."

"What?"

"You heard me. There are perhaps three or four women in this church who are interested in you, especially Betty."

"Who is Betty?"

"I'll show her to you and the others too on Sunday."

"Hey, hey. I guess I still got it, huh?"

"Yeah, either you got something or they're just desperate for a man." She laughed. "But I'll give you a call on Saturday. Talk to you later."

CHAPTER 6

Mayah's eyes flew wide open. She couldn't believe she had awakened prior to the alarm clock going off, especially on a Sunday. She got out of bed and ran a nice, hot tub of water. While basking in the tub, she thought of the women who had cornered her with reference to Kyle. She was truly hoping no one would be in their faces today, especially Betty.

She removed herself from the comfortable, hot bathtub and started getting dressed. Once again, she searched in her closet for something appropriate to wear. It wasn't that she didn't have any clothes; her problem was she had too many, and it made selecting clothes a lot harder. After getting dressed, she left to pick up Kyle. About five minutes away from his house, she telephoned him.

As Mayah approached his apartment, she couldn't believe her eyes. Lanky Kyle stood outside at the curb, dressed to the max in a dark suit with a sweater that accented his six-pack. She pulled up and Kyle hopped in the car.

"What's up with you?" she asked. "I don't think I've ever seen you this happy to go to church?"

"Hey, I want to see all these women who are so interested in me." He tugged on his jacket lapel and smiled.

"So that's why you're all dressed up and smelling so good?"

"Yep."

"I don't believe you."

"Girl, you got to meet them wherever you can, right? Church is probably one of the better places to meet women."

"I can't believe you said that. Don't say anything else, please. I don't have time to focus on your social life. I'm too excited about hearing this pastor again and not your foolishness."

From Church to Church

"Umm hmm. You're just jealous."

"Yeah, you're right. I'm just jealous that all these women want you," she smirked. "I don't think so. I'm going to church because I want to know more about Jesus and not about some man, nor am I interested in trying to get a date from the pool of men at church."

"To each his own."

Mayah pulled up in the tiny parking lot and it felt like all eyes were on her car. "What's going on out here? What's with all these women standing in the parking lot today? Kyle, this is crazy. This had better not be about you."

About four or five women came up to the car and stood right outside her door, waiting. She moaned under her breath, and inhaled deeply to prepare herself for the impending bombardment.

"Hello, Mayah."

"Hi."

"Hi, Kyle."

"Good morning, ladies. Do you all need an escort into the church?"

All the women giggled. "Yes, we do."

Mayah couldn't believe this. Here was Kyle, escorting these women into the church. They all walked in and the women sat by him. Mayah took a seat directly behind them on another row. Although she loved her brother, this was so typical of Kyle, the womanizer, and she didn't want anything to do with what was occurring.

The choir began singing. This time, Mayah was so focused on the women chasing Kyle that she couldn't hear what they were singing.

Pastor Jack got up and read his text for the day. Mayah was still so upset that she was unable to even get with his preaching. She couldn't believe the women were acting like that in church. The way they were chasing Kyle, someone would have thought the church

Jacqueline Jenkins

was a nightclub. And there her brother was, enjoying every bit of the attention they gave him.

Pastor Jack concluded his message with Mayah missing most of what he had said.

"We're so happy to see our visitors again. In fact, the young lady was out on Thursday night for Bible study. Oh, yes she was, and some of you have been here for over a year and haven't made it to Bible study yet. I pray I'll see all of you on Thursday night."

They collected the offering and dismissed church. All the ladies surrounding Kyle reminded Mayah of fleas on a dog. She headed out to the parking lot to wait on her brother. Her patience was being tried.

"Okay, ladies. I'll see you all real soon," Kyle told the entourage who'd followed him to the car. "Maybe I'll come back on Thursday night for Bible class. If so, I'll see you all then. You guys stay real." He flashed them one of his special smiles.

"Kyle, I'm so embarrassed! I can't believe you were flirting with all these women—and in church too!"

"Me? Flirting? Those ladies were all over me. I wasn't chasing them; they were chasing me."

"And what's up with, 'I might be back on Thursday night?' I thought our agreement was you'd only come with me on Sundays. So, because these women seem to be so enamored with you, you're considering attending Bible class just to set up some dates or hookups. I can't believe you."

"Mayah, they're running after me. I can't help it if I look good," he snickered.

"Alright. If you come here on Thursday, you'll be driving yourself." She gritted her teeth and shook her head. "I'm not going to pick you up so your ego can be stroked by these silly women."

"That's fine. If I come on Thursday, I'll drive myself."

From Church to Church

As Mayah drove Kyle home, the car became a traveling tomb, as there was no conversation. She dropped him off—neither said goodbye—and she sped off toward home.

"I can't believe any of this. They act as if he's the last piece of rich, tasty candy in a candy store. I was optimistic about this church, but I see the women are fools; that is, desperate fools. Maybe not all of them, but it's enough to make me not want to be a member here, and Kyle is no better—"

Mayah slammed on her brakes and skidded to a stop. *Oh no! I almost ran through that stop sign focusing on this madness.*

* * * *

Mayah hadn't spoken to Kyle since Sunday. Now she was on her way to The Church of Blessings for Bible study. As she pulled into the parking lot, she moaned in disgust when she saw Kyle's car. She let out a long sigh, got out of the car, walked into church, and took a seat toward the front of the sanctuary so she wouldn't have to see the women acting like idiots, nor would she have to see Kyle flirting shamelessly with them.

Pastor Jack approached the podium. He looked surprised to see the increased number of attendees that night. "Well, I see many of you took the challenge given to you on Sunday, and you're here tonight. Well, it's good to see all of you here. Let's continue discussing the *Fruit of the Spirit*. Let me pick up where your teacher ended last week. You know, before I move forward covering the *Fruit of the Spirit*, can we look at Galatians 5:16-21? I want to talk about the *Works of the Flesh* for a moment." He read the passage aloud.

"Okay church. The Bible says if you walk in the Spirit, then your flesh won't be acting up; that's to say, you won't be committing adultery, fornication, being hateful, jealous, and selfish, being lewd, and downright nasty. You'll be able to control yourself and not give in to wicked and sinful desires."

"Alright, pastor! Amen!" yelled some of the members in agreement. Mayah didn't say a word, because she knew her beloved brother was truly operating in the works of the flesh, as were those women, and although he was wrong, she didn't want to say anything in agreement with the others. The pastor completed his study and dismissed Bible class.

Mayah tried to walk pass Kyle without saying a word, but she couldn't hold her tongue. "Hey, Kyle. Now you be safe. Remember what the pastor preached on tonight," she said as she smiled dryly.

"Alright, sis. I'll chat with you later."

She was almost home when her cell phone rang. "Hello."

"Hey, sis. You mad at me?"

"I just can't believe you came to church tonight solely to meet women."

"I know. But you should know that I didn't do anything. I didn't give anyone a ride home, nor did I take anyone out to eat. Hey, I didn't even give my number out to anyone, nor did I get any."

"Good. I can't believe the women in this church are so man-hungry. You would think you were the last man on earth."

"I know. I'm really sorry. I'll stick to the agreement. If you don't want me to come to this church on Sunday, I'll stay home."

"No, I want you to come to church with me. I'll pick you up and we'll go together. I really need one more week at this church, if you don't mind, because I blew one service just focusing on dumb stuff."

"Alright. I love you and I'm sorry."

"Likewise Kyle. Please forgive me for being mad at you."

"No problem sis. I know some of this was my fault. I don't mind coming here another week. I'll talk to you later. Bye."

"Bye." She never could stay mad at her brother for very long. They were too close to hold a grudge. Mayah adored him. She also wanted to throw things at him sometimes.

CHAPTER 7

Mayah reclined in bed for a few moments, mulling over some things before getting up. It was Sunday again. She hoped she'd be able to hear Pastor Jack this morning and not focus on those silly women. She liked the way this pastor preaches, but didn't like the way some of the women act in this church. *What if I got married; I don't know if I would ever bring my husband around them. They just seem so man hungry.* She laughed at herself for her musings and shook off the thoughts.

Mayah climbed out of bed and rummaged through her closet. She picked out a gorgeous, teal colored suit and dressed quickly as she was running a little behind schedule.

As she neared Kyle's apartment, she phoned him. He promised to be downstairs and ready to go so they wouldn't be late. There he was, all dressed up and waiting on her.

"Hey sis. I'm so glad that we've ironed all that stuff out. I'm sorry."

"Think nothing about it. Let's just put that behind us."

As they turned the corner approaching the parking lot, Mayah was blown away by what she saw. There were even more women in the parking lot than before.

"Kyle, do you see what you've started? Look at these women. I guess they're all competing to see who'll get you, huh? This is ridiculous!"

"Don't worry, sis. Follow my lead."

They slowly got out of the car and many of the women approached Kyle.

"Good morning, ladies. Didn't the pastor teach a good lesson this past Thursday night, talking about our flesh? Isn't it good that we've all learned how to control it?"

"Yes," they all proclaimed.

"Well, I'll see you all in church. I need to sit with my sister today."

In total amazement, Mayah looked over at Kyle. "Good job, Kyle."

They walked into the sanctuary, looked around for some seats up close, and sat near the front of the church just as the choir began to sing a very upbeat song.

> "Who is like Thee, among the gods, oh, Lord, who is like Thee majestic in holiness? Awesome in praises, working wonders, who is like Thee, oh, Lord. There is none like You, Lord. There is none like You, Lord. Awesome in praises, working wonders. There is none like, none like You."

After the choir concluded their number, another soloist stood up and sung. Pastor Jack then walked up to the podium, paused for a moment or two, and then spoke.

"Church, I want to say that I'm glad that our visitors have returned. However, I do need to say something to all of you, especially to those who were at Bible study last week. I hope to see you all this Thursday night too. I pray that when you come out, you'll be here to meet with Jesus and not with any other person."

Mayah's ears perked up when she heard this. Had he noticed the appalling behavior of some of his female congregation? She found herself shutting out everything else and concentrated on his words.

"As the song says, 'Who is like Him?' Don't you know that there is *no* one like Him? No one can satisfy the longing of your souls, but Him. Don't you know that His Spirit—that is, the Holy Spirit —is the only One who can keep your flesh under control? He's also the One who leads and guides us into all truth. He's the One who convicts us of all unrighteousness. Now, I appreciate all of you coming out this past Thursday night, but this week, come out to meet Jesus. Some of you are undergoing tests and trials right now. But you can't say you're holy and set apart and be doing all kind of evil, sinful stuff. That would make you a hypocrite and a liar. We have to learn how to overcome all manner of evil as well as discipline our flesh."

Mayah nodded her head repeatedly. *Oooo weee! This preacher is on it! I bet these women are feeling real stupid right about now.* She knew it wasn't all of them who were chasing Kyle, but there were way too many. Mayah glanced over at Kyle, whose head was bowed. If she knew him, and she did, he felt embarrassed.

Pastor Jack concluded his message, the offering was taken, and church was dismissed. Kyle and Mayah left the sanctuary and headed out to the car, and not one of the women said a word to him; however, they all did say goodbye to Mayah.

Mayah pulled out of the parking lot and Kyle's eyes dropped.

"Mayah, I feel so bad. The pastor was right. Some of those women did come out on Thursday because I said I was possibly coming. I think when I get home I just may have to pray a little prayer to God, because I was wrong. I had an ulterior motive for coming out on Thursday night too."

"What? You're praying now? That's pretty good. Yes, you were wrong, and so were they. You're just getting started in this church thing, but they should've known better. I was so angry at you. I guess I'll need to offer up a prayer to God too for being so mad at you and the ladies." She laughed quietly.

As she approached Kyle's apartment, he was still apologizing, saying he was so ashamed of himself. But Mayah was equally ashamed for her attitude against him and the ladies.

"Okay. You've apologized enough. Go in your apartment, and pray a prayer to God. Give me a hug; we're still cool with each other. No problem."

Jacqueline Jenkins

Mayah drove off. Upon arriving home, she immediately repented to God for her negative attitude. Later that day, after eating dinner, she put on her pajamas and picked up Nan's Bible. She'd been sensing a real comfort as she read Nan's Bible. Having the precious Book also made her feel close to her Nan. She must have read for hours before drifting off to sleep.

Mayah awoke before daybreak thinking about the second church. Although she liked the preaching, she wasn't sure if she wanted to be a member. However, she still had one more Thursday night to go. She drifted back to sleep and was later startled by her telephone.

"Hello."

"Hey, Mayah, it's Tia. Well, I'm calling about your birthday. Have you thought of what you want to do?"

Looking at the clock, she realized it was time to get up and go to work; therefore, she decided not to scold Tia for calling so early. "Hmmm. I'm going to be in church services this Thursday evening and Sunday morning. You know, Tia, I really don't feel like going out partying right now. Maybe on Friday evening a few of us can go out to dinner."

"Dinner? You're joking, right? That's not what I just heard you say, is it?"

"Tia, I'm changing. I'm not interested in running around trying to find somebody to date. Nor am I interested in sitting in some club right about now. I will be twenty-one soon, and I want my life to count for something. It's time for me to get serious about the remainder of my life. Although I'm not married and don't have any children, I still have expenses, and I'm saving to buy a house. I don't want to be wasting my money out there in those streets either."

"Girl, you're right. You have definitely changed. Mayah, you're still young just like me, and this is the time where we can really enjoy life before we settle down, get married, and have a few kids."

"Do you honestly think I want to meet my future husband in a club? When I find or meet my intended, I want him to be doing something productive like working, or in church, in the library, at the cleaners, or at some type of a seminar or conference, and not drunk. I'm not saying that there aren't any good men in clubs. I'm merely saying that's not the type of man for me. I don't plan on running to clubs every weekend trying to see if Mr. Right or Mr. Wonderful is there. Most of those men are just looking for someone—that is, a one-night stand—and that someone is *not me*."

"So you plan on finding some man at church? Is that why you're going to church now, trying to hook-up with some church man?"

"No! I'm going to church because of the dream I had, and mostly because I now realize that I'm missing something in my life. My life just seems incomplete, and maybe it's because of how I've been 'content with the shallow things of this world' as one of the singers said in church. I haven't determined exactly what it is, but when I find it or realize what it is, I'll let you know. But for sure, it's not the club scene or a man."

"Girl, I don't know what's happening to you. It's like you're not any fun anymore ever since I celebrated my birthday and you didn't come."

"So what are you trying say? You think I was jealous because you and some of the girls went to a club and I couldn't because I wasn't twenty-one? You've got to be kidding! I was a little upset for a moment because everyone was going except me, but I got over that real quick. I told you about the dream that I had and the quest that I'm on right now. Tia, we've been friends for years. If you don't know me by now, you never will."

"Mayah, I'm saying that's what it looked like, and you've been a different person ever since then."

"I know. I just want to find a good church and start attending. Again, I don't want to be running the streets looking for no man or have some drunk man up in my face. You know, I want to be close to someone, but it's like this song that I heard, I want to be closer to God right now, and I'm trying to do what I can to accomplish that.

So, if you want to chill out for a while and do your own thing apart from me, I understand. Just like you don't want to go to church with me, I don't want to go to the club with you. So we're even, right?"

"I guess so Mayah," she said and then paused for a moment. "I just miss you."

"I miss you too, but we can still talk on the phone and go out to eat, but I just don't want to be hanging out right now. Please try to understand," Mayah said tiredly.

"I'm trying, Mayah. This is all so abrupt. Give me a little while to get used to the new you in the making."

"Right now, let's just put my birthday dinner and everything on hold until next month. Tell the girls that we can all go out to dinner the end of the month or whenever. Alright?"

"Okay. I'll talk to you later, Mayah."

"Alright. If you can't reach me by phone, send me an email, okay? I love ya, girl."

"Me too."

Mayah gently slid back into bed, and took a deep breath. That was an interesting call. Tia almost wore her out. She realized that she's changing on the inside; maybe it's stemming from going to church or from reading Nan's Bible. She didn't know. But whatever it was, she sure felt good right about now. If Tia couldn't get with her new program, they're going to have some friendship issues. She'd been her friend for fifteen years and she'd sure hate to lose her as a friend. *What am I thinking? She'll get with the program.*

CHAPTER 8

Instead of rushing home trying to cook something after work, Mayah stopped at a restaurant, and planned to go directly to church from there. She found an upscale restaurant about half a mile from the church. After parking her car, she noticed a few women from the church in the restaurant. Groaning inwardly, she headed for the restaurant, not wanting to eat with the women. She merely wanted to be left alone. The ladies had really gotten on her nerves by chasing after Kyle. They should've been ashamed of themselves. She approached the Hostess Station.

"How many in your party?" the hostess asked with a smile.

"Just one."

"Follow me please."

Mayah followed the hostess who walked right pass the women from the church.

"Hi, Mayah. Come sit with us."

"No, no, no. It's okay. I'm sure you guys have a lot to talk about, and I don't want to interrupt your conversation," she said as she attempted to get pass them without a scene.

"Mayah, you wouldn't be interrupting anything. We usually come here every Thursday night prior to Bible study and have dinner. You wouldn't be interrupting a thing."

Mayah bit her tongue, and her stomach turned flips from the acid that was churning. She was stuck and had no choice, and succumbed to their invitation.

"Okay ladies, if you're sure that I'm not intruding."

"No, you're fine, Mayah."

Mayah took her seat and the waiter came right over to take her order.

"I'll just have half a Caesar's Salad, please."

"Thank you for your order, ma'am."

As the waiter walked away, she mumbled within, *Ma'am, I hate it when people say that. I know he's just being courteous, but he's older than I am.*

"Mayah, is that all you're eating? No wonder you're so skinny."

Mayah stood five feet, five inches tall and weighed one hundred-thirty-five pounds, so she knew she wasn't actually skinny, but just right for her height. Many of the ladies were slightly overweight and somewhat shorter than Mayah. Perhaps that was why they thought she was so skinny.

"I'm really not that hungry, and I don't want to eat anything heavy because I don't want to fall asleep in Bible study."

"Girl, you wouldn't be the first one to fall asleep on Pastor Jack." The other women giggled. "All of us have." The women laughed even louder now.

"But that's rude," Mayah exclaimed, feeling a tinge of remorse for being so judgmental toward them.

"Girl, you don't know rude. Rude is making us sit up in that class listening to that boring teaching."

"Boring?" Mayah blurted out before she knew it.

"Yes, B-O-R-I-N-G," one of the women said loudly.

"See, Mayah, you're new. You haven't been at our church long enough to know everything."

"Like what?"

"We've gone through a lot in that church. All kinds of so-called Christians have come against us. We've been persecuted, ridiculed, and everything else and Pastor Jack didn't say or do a thing."

Their comments puzzled her. "Well, what was Pastor Jack supposed to do that he didn't do?"

"He should have defended us so those people would know that we have some backbone. He simply said that God would avenge us

From Church to Church

and we didn't have to say or do a thing. You know, like turn the other cheek type of thing."

Mayah was more upset than ever, and she just had to say something to these rude, man-chasing women. "You know, all of this is very new to me and Kyle. I never thought Christians hurt each other like this. From the way everyone responds to Pastor Jack, I assumed everyone—all of you—loved him and this church. Is it two-faced to talk bad about your pastor or your church and then sit up in church as if nothing's wrong? Where's the love in this church? I really like Pastor Jack and enjoy his preaching. I think he's a great teacher too. One more thing, my grandmother always told me that the truth will always stand on its own, but you'll always have to defend a lie. So, why would he waste his energy defending the lies being told about the church?" She quickly bowed her head. Her face slightly moistened and felt as if it was on fire.

The entire table went silent—dead silent. One by one, the women dropped their heads. The soundlessness went on for several uncomfortable seconds.

"Excuse me, ladies," Mayah finally said as she stood. "But I think I just lost my appetite. Here's my money for my meal. Can you please pay the waiter when he brings the bill? Oh, and if any of you are still hungry, you can eat my salad."

Mayah, graciously dismissed herself, headed to her car, and drove to church. She got there some forty-five minutes early, so she just sat in her car, with thoughts of what just occurred bombarding her mind.

"I never would've known that they were so two-faced. They be all up in the pastor's face, and then talking about him behind his back. I don't get it." She shook her head in disbelief. "I thought Christians were supposed to be a little different than this. Well, this is my last night here, and I'll be visiting church number three soon. I can't even remember the name of that church right now because I'm so perturbed, but Kyle and I will be there on Sunday."

As she continued speaking to herself, the church door swung open and Mayah quickly got out of her car and walked in.

"You're here a little early, Sister Johnson. Is everything alright?" Pastor Jack said as he greeted her with a warm smile and firm handshake.

"Good evening, Pastor Jack. Yes, everything is fine with me. I just want you to know that I've really enjoyed your preaching and the singing. My brother and I will be visiting a few other churches, and then I'll have to make a decision as to which church I'm supposed to be at. I have five others to visit."

"Okay, Sister Johnson. We've really enjoyed the two of you, and if God leads you back, we'll love to have you as members. Make sure that you follow the leading of the Holy Spirit. He knows what's best for you. Promise me that you'll do that."

Mayah thought about what Pastor Jack had said, and although she didn't thoroughly understand what he meant, she told him she'd do just that.

At this juncture, the ladies from the restaurant walked in. They viewed Pastor Jack shaking Mayah's hand. The way they looked at Mayah, it was obvious to her that they thought she had divulged to him what they had said.

Someone sung a short chorus and Pastor Jack stood up and started to pray; after which, he began fumbling with his Bible. "I was going to continue my teaching on the *Fruit of the Spirit*, but I feel a nudge in my spirit to talk about brotherly love on tonight. I want to talk about us loving our neighbors as we love ourselves."

The ladies from the restaurant were all sitting there quiet as a church mouse, with obvious bad attitudes. They kept rolling their eyes up toward the ceiling while they slowly shook their heads. Mayah did her best to ignore them, and concentrate on the Pastor's words.

From Church to Church

    Pastor Jack started expounding upon his lesson. As he neared its conclusion, all of a sudden, he asked Mayah to please stand. With great hesitancy, she obeyed.

    "Church, I want you to know that tonight is Sister Johnson's last night here. She and her brother have been with us for a few weeks now, and I want to thank you all for the love that you've shown them during their brief visit here. Sister Johnson, is there something that you'd like to say to the church? Why don't you come up front?" He then extended the microphone to her.

    Mayah gingerly walked up to the pulpit and cleared her throat. Her hands were perspiring and trembling as she slowly gripped the microphone. She gradually turned and faced the class. "Uhmm, I'm real nervous, so pray for me. This is my first time as an adult speaking in church, so please bear with me. I just want to say that I've really enjoyed my visit here. I mostly enjoyed listening to your teaching, Pastor Jack. It's so practical and easy to understand. I've seen and encountered many things while here, and your messages have become life lessons for me. In addition, I want to thank all of those who befriended both Kyle and me." She turned to face the pastor. "Pastor Jack, my father died in an automobile accident many years ago, and you've been such a good example of a father to me. Thank you. You say things and I hear my father's voice through you. Oh, and one more thing…"

    Mayah eyed the ladies from the restaurant. They leaned forward, the looks on their faces daring her to say something about what they told her at dinner.

    "When I was a little girl, my grandmother brought both my brother and me to a church similar to this one. I'm so thankful that those memories we once shared with her were stirred in my heart. Pastor Jack, I've learned from the Bible class and from your teaching that we're supposed to love one another in spite of all things. I just want everyone to know that my brother and I love all of you. Please pray for him and me. I think that's it, Pastor Jack."

He embraced Mayah as she handed him the microphone. "Sister Johnson, we'll continue to pray for you and your brother and for God to keep a hedge of protection around you both as you continue your search for a church home. I want you to know that we're here for you. It's been a pleasure fellowshipping with the two of you."

The four ladies whispered to each other. Mayah could only guess at what they might be saying. Perhaps they thought she was leaving church because of them. Maybe not. It didn't matter. She knew the truth, and merely wanted to continue with her original plan of checking out all seven churches before making a decision.

Bible study ended and all the members, with the exception of those four ladies who were at the restaurant, said their farewells to Mayah. After embracing Pastor Jack again, she picked up her Bible and Coach purse and walked slowly toward the exit. She felt as if she was leaving a part of Nan, at least some of their church memories, there in that tiny, wonderful church. As she departed, she knew she'd always remember Pastor Jack and his warm spirit, and superb teaching.

The ladies from the restaurant approached her, but only Debbie spoke.

"Mayah, why are you leaving? Is it due to what was said at the restaurant?"

"Debbie, I was truly disappointed by what you all were saying about Pastor Jack. What if I had considered joining this church tonight? I could've changed my mind based upon what you all were saying. I just came back to church after being absent for years, and I never thought Christians could be so cruel and say such negative things about one another. But you know what, I was reading my grandmother's Bible, and I realize that everyone who proclaims to be a Christian don't always have Christianly ways. So, I'll be praying for you ladies. What you said was mean and unchristian-like. You should have love for your pastor, and if you don't, perhaps you need to be at another church."

"Mayah, you're right. We get so tired of the way Pastor Jack preaches at times," Betty said sadly.

"Then why are you here possibly poisoning others who might want to come?"

"I didn't think we were poisoning you. But please forgive us."

"No problem," Mayah said. "I do want you all to know that I *do* love you, and our leaving has nothing to do with you. I'm on a quest trying to find a church to join, and I have several others to visit before making a decision. I'm sorry if I appear to be so hard. That's really not who I am. Although I've only been in this church for a few weeks, I've grown very fond of the pastor. He reminds me a lot of my father, and like any daughter, when something negative is said about her father, she wants to defend him. Please forgive me for being so blunt. I realize that we all have issues and we don't always say and do the right thing. Hey, that's why Jesus had to die for us, huh?"

"Yeah, Mayah. We were talking among ourselves when you left the restaurant and regretted the remarks we made. We love Pastor Jack too. God has used you to open our eyes to some character deficiencies dwelling in us. It took you, a baby saint, to point them out. We love you and if God sends you back, we'll do right by you," Betty said.

She hugged all four of them and slowly walked to her car.

As Mayah drove home, she called Kyle.

"Hello."

"Hey, Kyle."

"Well, how did it go? Did you join?"

"No. I decided to wait until after we visit all seven churches before making a decision. Like I said before, what if I think I've found the right church and discover later it was the wrong one? But don't worry, brother, I'm taking notes on the church's strengths and weaknesses, my likes and dislikes about them, so I can make a conscious decision in the end. I really do like this church, Kyle. I really like Pastor Jack. He reminds me so much of Dad. I didn't like all the foolishness, but I like the church."

"Uh, I thought you liked this church and you would be staying." He sounded disappointed.

"I do like it. I'm really tired right now and I'm about to park. Let me call you on tomorrow and I'll advise you where we'll be on Sunday. Thanks again for going with me."

"No problem, sis," he said and let out a huge sigh. "I'll be ready when you get here on Sunday. Goodnight and love ya."

"Goodnight. I'll talk to you tomorrow."

Mayah arrived home and headed straight to her bedroom.

"Let me take my hungry self to sleep," she said as she got ready for bed. "I can't believe that I walked away from my meal—in fact, I walked away before it even arrived. I wonder if one of those ladies ate my salad." She laughed and jumped into the bed.

* * * *

Mayah awoke a couple seconds before the alarm clock went off. She showered, dressed, and rushed out to work. While at work, she called Kyle.

"Hello. This is Kyle Johnson. May I help you?"

"Hey, Kyle, it's me. Well the church that we'll be going to on Sunday is The Church of Righteousness. Their service starts at eleven o'clock."

"Wow, they sure start late. I rather enjoy going early because I have my whole day ahead of me after church. Eleven o'clock? So that means I might not return home until two or three o'clock?"

"Probably. I'll pick you up around ten-twenty."

"Alright, Mayah, I'll see you then."

Mayah was fond of the name of the next church, *The Church of Righteousness*. She could hardly wait for Sunday's arrival, as she knew it would be another blissful adventure in both her and Kyle's lives.

CHAPTER 9

"Oh my. It's time to get up for church, and I didn't even read my Bible this weekend. I guess I'll have to do make-up reading all this week," Mayah said as she yawned and attempted to get out of bed for the third time.

She stood to her feet and searched through her closets, pushing garments to the left and right, trying to locate something classy or real nice to wear. The church they'd be visiting that morning was in an upscale neighborhood with an abundance of influential people in attendance. She thought she'd better dress to fit into that church's environment.

Mayah frantically sifted through two of the closets in her apartment that housed her extensive collection of clothes and found the perfect outfit. Being fatigued, she decided to take a bubble bath instead of a shower, so she turned on the faucet to fill up the bathtub. She grabbed her favorite rose herbal bath products and poured them into the foaming bathwater. She stood still, inhaling the fragrance for a moment as the smell of rose petals permeated the bathroom. As she slid into the water, her muscles spontaneously relaxed.

She mused over the two previous churches they had visited, surmising that if she had to make an immediate assessment, more than likely, she would join The Church of Blessings with Pastor Jack. She felt a connection with him, as well as the church. That probably was because it brought back childhood church memories of Nan. The women chasing Kyle and their backbiting personalities annoyed her. Realizing only four or five women were involved and not the entire female population of the church, she'd be able to dismiss what they did. Also, even though this little church suffered undue persecution, due to Pastor Jack's messages regarding holiness, she felt she could even endure the persecution, should she join.

After soaking for about fifteen minutes, she knew if she lingered any longer, both she and Kyle would be late for church. Slowly, she lifted herself out of her rose spa, and began getting dressed; after which, she drove to Kyle's apartment. While driving, she called so as not to disturb his neighbors.

Kyle answered the telephone, and Mayah heard him yawn. "Hey, Mayah." He yawned again. "Give me about five minutes. I overslept."

"Okay."

She turned on the radio while she waited, and before long, Kyle appeared at the passenger side of the car. She noticed how terrible he looked.

"What's wrong with you?"

"Oh, I went out last night and I'm worn out and sleepy," he said as he yawned again.

"You look awful."

"Well thanks a lot, little sis, that's exactly what I need to hear this morning. Just drive to church, girl."

"Alright. Why don't you just recline the seat, lay your head back on the headrest, and I'll wake you up when we get close to the church. You have about fifteen minutes or so to snooze."

He laid his head back and fell asleep almost immediately.

As Mayah neared The Church of Righteousness, she was amazed at the perfectly manicured lawn, extensive and elaborate landscape work, and the breathtaking, enormous stucco and stone edifice. There were cars in the parking lot that people she knew could only dream about driving, let alone owning.

"Wake up, Kyle, we're here. This is a nice church."

Kyle rubbed his eyes, yawned, and stretched. "Girl, where are we?" he asked as he stepped out of the car and scrutinized his surroundings. "This church is something else. Look at all these

Bentley's, BMW's, Benz's, and Rolls' up in this lot. Where are we? I don't think I've ever been over here."

Mayah surveyed the area. "You're probably right. This entire area is full of professional, influential, high upper class people. I think Congressman Taylor is a member here."

"Oh, we're with the *elite* class, are we, sis? Or should I say the *uppity* folks today. Hmm."

"Kyle, be quiet and let's locate the entrance to this church. Oh, there it is."

"Wait, wait," he said as he grabbed hold of her arm, keeping his voice down so as not to draw attention.

"What's the matter?"

"How do I look, sis? You know I just might meet my next girl in here."

Mayah's jaw dropped. "Is that all you can think about? Didn't you learn anything from the last church? Ugh!"

As they approached the entrance, greeters stood outside opening the doors for everyone, greeting them, and shaking their hands.

"Girl, this is really ritzy," Kyle said, obviously impressed.

The ushers inside the foyer led them to the balcony that seated thousands; the sanctuary floor had already filled to capacity. As they walked up the balcony stairs, they were able to view the large, ten-thousand-seat main sanctuary, with rich deep purple padded pews. The two quickly found a seat in the large balcony. A gentleman stood behind the pulpit, speaking, and Mayah strained to hear every word because Kyle wouldn't shut up about this "high-class" church. Finally, the choir stood to sing.

> "Changing directions, Lord. Fixing my eyes upon You, Lord. Turning around, setting my affections on You."

The heavenly harmony of the humongous choir completely captivated Mayah, and the song's lyrics filled her soul with awe. The choir continued.

From Church to Church

"Seeking Your face each day. Back on the throne of my heart will You stay. I'm changing my focus, setting my heart towards You. Back on the throne of my heart will You stay. I've changed my focus today. Back on the throne of my heart will You stay. I've changed my focus today. I've changed my focus today."

Tears trickled down her cheeks. Trying to conceal the fact that she was crying, she postured herself so Kyle couldn't see her face. However, it was too late; his piercing stare and look of pure shock emanating from his face as she attempted to mask her tears, told her he had already seen them.

"Mayah, are you alright? What's wrong?" He whispered.

"Nothing. That song is so beautiful. We'll talk about it later in the car. Be quiet so people can hear," she said, attempting to compose herself.

That song was an eye-opener for Mayah. It related exactly what she was doing—changing her focus. She felt her friends and brother possibly couldn't grasp the internal transformation that was slowly occurring. However, she was pleased with what was transpiring inwardly.

The choir director approached the pulpit and spoke out in a smooth, masculine voice. "Saints, it's time for us to get our minds back on God. I know and I can see how God is really blessing us, but we need to bless Him too. Many of us have put so many other things on the throne of our hearts that we no longer have room for the Lord Jesus Christ. The Holy Spirit isn't even welcome in some of our temples. Some of us have even kicked Him out and replaced Him with idols—that is, things that can't even satisfy our spirits. We need to repent this morning for allowing *things* to take His place in our lives."

Mayah was stunned. She'd never heard anyone say anything like this before. This man was going to have her breakdown right here in church. For so many years, she'd been guilty of putting other things on the throne of her heart, just like he said. Warm tears streamed down her cheeks once again. As she patted her face dry with tissue removed from her purse, remnants of makeup stained the once white tissue. However, she continued to listen very intently.

"Church, what I want you to do right now is this; if you know that you've drifted away from the Lord and He's no longer on the throne of your heart, or if you know you need to change your focus and/or the direction you're headed, I need you to jump to your feet right now."

Instantaneously, Mayah leapt to her feet. She gave no thought to anyone or anything. She didn't even look to ascertain if Kyle had risen. Her utmost concern was how *she* had drifted far away from God and had permitted other things to take His place in her life.

The director invited those who were standing to repeat a prayer after him. "Lord, I repent today." He paused to allow the people to replicate his words. "For having the wrong mindset… I repent for having other gods before You… I realize that the throne of my heart… is reserved for You… and You alone."

At that juncture, all Mayah heard was a loud echo resounding in the atmosphere of the sanctuary as all those who were on their feet repeated the prayer. People sniffed, sobbed, confessed, and repented to God for taking Him off the throne of their hearts.

After everyone finished reciting the prayer, Mayah eased back into her seat and whispered to Kyle, "I feel so light—as if a heavy load or weight has been lifted off me." She exhaled and wiped the tears off her chin.

The director signaled the pastor to come and take the microphone. Pastor Bob leapt to his feet, swaying from side to side for about fifteen seconds. He opened his mouth, and in almost a whisper he gently said, "I feel like the text has already been taken today. Choir, I thank you. I thank you Brother Brian for leading us into the very throne room of God. I'd like to keep speaking from where we are right now."

From Church to Church

The pastor picked up where Brother Brian left off, and his tone grew louder and stronger as he spoke. He ministered about the congregants changing their focus and allowing God to take His proper place back on the throne of their hearts.

Mayah hung onto every word, and before she knew it, he finished and sat down. Due to thousands in attendance, the ushers passed the offertory baskets from row to row. After which, Pastor Bob made some additional comments about people attending Bible class on Wednesday night, and then dismissed church.

As Mayah and Kyle stepped downstairs, Kyle shook his head. "Girl, you almost had me crying up in here today."

"Shhh. Wait until we get inside the car and let's talk then."

"Okay, sis. It's some fine women up in *here*."

"Shhh."

As they were walking to the car, they noticed a man and woman on the side of the church building, embracing each other—well, not just embracing, but exchanging a brief kiss. She recalled the gentleman as being Minister McIntyre who was in the pulpit earlier.

Before pulling out of the parking lot, Mayah looked over at Kyle. "This was really a unique experience today. I don't think I've ever felt such intense emotions—ever. I feel as if I just took a bath and someone washed and scrubbed all of my insides—clean!"

"Really?"

"Yes, I can't describe how I feel. I just feel light and clean."

"Alright, Ms. Bubbles." Kyle laughed so hard he could hardly catch his breath.

"Go ahead and laugh. This is real. I can't wait to go to Bible class on Wednesday night. Do you want to come?"

"Nope." Kyle shook his head. "Remember, I'm only coming on Sundays."

"Alright. I feel so good right now; I won't even debate with you."

"That's good. I think I could get used to this church. They have a lot of things going on, and the women, the ladies—Oooo weee!"

"Kyle, didn't you hear what the director and the preacher said today? You need to change your focus and the direction that you're headed."

"I've already been preached to today—don't you start up."

Mayah giggled as did Kyle.

On the ride to her brother's apartment, they didn't speak. Mayah reflected on all that happened and was still experiencing the affects of that life-altering service. Realizing that something had transpired or changed in her inner most being, she didn't know how to articulate what she was experiencing. She simply knew she felt different—in a good way.

Mayah dropped Kyle off at his apartment and headed home, trying to recall the song and the sermon. She wondered if they taped everything on Sundays. If so, when she returned on Wednesday night, she would purchase the tape.

Words of the song permeated her mind, and she began singing one of the lines that so moved her. "I've changed my focus today." She kept singing that same line over and over until once again, tears gushed out of her eyes, streamed down her face, and dripped from her chin onto her clothes. She didn't even care who was watching as she drove down the public street.

When she arrived home, still in what she deemed a spiritual, euphoric state, she felt as if she was floating on clouds of marshmallows—all light and fluffy. She peeled off her clothes so as to get more comfortable. After putting on her favorite sweat suit, she exhaled repeatedly and sat down just to relive the service. Never in her life could she remember crying in public except the three occasions when her father, Pops, and Nan died. However, she did remember Nan crying in church numerous times.

She exhaled again. "God, I don't know what's happening to me or in me," she said aloud. "I only know that I'm starting to feel real good about some things and saddened by other things that I've allowed to transpire in my life. I'm devastated how I've put You and church on the back burner of my life for so many years." She sobbed. "I don't know why You would even love someone like me, but I truly believe that You do. I know I haven't been reading my Bible like I should, but if You can, please forgive me. I'll do better. I promise." She wiped tears from her eyes for the third time that day.

Startled by her phone ringing, she looked at the caller ID and saw that it was Tia. She let out a long sigh and questioned whether she wanted to deal with Tia right then. She contemplated not answering the phone, as she didn't want Tia to disturb what she was feeling. However, after a short debate within, she took a deep breath and answered the phone.

"Hello, Tia."

"Hey, Mayah. What's up?"

"Nothing much, and then again—everything," she couldn't contain her excitement.

"What do you mean by that?"

Mayah sat down on her bed, as she knew this conversation could probably go on for quite some time.

"Well, I know you don't want to hear about all my church stuff, but I need to tell you what happened to me today. I mean, let me tell you the part that I understand, because there's some things that I don't even comprehend right now."

"Okay, Mayah. Give me the four-one-one."

"Well, girl, this is what happened. I was at church and this choir was singing, and all of a sudden, I just started crying. I don't know why, but tears started flowing down my cheeks."

"You were crying?" she asked as if she was unable to believe what she had just heard.

"Yes, me crying, and in public. I know that's a real shock, isn't it? But, it was more than that. It was as if each tear that fell scrubbed and cleansed my entire insides from all the dirt or debris that had accumulated over the years."

"I wish I could pretend to understand what you're talking about, but I can't. I can't even envision what you're saying. So, this scrubbing thing, did it hurt?"

"No, Tia," Mayah tittered. "It didn't hurt in terms of real human pain, but it hurt when I realized I really had some negative issues going on inside of me that I was totally unaware of. Just like the lyrics that I heard this morning, it caused me to recognize that I've been focused on too many unimportant things and not on God. I had become 'Ms. Corporate America' chasing the mighty dollar and prestige. I think that's what was scrubbed out of me today—my focus on self-ambition, self this, self that, and personal image. From what transpired, I believe I'm becoming a cured workaholic and self-aholic. That's the best way I can describe what I'm feeling."

"So, are you saying that you aren't interested in promotions and all the perks that go along with your job?"

"No," Mayah scratched her head. "That's not what I'm saying. I guess I no longer feel that I have to spend my entire life at work, trying to impress folks and climbing up the corporate ladder. Nor do I have to make work my life. I used to put in fifty to sixty hours or more a week. I would even go in on weekends, but that's not what I plan on doing in the near future. I'm going to do my forty, and if needed, I might do an extra hour here and there, but I'm going to make room for church and God in my life."

"So, how long is this phase going to last? Do you really—"

"Hold on, Tia. I don't believe this is a phase. I know in my heart this is something I want to do and something that's needed. I also know, at least now I know, I was placing my career before God and everything else. One of the preachers asked, 'If you were to die today, what natural thing or things that you've placed all your focus on or that you've made an idol in your life could you take with you?' Then he asked, 'And if you died today, where do you think your

From Church to Church

spirit will go—to heaven or hell?' Lastly, he asked, 'And why do you believe your spirit would rest there?' I really had to—"

"Wait a minute, Mayah. Spirit? Soul? I don't know the difference between the two."

"That's why you need to come with me and Kyle to church on Sundays, or if you like, you can come with me to Bible class during the week; that way, it won't interfere with your weekends."

Tia took an extremely long pause.

"Hello. Tia, are you still here?"

"Yes. I'm here. I was just thinking about what you said. Let me think about it and I'll let you know."

"Fair enough. Look, I need to get back to my reading. Can we pick up this conversation at a later date?"

"That's fine, Mayah. We'll talk about this later. Seems like that's all we do now is talk on the phone because you're always going to church."

"I know. But we'll get together soon. I love you."

"I love you too."

She took a moment to reflect on their conversation. Tia was thinking about what she'd said. But what had she really said? Mayah felt she didn't understand much; however, she was going to study so she could help Tia, Kyle, herself, and perhaps even her mother.

Then she had another "aha" moment. Tia didn't reject the idea of attending church as she had done previously. This time she said she would think about it. That's progress!

CHAPTER 10

Mayah cleared off her desk, trying to get out of the office so she could attend Bible class. She knew she had better hurry so as not to be late. At first, she wondered if she should call Tia, but decided to wait until after attending her first Bible class.

Realizing she wouldn't have sufficient time to drive home, prepare a meal, and arrive on time for class, she stopped at a restaurant on the way to church. As she entered the restaurant, she recognized the couple who were all lovey-dovey in the church parking lot that past Sunday. As she approached the booth where they were seated, she greeted them.

"Hello. How are you two?"

"We are just fine," Minister McIntyre responded, eyeing her suspiciously.

"I think I saw you two this past Sunday at The Church of Righteousness," she explained, realizing many people see her as overly friendly.

"Where did you see us?" he asked in a quizzical tone.

"In the parking lot on the far side of the church building."

Both his and the woman's eyes resembled those of owls.

"I got to go," the woman hastily said to the man.

"No, no." Mayah said, shaking her head. "You don't have to leave on my account."

"Oh no, I need to prepare myself for service." The woman said.

Minister McIntyre also stood up to leave.

They all said their goodbyes and the waiter sat Mayah at her own table. She wondered what was up with that couple. They hastily got up from the table, leaving the majority of their food in their plates.

From Church to Church

Additionally, Minister McIntyre had to run back to the table and grab the car keys he'd left behind.

Mayah ordered her meal and reflected on the goodness of God. She so desired to alter her focus and set her affections on Him. Her food arrived; she finished her meal and drove to church. Upon her arrival, the friendly greeters were back at their posts. They shook her hand and ushered her into the sanctuary, this time on the main floor.

Being seated on the main floor gave Mayah a different perspective. She'd get a better look at the pastor's face too. There weren't as many people in the church tonight as there were on Sunday morning.

Shortly after taking her seat, the worship team took their place on the massive stage, posturing themselves to sing their first song. The worship leader walked up to the podium.

"How many of you have made Jesus Lord of your life?" he asked. "How many are willing to make that declaration if you're on the mountaintop or in the valley? How many recognize that He is still Lord even during times of trials or when adversity strikes?"

The church responded with "Amen," and others were raising and waving their hands, as he queried them.

"Okay. Let's all stand to our feet and declare His Lordship on tonight."

They put the song upon three, huge overhead screens, and the worship team began singing.

> "Shout it from the mountaintop. Shout it from the valley low. Shout it everywhere you go, that Jesus Christ is Lord. Jesus, awesome and mighty Jesus. Jesus, Jesus Christ is Lord."

Although she was not a public singer, Mayah could hit notes with the best of them. As a child, Nan would periodically have her sing a solo in church, and the people loved her singing. She had a well-tuned, angelic voice. Mayah remembered this song from a previous church, and joined in with the congregation, singing with great confidence.

> "He is Lord. He is Lord. Jesus Christ is Lord. He is Lord. He is Lord. Shout it everywhere you go, that Jesus Christ is Lord. Jesus."

When the singing subsided, Pastor Bob approached the pulpit. He was a giant of a man, neatly dressed, and very articulate. He made a few announcements, and invited Minister McIntyre to come forth and teach the lesson for the night. Mayah recognized Minister McIntyre as the man she met at the restaurant and the same man she saw after Sunday morning's service all lovey-dovey with his wife.

Minister McIntyre slowly approached the podium, carefully lifted the microphone off the stand, and asked his wife, who was seated on the front row of the church pews, to please stand and greet the people.

The lady who stood up was not the woman Mayah saw him with in the parking lot or in the restaurant. *If this is his wife, then who is that other woman that I've seen him with?*

In a smooth, baritone voice, Minister McIntyre commenced teaching. "Tonight I want to talk about *How To Live Without Compromise*."

"What? Living without compromise? If who I thought he was with was not his wife, then how can he tell others how to live without compromise, as it seems he and that lady have something going on? Maybe it's his sister or another relative." Mayah mulled over the incident behind the building, and she also reflected on the two of them sitting in the restaurant and how familiar they were with each other. No, she couldn't be his sister, which left her more confused.

He had already begun teaching, and Mayah missed his introduction because she was distracted and extremely disturbed about how he could be ministering on *How To Live Without Compromise* while it appeared his life was full of compromise. As

From Church to Church

she regained control of her thoughts, she tuned in to what he said next.

"Don't you know God will give us the ability to overcome and thwart off anything and everything unlike Him? Don't you know that for every temptation, a way of escape has already been made? Turn your Bibles to 1 Corinthians 10:13."

Mayah heard Bible pages turning as the people located the scripture.

"My brothers and my sisters, the scripture alone lets us know that no matter what situation we find ourselves in, God will not allow us to be tempted above human resistance—we can resist! The Bible states we're to submit ourselves to God and resist the devil..."

At this juncture, someone could have driven a Mack truck through Mayah's mouth. She didn't want to make any assumptions. Maybe the woman was his sister or another relative or something. Perhaps what she thought she saw was innocent. *But why did they both want to vacate that restaurant when I told them that I saw them in the parking lot on that past Sunday?* She shook herself and attempted to refocus, but Minister McIntyre concluded his teaching. The pastor stood, and most of the congregants stood, cheering, and applauding Minister McIntyre for such a great message.

Mayah must have gotten everything wrong about him. She decided to put that situation out of her mind, as it wasn't her business anyway.

The worship team gracefully returned to the platform and began singing a very slow tempo song.

> "In Your presence, Lord, is where I long to be. In Your presence, Lord, is where I want to be. Basking and dwelling and just loving You. I'm determined, Lord, to always be with You."

The pastor extended an invitation to anyone who desired to become a new member. No one approached the altar; therefore, church was over.

Mayah berated herself because she probably missed half of the teaching that night as she dwelt on something that wasn't even her business. She figured she'd just wait until Sunday to talk to Kyle about class and she wouldn't say very much to him about what she thought was going on. She'd just leave it alone. On her way out, she noticed the tape nook was open, so she stopped by and purchased Sunday morning's message as well as the singing tapes.

* * * *

Over the next few days, Mayah didn't want to reflect on Minister McIntyre and the other lady, but she couldn't help herself. Almost every time her mind went idle, she focused on them all the more.

On Friday night, Mayah decided to go across town to visit Tia. While driving down Peachtree Blvd., in a very secluded part of town, she saw Minister McIntyre and that woman holding hands. She was livid and acutely aware that they were involved with each other, at least in some capacity. In fact, judging the appearance of things, they were real close, and this ticked her off.

How could this man tell her anything? How could he be in the pulpit one moment teaching the Bible and later on cheating on his wife? That was scandalous and disgraceful. She felt so sorry for his wife, who possibly had no knowledge of his affair.

Agitated and upset by their actions, instead of surprising Tia with a visit, she decided to park her car and casually approach him and the woman. She wanted to let them know that she saw them and knew what was going on. After parking her car, she quickly walked down Peachtree Blvd. It took her a moment, but she found them, laughing and holding hands.

Mayah made eye contact with Minister McIntyre as she drew near. His eyes were bulging out of his head. Quickly he turned to his female companion and they abruptly let go of each other's hands.

Mayah hoped they didn't think she was stalking them as she approached them.

"Hello, you two. I just seem to keep bumping into you. Who would've thought our paths would cross on tonight and in this part of town?" she said somewhat sarcastically.

Brother McIntyre managed to force something out of his mouth. "How are you doing, young lady? Yes, it seems we travel to some of the same places."

He then turned to the somewhat jumpy, older woman accompanying him. "Brenda, you remember this young lady from the restaurant, right? She just started attending our church."

Brenda nervously responded. "Yes, and how are you, dear?"

"I'm terrific," Mayah said, smiling, though she didn't feel like it. "Minister McIntyre, I was so inspired by your teaching the other night. Let me see if I remember your title. Hmmm, Oh yeah, 'How To Live Without Compromise.' I must admit, sometime I find that rather hard to do, but I'm trying to live that way. I guess we all are, huh? Well, I'll see you two on Sunday."

"Yes, young lady, we'll see you on Sunday," he responded as perspiration slowly beaded upon his brow and dripped down his face.

Mayah's sudden unwelcomed appearance must have ruined their evening, because when she turned back to take one last look at them, they both were heading toward different cars. She could only presume they were going home to their respective spouses.

Mayah was highly upset. She forgot about going to see Tia and headed home, unable to shake the vision of them having an affair. In spite of what she read in the newspapers, she didn't want to believe this type of thing really happened in church, especially not in the church that she was attending. This cheating man was a Bible teacher, and she still didn't know who Brenda was.

Did the pastor know what was going on? If he found out, would he be the kind of man who would do something about it, or would he turn his head the other way? Such questions were important enough to make a difference on whether or not Mayah decided to become a member of their church.

CHAPTER 11

Saturday breezed right on by, and before she knew it, Sunday morning had dawned bright and warm. Mayah leapt out of bed. She dashed to get dressed. Although it was really none of her business, she wanted to know what was going on in this church, and she wondered if Brenda was also married.

She left her apartment and telephoned Kyle, alerting him that she was five minutes away. He promised to be ready. She arrived and Kyle hopped into the car.

"Hey, Sis, what's up? I haven't heard from you but once this week. What's his name?"

"What do you mean, 'what's his name?' I'm not involved with anyone. I've been doing a lot of Bible reading and just going over some things that was said and occurred in church last week."

"Oh, I forgot to ask you about Bible class. How did it go?"

Trying not to reveal any of her suspicions, she had to really think how to respond. "Well, Bible study was okay. The teacher said a lot."

"What did he talk about?"

Becoming frustrated by all of Kyle's questions, as well as that affair, Mayah blurted out, "Why are you so interested in Bible class? If you want to know what's going on or what's being taught, you need to attend and quit interrogating or cross-examining me!"

Scratching his head and looking at Mayah in total shock, Kyle asked, "Did someone get up on the wrong side of the bed this morning?"

"No. I'm just saying if you're that interested in what's going on, you need to attend Bible class, that's all," she said as she calmed down.

"Okay, sis." He still had a strange look on his face, and she knew he was attempting to figure out what was really bothering her. Well, she wouldn't give him the satisfaction. If he wanted to know what goes on at church, he can just come and find out for himself.

They arrived at church, and once again, the parking lot was arrayed with luxury automobiles. Kyle's expression perked up.

"Hey, Mayah, one of these days, I'm going to get me one of those," he said as he pointed to a Bentley.

"That's good, Kyle. You already have a nice car, a BMW. Materialism isn't everything."

"Yeah. I have a five series; these in this lot are seven series. I know materialism isn't everything, but it sure makes life a whole lot easier, huh?"

"I guess."

The greeters met them at the door, and the moment they stepped inside, Mayah saw Brenda with some man. Her husband, maybe?

Brenda saw Mayah looking in her direction and turned her back toward her, but Mayah walked straight up to her.

"Hello, Brenda. How are you this morning?"

"Oh, hi." She hesitated for a moment. "I'm sorry, but I don't think you ever told me your name."

"It's Mayah. Mayah Johnson."

"It's good to formally meet you, Mayah Johnson. This is my husband, Bill."

Mayah wrestled within herself trying to keep her composure. "Hello, Bill. It's nice to meet you."

"It's good to meet you too, Ms. Johnson," he said, extending his hand out to her. "How do you and my wife know each other? Do you work together?"

"Oh no, sir. I met her here at church."

"Well, that's wonderful. There's nothing like having Christian friends."

From Church to Church

Mayah stared at Bill. She wanted to say, "Friends? By no means am I her friend." But she didn't; she just nodded her head and walked away slowly.

This time, Kyle and Mayah were led to the ground floor and they took a seat near the middle. Service started, and the worship leader spoke to the congregation. "I would like to teach you a new song this morning. Is that alright, church?"

The church went up in a roar, "Yes, teach us a new song. Go ahead," they shouted.

"Alright, put the words on the screens. We'll sing it through a couple of times, and then I want you to join in with us." The musicians played a tune with a lively, Latin-influenced beat. Then, the worship team sang out with strong voices.

> "We celebrate You Lord. We celebrate Your power. We celebrate Your love. We celebrate Your presence. We rejoice, Lord, in You. We rejoice, Lord, in You."

The leader shouted out, "Let's sing that part a couple more times," and they did. "Okay there is one more part to the song."

> "For this is the day the Lord has made, and we celebrate You, Lord. For You are worthy of honor, glory, and praise, and we will rejoice in You. We celebrate You, Lord."

Charged by the response of the people, he had them sing the song over and over again.

"I wish he'd sing something else. I'm about bored to death," Kyle said as he leaned over to Mayah.

"Can't you see how excited the people are when singing this song? Why don't you just get with the program and sing?" Mayah said in a low voice.

The song ended and the team sang two additional songs. However, when they got to their last song, after hearing just a few lines, Mayah was back in tears.

> "There are no words that could declare how much I love You. There's no tune, no melody within me. There is no

song that's pure enough to say how I truly feel. For the love I have is best expressed, by my spirit man. And in the spirit this is what can be heard. La la la... I love You. La la la... I do. La la la... I love You. My spirit's saying how I truly feel."

They sang that little tune repeatedly until weeping resounded throughout the sanctuary, and Mayah Johnson was one of those sobbing like a baby. She questioned God as to what was happening to her; why couldn't she stop crying? Once again, Kyle just stared at her and offered no conversation.

The well-dressed pastor arose and spoke while the worship team sung softly. "Church, you should all be grateful to God for how He's blessing you. He has truly allowed you to be prosperous. You have fine cars, extravagant houses, good paying jobs, etc. We have a wonderful edifice here with the best soundboard that money can buy, excellent equipment. We have the best musicians, singers, and preachers, some of the best tithers, and many members don't have to want for anything. We have the personal support of our community. Some of you don't even have to work because your spouse, partner, or significant other has blessed you so you can remain at home."

Mayah's tears immediately halted. She sensed something was wrong—significant others or partners? What was that all about?"

She stared at Kyle and whispered, "We need to talk in the car after church."

When the service concluded, Mayah grabbed Kyle's arm, nearly dragging him out to the car.

"Slow down, girl." He looked at her. "What's wrong with you?"

After taking several steps in the direction of the car, she responded. "Kyle, what did he mean when he said, significant others or partners? I know what we mean when we use that terminology, but what does the church mean?"

He shrugged his shoulders as he responded. "I don't know, Mayah. I don't know what he meant when he said that."

From Church to Church

"So, do you think people are shacking up in the church or involved in alternative lifestyles?"

"I don't know, Mayah. You need to ask someone who knows."

"Alright, when I get to work on tomorrow, I'm going to ask Lesley. She's a Christian. In fact, her church is on the list of churches we'll be attending."

"That's good, because I don't have a clue about what he meant."

Mayah pulled up in front of Kyle's house, dropped him off, and headed home. She still couldn't get over the last few remarks the pastor made. She entered her apartment and quickly threw down her keys, kicked off her shoes, and located her work directory for her Department. She found Lesley's number and called her.

"Praise the Lord," said the sweet, feminine voice on the other end of the phone.

"Hi, Lesley, this is Mayah from work."

"Hi, Mayah. Is there something wrong at work?"

"Oh, no. I know you're a Christian, and I need to ask you a few questions, if you have a moment."

"No problem; I have plenty of time. I hope I can answer them for you. What's on your mind?"

"I was visiting a church today, and the pastor said something that caught my attention. In fact, I was rather disturbed by his statement, and you're the only one I thought to call."

"What did he say?"

"He said that God was blessing some of the church members so that their spouses, partners, or significant others didn't have to work."

"*What?*"

"That's what I thought. What did he mean by that? I know how we use that terminology, and I want to make sure he isn't saying what I think he's saying."

"It means pretty much the same thing in the church and in the world."

"Why would the pastor say something like that, Lesley?"

"Let me ask you this before I answer your question; what church were you at?"

"The Church of Righteousness."

"Oh."

"What did you mean by that?"

"Well, I've been told that they have thousands of members, but their church is where there's a lot of satanic activity. A lot of the world's practices and standards have infiltrated that church. It all started when a couple of congressional representatives and high city officials joined. They were heavy tithers. After they became members, hundreds of other six-figure income people came, and little by little, the pastor began compromising the Word of God so as to keep them in attendance. There are multimillionaires in that church, but a lot of them are caught up in sin, and supposedly, no one's correcting them. Please understand that I'm not trying to put that church down as I hear they have awesome worship and a lot of the teaching is Bible-based; but you just have to be cautious about taking everything into your spirit as the gospel. If something sounds strange, you need to research it in the Bible or call someone who can point you to the scripture."

"Oh my, Lesley."

"Mayah, it started with a little compromise here and there. Now, get me right, there are many, perhaps thousands, of people living right in that church. It's just that some of their teaching has been compromised so as not to lose those who are financing that church's vision."

"It all makes sense now. I saw some things and wondered if the pastor knew what was happening. Lesley, I think I mentioned to you that I was looking for a church to attend. I have four other churches that I'll be visiting, one of which is yours."

"That's great. But what you need to realize is there's no perfect church. I'm glad that you're out there spying out the land before you join a church. However, every church that you'll attend will have some flaws. But you need to know this, if you have any questions about God or Christianity, I may not have all the answers, but I know enough Christians who I can call, and they can direct me to where the answers can be found in the Bible."

"Lesley," Mayah said with a long sigh of relief. "I'm so glad that you said that. I have so many questions. I really don't have anyone to call. So it'll be okay if I call you sometime?"

"Yes. You can call me anytime. Incidentally, I don't know what you do on your lunch hour, but we can even have Bible study during our lunch break, if you like, and you can ask me questions at that time too."

Mayah began sobbing. "You just don't know what this means to me. I've heard so much church terminology that I don't understand, and I'd love to study with you at lunchtime."

"Wonderful. When do you want to start?"

Mayah's tears dried and with a huge smile on her face, she replied, "Is tomorrow too soon? I must warn you. I have a lot of questions."

"That works for me. Meet me outside at the lunch tables at a quarter to twelve and we'll have Bible study. Why don't we just bring a bag lunch so we won't have to waste time going to grab something?"

"Ok. I'll meet you at a quarter to twelve. I'm so excited!"

"Alright, see you tomorrow, Mayah."

"Thanks for talking to me."

"No problem."

Mayah gently laid the telephone receiver down and communed with God. The words flowed out of her mouth without any thought. "Oh God, I'm so happy that You've given me someone who can help me understand a lot of things pertaining to You, the Bible, and church. I'm so grateful for Lesley agreeing to study with me. Thank you, God. You've already answered one of my prayers."

She retreated to her bedroom, crawled into the bed, and immediately fell asleep. However, because she fell asleep so early in the day, she awakened in the middle of the night and later drifted back to sleep. Before she knew it, it was time to get up for work.

Although her sleep was broken, she sensed a terrific day in the making, as she would be having Bible study with Lesley. She sat up in bed for a moment, and then jumped up to her feet and rushed downstairs to the kitchen to prepare some coffee as well as her lunch. She ran back upstairs to her bedroom to retrieve Nan's Bible and placed it on the kitchen table so she wouldn't forget it. She thought about Nan and reflected on some of the past treasured moments they once shared. Nan was an excellent example of a Christian woman. Mayah prayed that her new life and aspirations would be something that would've made Nan proud.

While at work that day, her attention span wasn't the greatest as she paid more attention to the clock than her workload. When eleven-thirty came, she hastened to get to the lunch tables in anticipation of her meeting with Lesley. It was incredible to have someone finally answer some of the questions that were burning in her heart.

"Hi, Mayah, you're early. You must really have some pressing questions to ask." Lesley said. "Okay. What do you want to know? I pray I can help you. If I can't, like I said previously, I'll get the answers for you."

"I heard a man sing a song which described how he *thirsts* for God. Could you please enlighten me on how one thirst for God? I know what it means to thirst for water, but not for a person, let alone God."

"Mayah, what the man was singing about is having a strong, unrelenting desire, a craving, hunger, or a longing for God. He yearns for God. Just like you get thirsty and crave water, that's the way he feels about God. He craves Him. That's what he was saying.

From Church to Church

"Whoa. That's deep. That makes sense. I didn't think of it that way. Have you heard the song before?"

"Yes, I have the CD. The song also relates that nothing can satisfy that thirst, craving, or longing—but God. There's absolutely nothing that can satisfy the spirit of man but God. God created us that way. Now, when it comes to our flesh, if you're hungry you feed your body. Every day, someone attempts to fill a craving in their spirit with something other than God, and that's called an 'idol' because it comes before God. But it'll never satisfy the craving in their spirit; only God can."

"Lesley, that's really good. I know in the past I've tried a few things to satisfy my thirst per se, but now I want to do it the correct way."

"Mayah, I have a question to ask you. Are you a Christian? I mean, have you accepted Jesus Christ as your Lord and Savior? Are you born again or have you ever been baptized?"

"Honestly, I haven't been in church since I was a young girl. My grandmother used to take my brother Kyle and me. However, when she died, we stopped going. I don't remember what was really going on because I was so young."

"Do you know what it means to accept Jesus as your Lord and Savior?"

"I guess," Mayah responded, with uncertainty.

"Okay. Let me explain it to you. Can you write these scriptures down: John 3:16; Romans 10:9-11; 1 John 1:7; Revelation 1:5-6; Romans 6:23; Isaiah 53:6; Jeremiah 17:9; and Romans 3:10-12. What I want you to do is study them tonight, and we can meet up again on tomorrow, if that's okay with you."

"Yes, that's fine. I'll be more than happy to meet with you on tomorrow. This is so exciting. I've never had a real Bible study like this. I've attended several Bible classes during these last few weeks, but this is an intimate setting, a one-on-one, and I think I'm really going to like it. Thank you, Lesley."

"There's no question that you can't ask me. I need to change something; I don't want to meet with you tomorrow. I want to meet with you Wednesday. The reason being, I want you to really meditate on these scriptures and write down what they mean to you. Can you do that?"

"I sure can. That's really a good idea. But can I ask you another question?"

"Sure."

"Once in church, or maybe a few times, I had to fight back some of my emotions, but here lately, when certain songs are being sung, tears just trickle down my face. I don't really understand that. It's as if I have no control over my tear ducts. Why is that?"

Lesley gave her several reasons why she's been bombarded with tears. She told her the words of the message or the songs might have awakened something in her spirit. Then she told her God might be dealing with her and opening up her understanding of where she was and how near she has come to Him. The next point Lesley made was that Mayah was experiencing the peace, joy, comfort, and love of God while the songs were being sung, and her response was a love response to Him. And lastly, she mentioned that the tears could be a result of sin and/or guilt over certain things that she had said or done, and now perhaps Mayah was not only remorseful, but was experiencing Godly sorrow.

"Mayah, you need to repent for all the sins of your past. I don't think I can wait until Wednesday. Do you want to accept Jesus Christ as your Lord and Savior right now? No one knows the day or the hour that they'll die. I don't think you'll die before Wednesday," she said as she smiled.

Lesley then explained exactly what it meant to accept Christ as her Savior. She had Mayah open her Bible and turn to Romans 10:9-11 and then John 3:16. Lesley then expounded upon the *Four Spiritual Laws* from a pamphlet that was tucked inside her Bible.

After she finished, she led Mayah in a prayer of repentance and Mayah accepted Christ that day as her Savior as they sat at the lunch table at work. Mayah once thought she had to be inside a church in order to receive Christ, but Lesley quickly cleared up that fallacy.

"Wow, Lesley. Is it that simple? All I had to do is believe, repent, say those words, and I'm saved?"

"Yes. Christ has already done all the work. All we have to do is confess our sins, and simply say 'yes' as we totally surrender to Him, and live in accordance to God's holy Word. We'll make mistakes and we'll even mess up, but the forgiveness of God is there. Romans 3: 23 states, we all have sinned and have fallen short of God's glory. Salvation makes us sin 'less' as our lives are transformed, especially when we're converted and filled. We'll talk about those things later because I don't want to overwhelm you with so much data. But let me say this, when we do mess up, we have to ask for forgiveness, and repent for our sin—that is, for whatever we've said, done and/or thought. You see, sometimes we sin with our thoughts. Our thought-life has to be kept in check; otherwise, negative thoughts will eventually enter into our hearts, and we'll begin to either act on them or speak them.

"Repentance means we change our direction, and literally do a complete turnaround and change our mindset and see sin as Christ and the Bible outlines it. If we repeatedly do the same act, after we say we've repented, that means we never totally turned away from that sin. We just feel guilty or sorry for the act. Mayah, we'll touch on these things in detail a little later. Let me stop here for today. But the important and fantastic thing is this; you've accepted Christ as your Lord and Savior. Praise God!"

The two returned to their desks. Mayah had that "light" feeling again. She couldn't remember if and when she had ever felt that good. The gift of salvation was greater than any gift she had ever received—greater than any promotion, bonus, material thing, or any man. She resolved not to call Kyle until she was at home. Mayah could hardly wait to hear his response.

Upon getting home from work, she quickly called Kyle, the somewhat reluctant participant in her church search.

"Hello."

"Hey, Kyle. I have some exciting news to tell you."

"Please, tell me that you've found a church," he said.

"No, I haven't found a church, but I found something greater—salvation. I got saved today at work."

"You got what?"

"Saved. I'm a Christian. I called Lesley after I dropped you off, and she and I had Bible study at lunch today. She led me to Christ and I'm saved."

"That's wonderful, Mayah." His pause let her know he was trying to process all this. "Have you thought about joining one of the churches yet?"

"Aren't you excited for me?" His lack of enthusiasm didn't surprise her. He told her from the start he'd be moral support for her in her search, but that was all. "Is that all you can think about—whether or not I've found a church? No, I haven't. Remember, I told you that I wanted to wait until I attended all seven of them. Are you tired of going with me?"

"Not really. I just want you to hurry up and find something especially since you're *saved* now," he chuckled.

"Kyle, this is serious. I don't know what that laugh is all about, but I'm serious about what I'm doing, and if you think this is all fun and games, you don't have to go to any more churches with me. I can go by myself," she blurted out.

"Hold on, little sis. I'm sorry. I wasn't trying to make fun of you. I gave you my word, and I'll hang in there until you've gone to the last church—that is, the last service at the last church. I'm sorry. I didn't mean to sound so flippant. You forgive me, right?"

"You know I do. I know this is not a priority for you, and the timing seems to be a little off for you, since it's football season; however, I do really appreciate the sacrifice that you're making. I think Nan would be so pleased that we're going to church together, don't you?"

"Yeah, I think she's probably jumping up and down, dancing in heaven because you got saved today." He laughed. "Now, before you ask me your next question, let me answer it, 'no' I'm not ready to get saved, so don't ask me. I'm having too much fun right now in my life, well, at least I used to have a whole lot of fun on the weekends, but we don't have too much longer to go. I just agreed to go on this church search thing with you and that's it. Don't push it."

"I wasn't going to ask you anything. I just wanted you to know that I love you, and I appreciate you taking time out of your life to go to church with me and that's it," she said softly.

"There you go, getting all mushy again. I love you too. I'll see you on Sunday."

"Bye for now."

Although Mayah was in high spirits about her life, she was somewhat saddened over Kyle not wanting to get saved or go to Bible study on Wednesday nights, so she began praying aloud. "God, I love my brother and I know You love him more. My desire is for him to get saved and change his life. It's not that he's a bad person; he'll do anything for almost anyone. He simply has some habits, as did I, that he needs to abandon. Can You please talk to him and let him know how much You love him? I'm not sure he really understands. Thank you God. Oh yeah, and I love You." She wiped the tears away from her chin and eyes.

CHAPTER 12

As Mayah drove to church for Bible study that Wednesday, she thought about what might take place tonight. *I sure hope Minister McIntyre isn't teaching tonight. It's distracting and difficult for me to listen to him because I know he and Brenda are messing around.*

The greeters met her as she entered the foyer, and the ushers led her to a seat on the main floor. She was amazed at how few people attended Bible study during the week, which seemed to be a common occurrence at all the churches she had previously visited.

As Mayah took her seat, a woman walked the floor in front of the altar with a microphone in hand, praying aloud prior to Bible study. Mayah listened intently to the words of her prayer. She hadn't heard anyone pray like her before. She prayed with such force and power. Mayah wondered how long she'd been in this church and how many years she'd been praying.

Shortly, Pastor Bob stepped up to the podium with a heartrending look on his face. He took a deep breath and said, "I'd like for you all to be patient for a moment. Minister McIntyre has something to say to the congregation."

Mayah's palms were sweating, and she felt a bit uneasy about what he might have to say.

Minister McIntyre stood and nervously took the microphone from Pastor Bob. He kept fidgeting with the microphone as though he thought it was malfunctioning or something. He cleared his throat and then spoke.

"My sisters and my brothers, I'm standing here repenting to all of you as well as to my wife, who I have already spoken to this afternoon. I haven't been the best husband one could be."

From Church to Church

Mayah could hardly believe her ears. Was he actually about to confess his sins before the congregation?

"I've made some serious mistakes. God has been dealing with me for quite some time now. However, I refused on numerous occasions to listen to Him. Well, He really got my attention last night. I was up all night. God began telling and showing me my life and the things that He was and wasn't pleased with in terms of my Christian walk. Like I said, I've already repented to my wife, and now I'm asking the church for forgiveness. I've also spoken with Pastor Bob and have decided to take a seat in the congregation until God releases me to minister again. I also want to apologize if I've been a stumbling block in anyone's way. Please forgive me."

Tears were flowing down the cheeks of many and some whispered among themselves. Mayah felt great remorse for the numerous negative thoughts and comments she had mentally launched against him. Even she was crying. Through her tears, she thought what courage it took for him to tell his wife as well as Pastor Bob and the congregation that he had done wrong. She didn't know if she'd ever have the courage to stand up and tell an entire church that God wasn't pleased with her.

After Minister McIntyre concluded his apology to the church, Pastor Bob embraced him and took the microphone. "There will be no Bible study on tonight. In lieu of class, I want to have an altar call. If you're aware that you're not living right or doing what God has called you to do, please make your way down to this altar, repent to God, and get free. It's *nobody's* business what you've done; that's between *you* and God."

One by one, people gently eased out of their seats and approached the altar; in the midst of that long caravan of people was Mayah. She felt convicted of some things, one of them being her attitude toward Minister McIntyre.

As the people gathered at the altar, they promptly knelt, covered their faces, and sobbed. Mayah knelt as well and started praying under her breath. "God, once again I'm sorry for all the wrongs that I've done in my life. I'm relatively a good person, but my thoughts and actions haven't always been pure. Even tonight, when Minister McIntyre arose from his seat, my first thought was, 'He can't tell me a thing,' but I was so wrong. I learned a lot from him on tonight. It took so much courage for him to do what he did. I'm sorry that I judged him." She then recalled what Lesley had previously told her; she had to guard her thought life. She now comprehended exactly what she meant.

About an hour or so later, people dismissed themselves from the altar. They gathered their personal belongings and quietly left the sanctuary. Mayah also arose and was in the process of walking toward her seat to get her belongings when suddenly Minister McIntyre approached her and asked if he could see her outside in the foyer. She agreed.

After clearing his throat numerous times, he was able to speak. "Young lady, I need to apologize to you."

"Apologize to me?" He'd caught her off guard. "I don't understand, Minister McIntyre."

"I'm sorry. I can't think of your name right now, but I do know you by your face."

"My name is Mayah Johnson, sir."

"Ms. Johnson, I'm sorry that I wasn't a good example for you and you know what I mean. I have repented to God, my wife, the pastor, the church, and now I want to personally repent to you. You're a new saint and I could've been a stumbling block in your way. I could've caused you to turn your back on the church and God, and for that, I'm sorry. There's a lot I could say. I could even attempt to justify what I was doing, but there's no justification for sin. Can you please forgive me, Ms. Johnson?"

"Yes, sir. I can and do forgive you. I need to ask your forgiveness too, because I've made some negative remarks about you in my heart."

Minister McIntyre shook Mayah's hand and said, "God has forgiven you. I hope you'll return to this church on Sunday."

"No, sir. I won't be back on Sunday." Mayah dropped her head. "You see, I've been on a quest to find the perfect church for me. I have seven churches that I'm visiting. I'm only spending two weeks at each one, and this would be the end of my two weeks here."

"Ms. Johnson, I pray that nothing I did will deter you from returning to this church or from joining it."

"Minister McIntyre, I don't know what church I'll be joining at the end of my quest. However, because of what you did tonight as well as others in this church, I haven't written this church off my list. I'm so glad you took the time to come and speak to me. You're not a bad man; you just made some mistakes like the rest of us. I was having Bible study with one of my coworkers, and she gave me a scripture that has stayed with me. I can't say it verbatim, but it goes something like this. We have all sinned and have failed God miserably, but He still loves us and forgives us."

"Thank you, Ms. Johnson," he sighed. "You have a blessed night and I hope to see you soon. I was so afraid that my failure could've caused you to turn your back on God and the church. I'm so grateful to know that it didn't. Be blessed, Ms. Johnson."

"Thank you, sir."

Mayah gathered her belongings and walked toward her car; once again, tears streamed down her face. Although she would've loved to share with Kyle what occurred at study that night, she decided against it. He already had a low opinion about preachers, and she didn't want to add fuel to the fire.

On her drive home, she mulled over many things that she'd done in her life. She began to see how she too had fallen short of the glory of God. So how could she judge Minister McIntyre, who had stood before the entire church and repented? She clearly understood what Lesley meant about true repentance.

The following morning she arrived at work and couldn't wait to see Lesley to tell her what occurred at Bible study. While she was in the break room, Lesley walked in. Mayah ran over and asked if she could meet her at the bench on her lunch hour. Lesley agreed.

Later at the lunch table, Mayah shared everything that occurred at Bible study the previous night.

Lesley's eyes welled up and a few tears rolled down her cheeks. "Mayah, that's beautiful. That's what repentance is all about. I'm so ecstatic that he came to you and asked for your forgiveness. How awesome. You don't see that very often, but it does happen in churches, marriages, and friendships. I'm so happy God is really dealing with some things, not only in His churches, but in His temples. Did you know that you're the temple of God?"

"No, I didn't."

"When you get home, I want you to read 1 Corinthians 3:16. Let's talk about that next. I want you to really study that, as well as those other scriptures, and we'll talk at lunch on tomorrow, okay?"

"Lesley, how about you coming over for dinner on tomorrow instead; we'll have more time to talk?"

"That's great. Email me your address, and I'll be there right after work, if that's okay."

"Of course. I'll see you then, and don't worry about bringing anything. I'll prepare a meal."

* * * *

Mayah had a long day. Lesley came over after work and they both had a wonderful time studying the Bible. Lesley was able to answer most questions burning in Mayah's heart. Those that Lesley couldn't answer, she made telephone calls to her Christian friends for scripture references. Mayah's spirit was content with the responses she received, especially since they were Bible-based.

From Church to Church

Friday came rather quickly, and Mayah was thankful her week had come to an end. They worked her hard that week. Aside from being a Paralegal, Mayah held a Bachelor's Degree and was proficient in accounting. As she walked out of her work building, she decided to call Kyle to let him know which church was next on her list. He didn't answer so she left him a voicemail.

"Hey, Kyle, I guess you're out doing your thang. Listen, I'll be picking you up at seven-thirty on Sunday morning. We'll be attending The Church of Faithfulness. It'll take us about twenty-five minutes to get there. So be ready. We'll be going to their first service. Oh, and guess what? You'll be able to watch your sports afterwards." Mayah laughed and hung up the phone.

CHAPTER 13

Mayah was on her way to pick up Kyle for church. As had become the customary pattern, she telephoned him. He immediately came downstairs and jumped into her car.

"Hey, Kyle."

"Hi, Mayah."

"Well, are you excited about the new church we're going to this morning?"

Kyle paused before responding, as if he didn't know exactly what to say. "Not really, but I'm keeping my end of the bargain. In fact, after this is over, you need to finance me a well-needed and well-deserved vacation somewhere. My social life has been cut to a minimum, and I need a break from a lot of things. How does that sound to you, little sis?"

"Hmm. I need a vacation myself, not from attending these churches, but to assimilate all the data I've gleaned thus far. But you know what, after all this is over, because you've sacrificed a great portion of your social life, I'll gift one thousand dollars toward any trip of your choice. How does that sound, brother dear?"

"Sounds like a plan to me, and don't think I'm too proud to take your money either. I've *earned* this." He chuckled.

As they pulled up in front of The Church of Faithfulness, they stared at the church for a moment, glanced at each other, and then broke out into laughter.

"Well, brother, this church is a far cry from the last one we visited, but let's find the parking lot."

"Find the parking lot is right. I don't think they have one, girl."

Mayah glanced all around the church and saw approximately ten occupied parking stalls.

From Church to Church

"Well, Kyle. We might as well try to find a spot to park on the street somewhere."

She found a place to park about a block from the church, and they walked to the main entrance. As they approached the church, they saw several men standing beside the building, crushing cigarette butts on the pavement with their shiny, well-polished, black shoes.

"Man, I sure hate the smell of those things. But let's just go in, Kyle."

"Alright, sis, but I don't have a good feeling about this church."

Several small children between the ages of eight and twelve greeted them at the door and escorted them to their seats.

"Ain't that cute? They have children ushers," Mayah said.

"Yeah. It's cute, but I still don't have a good feeling about this church."

"Don't prejudge it before we even step foot into it or hear a song or sermon. That's not fair."

"I hear what you're saying, but I still don't have a good feeling about this."

They took their seats. Mayah looked around the nearly filled sanctuary; most of the congregants were young adults. There were perhaps three hundred or so. A group of singers stood in a uniformed line in front of the pulpit, looking around as if someone or something was missing. Suddenly, a fortyish, stocky, well-dressed woman took her position at the organ and began playing. The singers joined in.

> "So caught up with man's tradition and with man's opinion. Heeding the voice of everyone except the voice of the Lord. Give God what He wants. Give God what He's due. Honor, Glory, and Adoration, just worship Him today."

The singers and lyrics grabbed Mayah's undivided attention.

> "Give God your heart, pour your affections out on Him; He's truly waiting. For the fragrance of our worship to ascend up to Him, He's truly waiting."

The woman on the organ began speaking, initially in a rather soft voice. However, at some point, when the singers ceased singing, she got excited or agitated as her voice ascended to a thunderous level.

"We're here to give God what He wants. He wants our praise and our worship. We need to surrender to His will—not just on this morning, but every day. I know some of you possibly had some challenges last week. Some are caught up in the economics of this day. Many may be unemployed, but let's just forget about those things and worship God this morning. Now, we need to worship Him not only in song but in deeds also. So as the team continues to sing, I want the ushers to come forward and take our tithe and offering for today. Let's also worship Him with the giving of our tithes and offerings."

The ushers stepped forward, and everyone walked to where they were stationed up front and placed their money in the offering baskets. The woman on the organ kept playing and talking while the singers decreased their volume as she spoke.

Mayah glanced over at Kyle and whispered, "See, it's not that bad."

"I still don't have a good feeling about this church," he responded quietly, "but I'll hold on until the service ends."

The woman ascended from the organ seat and welcomed the visitors. A young man rapidly slid onto the organ bench and continued playing the previous tune. He was one of the young men whom they had seen on the side of the church smoking.

Kyle rolled his eyes toward Mayah, and didn't say a word. Subsequently, he quickly closed his eyes, bowed, and shook his head. Mayah knew he was displeased with the young man on the organ because of his smoking before church.

Many young people were present in this service from the ages of eighteen to thirty-five. The service was very lively, but for some reason, Kyle shifted in his seat as if trying to get comfortable. He acted unnaturally restless, and Mayah wanted to ask him about it.

From Church to Church

Just then, a nicely dressed, beautifully shaped, young lady walked to the front of the church, clutched the microphone, and began to sing.

Kyle's eyes got as big as two giant cantaloupes. "Oh, no." he said as he leaned toward Mayah.

"What?" she asked.

"I met this girl a few weeks ago—at the club," he told her. "I never would've known it was the same girl because she's fully clothed on today, but at the club she was hardly dressed at all." Kyle just sat there with an unusually perplexed look on his face.

"Be quiet Kyle and we'll talk after church."

He didn't take his eyes off the young lady. She never made eye contact with him, since she sung with her eyes shut. She ended the song and took her seat; however, Kyle continued to be distracted.

The organist commenced speaking again. "Church, the pastor is out of town today; however, he'll be back for Bible study on Tuesday night. But we have a real treat for you today. In his place, one of our own will be delivering the gospel. Come on up here Minister Erick."

The congregation stood on their feet and applauded. Minister Erick was well-dressed and well-groomed: perhaps in his late twenties. As he made his way to the podium, Kyle's eyes bulged.

"You got to be kidding," Kyle whispered. "This man is a preacher. I just saw him in the nightclub a few weeks ago too. What's going on in here?" His agitated demeanor rose to a greater level.

Minister Erick read his text. His diction was impressive as he ministered to the people. Kyle fidgeted and shifted in his seat often, apparently having a difficult time getting into the message. Mayah tried to ignore him.

Minister Erick stepped up his preaching and the congregants got even more stimulated. They were upon their feet, applauding, and shouting, "You better preach up in here!"

Mayah was still trying to hear the sermon over all the loud applause and noise coming from the people. She then glanced over at an uneasy Kyle.

"I need to get out of here—now," he said through a clenched jaw.

"Why?"

"Just trust me, girl. Let's go right *now*," he said firmly.

Kyle got up and walked toward the exit. In total shock and amazement, Mayah followed.

They rushed out of the sanctuary and Kyle picked up speed. He walked as if he had just begun his first leg of a speed walkathon.

"Hold up, Kyle," Mayah yelled as she attempted to catch up with him. "What's the matter with you? I've never seen you like this before, especially in church. What's wrong? You seem spooked."

"I was at this club a few weeks ago and I met Sharon, the girl that was singing."

"And?"

"And I got her number and we're supposed to be going out this Friday night. Also, the dude that was up preaching, he was dancing in the club that same night."

"Are you sure? Maybe they just look like someone else. You know the lighting isn't always clear and bright in clubs, so I'm told, and maybe you met someone who resembled them."

"No way! It's them!" He blurted out.

"Wow. I'm at a loss for words."

"Don't say anything. Let's just get in the car and you can just take me home. I never thought I'd run into someone I just met in a club singing and preaching in church."

"Well, think about it, Kyle. You were in the same club with them. Maybe they were thinking the same thing when they saw you. Maybe they just started going to church like us."

"Mayah, you can make all the excuses you want, but *dude* didn't just start preaching two weeks ago."

"Hmm. That's probably true."

They arrived at the car and they both got in. Neither said a word, as they were both speechless. Kyle stared out the passenger's window and then said, "Yeah, it's her."

"Well, are you still going to take her out on Friday?"

"You know, Mayah, I think I will. I just want to see her face when I tell her I was at her church and heard her sing. I just want to hear what she has to say."

"Kyle, no one is perfect."

"I know. But I didn't think that I'd run into someone in church who I just met in a club a few weeks ago."

Mayah knew her brother was still upset so she decided to drop the subject to help him calm down. "Well, I'm going to Bible class on Tuesday night to meet the pastor. The inside of the church is quite nice, and there's a lot of people our age at their first service. I like that. This church possibly caters to a younger crowd, or at least the eight o'clock service does."

"Yeah, you're right about that. But are you still thinking about going back, even though you saw the brothers outside the church smoking and the two people that I met at the club singing and preaching in church?" Kyle asked with a perplexed look on his face.

"Yes. These two have nothing to do with the pastor or anyone else in this church. Maybe they're just not that dedicated, or perhaps they think there's nothing wrong with smoking, dancing, drinking, and partying in the club and going to church. Maybe that's a personal issue that you have, and they don't share your opinion or conviction."

She couldn't believe what she'd just voiced to Kyle. Just a few weeks ago, she probably would've thought something all together different. Her mindset was slowly changing. Church was really making a huge difference in Mayah's life.

"Okay," he finally said in a calmer tone of voice. "I do all of that, you know; I drink a little and party; and I know I'm not a

Christian, but I thought Christians lived their lives in a totally different way. Isn't that what you thought too? Remember that church we visited and all those women were chasing me? Do you remember how upset you were? Well, didn't you think Christian ladies lived their lives differently from the ladies in the street?"

She let out a long sigh. "You've made your point. But I'm still going to church on Tuesday night to hear the pastor teach. I want to be fair to each church as I make this life-altering decision. I must say, I'm a little confounded over what you've said."

"Mayah, if I ever get in trouble, you're the one I'll definitely call, because you see good in everybody and everything." Kyle shook his head and let out a boisterous laugh.

"Alright. Here we are at your house. Call me after your date on Friday. I want to know what Sharon says after you tell her you saw her in church singing."

"Alright, baby girl. This is my stop." Kyle kissed Mayah on her cheek and stepped out of her car.

While driving home, she meditated on the church service and took inventory of all that transpired before their hasty departure. There were a lot of young people in this church, and she liked that because she'd be able to relate to them. Also, she loved that song, *Give God What He Wants*. She couldn't wait until she got home so she could look at the church's program to see those words again.

Mayah walked into her apartment, took off her shoes, and checked to see if she had any messages. There weren't any. She went upstairs and changed into some sweats, and opened up the church's program.

She searched for the words to the song. *Caught up with man's traditions and opinions*. Mayah thought about it a moment and realized that applied to many people. "Yes, we pay attention to the opinions and voices of our friends and the dictates of the media rather than what the Bible says. But this song says we pay more attention to all of that rather than *the voice of God*." She said aloud.

She felt another discussion coming on with Lesley. The voice of God? How could she hear the voice of God? How would she know if and when He spoke to her? Could she hear Him audibly? She needed answers to these questions. At this moment, she didn't want to disturb her friend; however, she would definitely ask her in the near future at work. She could hardly wait to visit Lesley's church.

She continued to try to sort things out. What did God want from her specifically? The song said, *Honor, Glory, and Adoration and to worship Him.* Perhaps that's what He desires from her too. She decided to look up those words to get a fuller understanding of what He required. Mayah grabbed her laptop and began Googling the words.

She sat back in her chair and mulled over the definitions for a moment. "This song is saying that I'm to respect, esteem, honor, and praise God: to give glory, worshipful praise, and thanksgiving to Him, and to have extravagant love and respect for God. Whew! I think I do respect Him. I have to work on publicly and privately displaying my worship, affection, and extravagant love to Him though." Initially, she felt this might be challenging, but soon realized it was something that she must do—in order to *give God what He wanted.*

CHAPTER 14

Mayah jumped to her feet and strolled into the kitchen to find something to eat. She didn't feel like cooking, and concluded that she'd order some food, lie across the bed, and read more of the highlighted verses in Nan's Bible.

Mayah called her favorite Chinese restaurant and placed an order over the phone. As she drove to the restaurant, she couldn't stop rehearsing the definitions of the words she previously studied. She arrived at the restaurant, paid for her food, and headed home. While driving home, she passed Tia who was traveling in the opposite direction. Tia called Mayah on her cell phone.

"Hey, Tia. What's up?"

"Girl, where are you headed?"

"Oh, I just left the Chinese restaurant. I didn't feel like cooking today."

"Me either. Hey, how about sharing some of your food with me or I can make a stop at the restaurant and pick up a few additional items and come over."

Mayah wasn't thrilled about having company, but she hadn't seen her friend for quite some time so she invited her over. "Okay, Tia, I may have enough for the both of us."

"Good. But I think I'll run back to the restaurant and pick up a few additional things. Tell me what you ordered so I can avoid duplicating them."

Mayah relayed what she'd ordered and Tia promised to be at her apartment shortly. Thirty minutes later, Tia arrived at Mayah's with a huge bag full of Chinese food.

"Tia, why did you get so much?"

"Well, since we haven't seen each other for quite some time, I thought I'd bring enough so we can spend some time catching up on what's going on in our lives."

"Girl, it looks like we're having a party!"

Tia said nothing, but she had this strange, guilty look on her face.

Just then, the doorbell rang.

"I wonder who that can be." Upon opening the door, Mayah saw more of their friends standing in the bright light of the hallway.

"What's going on here? Why is everyone coming over on today?" She then noticed that they too held a couple of bags in their hands.

She turned to Tia. "What's going on?"

"Well, Mayah, you know we've been trying to get together since your birthday, and you keep putting us off. Well, when I saw you driving down the street, I made a few calls to some of our girls, and they're coming over to celebrate your birthday with you."

"Tia you didn't—"

"Yes, I did." Tia smiled and batted her eyelashes.

Again, the doorbell rang. This time it was Margueritte, and she carried a birthday cake with numerous lit candles on it.

"I can't believe you guys are doing this," Mayah said, trying not to cry. Knowing her friends cared about her so much touched her heart.

Everyone laughed and sang the happy birthday song.

"What a pleasant surprise. I had planned on running out getting Chinese food and taking it easy on today—just studying the Bible."

"Studying the Bible?" Carmen asked.

Tia rolled her eyes toward the ceiling. "Yes, studying the Bible. Mayah is on this church kick thing—trying to find a church to go to or something."

"That's great, Mayah," Teria said. "I've been going to a church called The Church of Glory for some years and I love it."

"I have a coworker named Lesley who attends your church. I plan on visiting The Church of Glory in a few weeks. I would ask you some questions, but I've decided that I wouldn't ask any questions about a church until after I've attended—that is, should I have any questions. I want to formulate my own opinion based upon what I'm feeling or seeing. So far, I've only had to call someone once."

"I understand," Teria said. "But I *will* say this, I've been very happy and blessed there. I have no complaints." Teria took a seat right next to Mayah and Margueritte.

Mayah could hardly believe her ears. Right there under her nose all this time, one of her closest friends had been a churchgoer and never mentioned anything about it, at least she couldn't recall her saying anything. She questioned what other things she didn't know about her circle of girlfriends.

"Well, I didn't come over here to talk about this church stuff," Tia said. "I called all of you over to celebrate Mayah's birthday."

"Alrighty then. Let's get this celebration started!" Carmen shouted with great enthusiasm.

They dug into the food and laughed and talked as they caught up on each others' lives. Some shared information about the men they're dating. However, Mayah just sat and listened. She felt detached from the conversation. Tia noticed this and attempted to draw her back into the conversation.

"Hey Mayah, you seem to be a little distant on today," Tia chuckled. "What's going on in your life other than church?"

Mayah glanced at Tia and replied, "Not much. I guess I'm just a little tired."

"Girl, but we're here to celebrate your birthday."

"I know." Mayah sighed. "And I appreciate it. I guess I'm just more tired than what I thought."

From Church to Church

"I understand," Teria said. "There are days when I just want to come home from church or work and just crawl into bed and just 'veg' out. So I can truly relate to where you are."

"I have an idea," Tia said, apparently trying to stop any further talk about church. "Let's just pop open the wine, make a toast, eat some cake, and then we'll be on our way so my girl can get some rest. Oh, and don't worry, Mayah, we got some non-alcoholic wine because some of your girls don't drink." Tia then giggled as she jumped up off the couch and looked through a couple bags.

"Tia, that's great. I don't want you all feeling like I don't appreciate you coming over, but I'm so tired today. However, if you want to stay over for another hour or so, that'll be fine."

Tia shook her head once again. "No, Mayah. We'll be out of here real soon so you can get your rest. Girl, I don't know what's making you so tired. If running from this church to that church is tiring you out like this, you need to slow down."

"No, it's not the going to church that's tiring me out. You know how I am. I want to have a clear understanding of all things at that precise moment, and in the real world, it doesn't always happen that way. So when I left church today, I had a few questions in my heart that I was going to research while lying down reading Nan's Bible and munching on some Chinese food."

"Does everyone have their glass?" Teria said as she interrupted the ongoing conversation.

Everyone reached for their glass and toasts were made in honor of Mayah. One toast stood out from the rest—Teria's.

"Mayah," she said, lifting her glass of sparkling cider. "I pray that you'll know God in a way that brings joy to your soul. I pray that all unsettled questions will be answered and that you'll find the church He wants to plant you in. I pray there will be such intimacy between God and you that you'll know not only His voice, but His heartbeat. I pray worship and fellowship will be established in such a way that you'll know you can't live without Him nor will you be able to live without spending time on a regular basis in His presence. I pray you'll treasure the gift of salvation, the presence, and voice of God—"

"Okay, Teria," Tia exclaimed. "That's good enough. We didn't ask you to preach a sermon." She then giggled along with a couple others.

"Tia, you don't understand," Mayah sobbed. "Teria, thank you so much for that toast. I do want to know God like that. Your prayer is really my heart's desire, but I hadn't been able to really voice it." She paused and composed herself; however, the tears continued. "Thank you *all* for what you've said and for coming over to celebrate my belated birthday."

Everyone stared at Mayah as she sobbed and Yvonne embraced her.

"You know, I thought I needed to read Nan's Bible today, but your presence here has meant a lot to me. The words you've all spoken have really touched my heart."

"Mayah, we didn't mean to make you cry," Margueritte said. "We wanted to come over to make you laugh and smile."

"You all have done that and more. Tia called you, and all of you dropped what you were doing to come over and celebrate my birthday, and I'm so grateful for friends like all of you." Mayah reached out and hugged all of them.

"Girl, you're too funny," Tia said. "Let me get some foil so we can take our cake home with us and leave you to cry all by yourself." She paused a moment then giggled again. "Nah, I'm just kidding. We love you and we're going to be heading out so you can lie down and get some rest."

Everyone dashed to the kitchen, wrapped up their cake, and kissed Mayah goodbye. However, as Teria embraced her, Mayah couldn't help whispering something in her ear. "Thank you so much for that prayer. You really prayed what's in my heart. Tia doesn't

From Church to Church

understand this, but I thank God that you do. Please continue to pray for me and Tia."

Teria embraced Mayah and kissed her on the cheek. "Call me anytime you want to talk and I will be praying for you as well as the others."

One by one, they all took turns wishing Mayah a happy twenty-first birthday, and then they left.

She went about the apartment, straightening up and putting up all the leftover food as she lovingly thought about each of her dear friends. When she came to Teria, she teared up again. "That girl sure knew how to pray while making what was supposed to be a toast."

The toast was really something in light of the words she had just studied: *honor, glory, adoration, and worship.* Tucked inside Teria's honored salutation was a prayer for Mayah to have extravagant love, fellowship, knowledge, and worship toward God.

"That's awesome!" she said aloud.

She sat down and tears rolled down her cheeks. All of a sudden, she stopped crying. Mayah realized how much she'd grown since reading her Bible and attending church. Although a few of the girls spoke about their relationships with men, among other things, she had nothing to say. She was cognizant of how much she'd changed, because normally she would've been one of the first to speak, but not this time.

CHAPTER 15

Upon her arrival at Bible study the following Tuesday, Mayah had to park on the street due to limited parking. She made her way down the street and encountered others heading toward church. As some hastily passed her, they greeted her with a, "Good evening, sister." She responded kindly each time. This was so different from some of the previous churches she'd visited.

As Mayah stepped into the foyer, an elegantly dressed woman in her mid-forties approached her. "Hi, are you new here?"

"Yes, ma'am," Mayah answered.

"I've been here for quite some time. Would you like to sit with me?"

"That'll be great. Thank you." Mayah felt more welcomed here than at any of the previous churches.

"Oh, by the way, my name is Sylvia."

"And I'm Mayah."

"Okay, Mayah. Let's go in."

She followed Sylvia who headed toward the front of the church. In fact, Sylvia took Mayah to the front row with her. Confounded, Mayah panicked a little bit. Who was this woman and why did she want to sit on the front row with her? However, because Mayah said she'd sit with her, she didn't mumble a word.

The singers assumed their uniformed line again, the organist took her position, and a very distinguished, muscular, middle-aged man walked in through a side door.

"Is that the pastor?" Mayah asked Sylvia.

"Yes it is."

The worship team sung a few songs, and someone prayed, after which the pastor took the microphone. "For those of you who are visiting tonight, I'm Pastor Earl. It's a pleasure to see so many of you out tonight. I see my wife has a new friend. Stand up, honey, so everyone will know who you are, and please introduce your new friend."

Oh my goodness. I can't believe I'm sitting with the pastor's wife!

Sylvia stood. "Hi. You all know me and this young lady is a new visitor here. Why don't you stand up and introduce yourself, sweetie."

Mayah's nerves jittered inside her, but she managed to stand, release a rather sizeable smile, and recite her name.

Pastor Earl nodded and welcomed her as she dropped back into her seat. "Tonight, I'm going to speak on the *Fruit of the Spirit*. Please notice that I didn't say "fruits" as they're all in one large cluster. Therefore, the Bible calls them fruit."

He taught for an hour, and then it was time to dismiss the Bible class. As he concluded his teaching, he informed the members that next week Sister Samantha would be concluding the teaching on the subject matter, as he would be out of town.

As the class came to a conclusion, Sylvia gave Mayah a rather intense hug and told her to come back because God really wanted her to ingest the teaching on the *Fruit of the Spirit*. At this juncture, a young woman walked up to them. Sylvia introduced her as Sister Samantha to Mayah. They exchanged niceties and Mayah walked toward the exit when all of a sudden, Sister Samantha called out her name.

"Sister Mayah."

Mayah turned around wondering what this woman could possibly want with her. "Yes, Sister Samantha?"

"Is this your first time in our church?"

"No, ma'am. I was here on this past Sunday with my brother."

"Do you have a church home?"

"No, ma'am. I'm in the process of finding one."

"Well, I have a Women's study at one of the member's residence every Thursday night and I'd love to have you come. We talk about the Bible and about the Word that was preached on that previous Sunday. Can I give you the address? I hope you'll be able to come out this week. There are a lot of young adults who attend this class, and I really think you'll enjoy it."

Mayah thought about the invitation for a moment and decided it would be a good way for her to get to know more about the church and the ladies. "Yes, ma'am, I think I can possibly come out. I don't have any plans on Thursday so if the class isn't too far from my home, I'd love to attend."

Sister Samantha gave Mayah the address, and they said their farewells until Thursday night.

Mayah proceeded toward her car, thinking how nice it will be to meet some of the young adults in the church. She had hopes of making a new friend or two.

* * * *

When Thursday arrived, it surprised Mayah at how excited she was about attending the Women's study. When her workday ended, she knew she'd have to rush home, change her clothes, and find something to eat, and she did just that.

On her way to the Women's study, she called Kyle.

"Hey, Mayah, what's up?"

"I just thought I'd let you know that I'm going to a Women's Bible class on tonight. I met a lady at church on Tuesday and she invited me. There should be a lot of young adults at this study."

"That's great, sis; sounds like I need to be at that *Women's* class." He chuckled.

"I don't know what I'm going to do with you. I'll be so glad when you finally find someone and settle down with her."

"Who, me?"

"Yes, you."

"Girl, don't you know that I enjoy being single too much to get married?"

"Yeah, but at some point, you'll need to settle down with *one* woman, marry her, and have some babies. I'm looking forward to becoming an aunt."

"Girl, you're dreaming. What you need to do is meet some dude, settle down, and have your *own* babies." He laughed.

"Alright, I just wanted to let you know what was up, just in case you called. I'll give you a call on tomorrow."

"Have a good time at class with all the *ladies*."

"You're so crazy, but I love you anyway. Bye, Kyle."

Mayah reached her destination and while parking, she noticed many young women walking toward the Bible study residence. There were so many cars on the street, and she wondered whether they all belonged to women attending the class.

She exited her car and started her walk toward the house, when some women inquired if she was going to Bible study. Mayah advised them she was. They exchanged names and all walked up to the door together: one of them rang the doorbell.

As they walked in, Mayah could hardly believe how many women were there; around fifty women or so were in attendance. She was so excited to be at a Women's class. At that juncture, she made eye contact with Sister Samantha, who slowly nodded her head toward her.

Someone prayed, followed by a short chorus of a song, and Sister Samantha took over.

"First of all, I'd like to thank all of you for coming out to class tonight. I see we have two visitors. One of them I invited on Tuesday night and she's here. Mayah, why don't you stand up and tell the group who you are and whatever else you'd like to say."

Mayah nervously stood. "Well, my name is Mayah Johnson. I live about fifteen minutes from here. I visited the church on Sunday and went to Bible class on Tuesday, and that's where I met Sister Samantha who invited me here tonight—and here I am." She quickly sat down.

Everyone applauded Mayah and told her how glad they were to have her there. They did likewise with the other visitor.

Sister Samantha started out by saying, "For those of you who don't know me, I am Minister/Prophetess/Teacher Samantha. I've been at the Church of Faithfulness for ten years. You can just call me Minister Samantha." She went on to give all her credentials, and then the teaching began.

"How many of you are single women?" She asked.

All but two women raised their hands.

"Okay, I'm in the right house tonight."

Mayah didn't quite understand what she meant by that. Since there were only two visitors, wouldn't she already know how many single and married women were in attendance? There was something about Minister Samantha that made Mayah a little uneasy. Minister Samantha was somewhat of an attractive, freckled-faced woman who wore rather clumsy, oversized clothing. She was in her early thirties and spoke very stern. Mayah refocused and lent an ear to the teaching.

Minister Samantha spoke to the young women about what it meant to be single and what God was expecting from each of them as they patiently waited for their potential spouse. Subsequently, she called numerous women forward and prophesied over them. Mayah sat with her eyes fixed on her, absorbing every word.

Minister Samantha informed one young lady that she was dating a man who wasn't a Christian. She further advised her that she'd been contemplating whether or not she should marry the man. Then she conveyed to the young woman that God said to go ahead, because He would be changing his heart.

The young lady, consumed with joy, responded, "Good, then I'll call him tonight and accept his proposal of marriage."

Mayah sat there wondering how Minister Samantha knew what God was saying and how she knew it was God.

"Some of you feel that your boyfriend has to be saved before you marry him, but that's not so. God can and will change who he is, either before or after you're married. So don't be afraid; it's alright," the minister said.

Many of the women applauded and others shouted out, "That's right!" However, Mayah and a few other women sat in silence with bewildered looks on their faces.

Three more women were ministered to, and then she brought her teaching to a close. "Well, I believe I've said and done all that God has ordained me to say and do, and we can now fellowship with each other. There are snacks on the dining room table, but first let me pray over the food." She prayed and everyone congregated in the dining room.

One of the women approached Mayah and introduced herself. "Hi, my name is Jan and I'm sorry, I forgot your name. Please forgive me."

Mayah smiled and replied, "My name is Mayah."

"So how did you enjoy the class, Mayah?"

"It was fine," she said, avoiding saying what she really thought.

"You really didn't understand all that was going on, did you?"

Jan must have seen the confused look on Mayah's face while the teaching and prophesying were going on.

"Not all of it," she nervously admitted.

"I know. I was watching you. Well, that's the same way I was when I first started coming. I've been coming for two weeks."

"Jan, I guess I do have a question, but I really don't want to ask it out loud."

"Why don't I write my number down, and you can call me tonight or tomorrow morning, if you like? I hope I can answer it. Or would you rather Minister Samantha answer it?"

The question she wanted to ask pertained to Minister Samantha's teaching, so no way did Mayah want to ask her.

"Oh, no. You'll do just fine," she quickly replied.

"If it's a really pressing question, why don't you give me a call when you arrive home tonight or if you have a cell phone, call me when you leave? I reside three houses down, in walking distance, and I'll be up for quite some time."

"Thanks, Jan. I'll give you a call."

"Very good, Mayah."

Minister Samantha approached Mayah and thanked her for coming. She also inquired how she enjoyed the class. Mayah clearly didn't know how to respond. There were some things she was unfamiliar with and they puzzled her. However, she managed to release a truthful response without offending her.

"The class was very interesting and insightful."

Minister Samantha smiled with a somewhat self-righteous, smug look on her face. "Yes, God is good and He's truly using me in this hour to speak to His people. I hope to see you next week. You're coming back next week, aren't you?"

Being put on the spot, Mayah wanted to say she didn't know, but instead, and to her own surprise, she said something entirely different. "Yes, I'll see you next week."

Minister Samantha embraced Mayah and told her she'd see her at church on Sunday. Mayah nodded her head and made her departure, as she wanted to call Jan.

While walking down the street under the moonlit sky, she reflected on the lesson and the things that Minister Samantha taught and did. A Christian marrying a non-Christian was contrary to what she'd heard in various other churches as well as what Lesley and she had discussed. She felt inadequate, though, as she didn't know enough Word to challenge Minister Samantha. However, she *would* be calling both Jan and Lesley to get their opinions on the matter.

From Church to Church

Mayah got in her car and drove for about two minutes. Realizing that patience wasn't one of her virtues, she reached into her purse to locate Jan's phone number and her cell phone so she could call her. She carefully pulled over and parked at the curb, just long enough to read the number and called Jan.

"Hello."

"Hi, Jan, it's Mayah from the study. I couldn't wait until I arrived home. I was so eager to call. Here's my question. I've attended a few churches and Bible studies and was taught Christians couldn't and/or shouldn't marry a non-Christian. Tonight, I heard differently. Which is it? Is it or is it not okay to marry someone who is not a Christian?" She asked as she pulled back into traffic.

Jan paused. "Mayah, there are a lot of people who argue in favor of one opinion and others in favor of the other. However, the Bible says we're not to be unequally yoked with unbelievers. Do you know what that means?"

"I think so." Mayah sighed. "It means we're not to marry anyone who is not a Christian, right?"

"That's correct."

"Well if you know that's true, and other people in the class probably knew likewise, why didn't someone speak up?" Mayah gingerly inquired.

Jan remained quiet for a moment before answering. "Well, no one wants to confront Minister Samantha. She's been saved for such a long time. She is a teacher, preacher—you heard her outline her credentials—and no one wants to challenge her."

"Jan, is that the correct thing to do? If she's wrong, she's just wrong, right?"

"You're right. And to answer the other part of your question, no, it's not acceptable for us to not question her openly, because improper or erroneous teaching and incorrect doctrine cause weak or new saints to err. I think I owe you an apology. I should've said something myself. But I'm relatively new too, and like many of the others in attendance, I'm somewhat intimidated by Minister Samantha, nor do I want to rock the boat."

"Jan, thank you for speaking to me and for helping me understand the truth of that statement. I'm pulling up in front of my house, and perhaps I'll see you on Sunday morning or in Bible class next week."

"You're coming back?"

"Well, I kind of promised Minister Samantha that I'd be back so I need to keep my word."

"That's good, Mayah. Keep my number, and you can call me anytime; it doesn't have to be about this or church either. Perhaps we can have lunch some time."

"Thanks. More than likely, I'll take you up on that."

Mayah arrived home and went straight to bed.

* * * *

Since things were going at a snail's pace at work, Mayah called in the next morning and took a vacation day to just chill out and clean her cluttered closets. They wouldn't need her, and she hadn't taken any of her personal days yet. Her self-imposed assignment for that day was cleaning out two of her closets and taking clothes to the Goodwill Store. Besides, she needed time to sort out some things she'd learned about God and church these past weeks, and that was going to take at least a day.

CHAPTER 16

Mayah awakened on Sunday morning, excited about going to church. She put on a red silk dress, which complemented her thin frame, and grabbed a cup of coffee. She immediately left home to pick up Kyle, eager to hear about his date with the singer. She telephoned him, as was her usual custom.

"Hey, Mayah," he said in a slow, soft voice.

"I'm on my way. What's up with you? I've been trying to call you since yesterday."

"Mayah, I'm not feeling very well. I'm sorry but I've been taking a lot of medication since yesterday, and all I've been doing is sleeping. I need to pass on church today. There's no way I can sit in service without getting sick, if you know what I mean."

"Okay. Stay in bed. When I leave church, I can stop and get you some soup, juice, and ale, if you like."

"That would be great. I'm sorry I forgot to call you."

"No problem. Just stay in bed, and I'll come over after church, unless you need something right now."

"No. I'm okay for now. I'm just gonna roll back over and go to sleep. Do you still have your key to my place?"

"Yes."

"Go ahead and use it when you come over, just in case I'm asleep when you arrive."

"Alright. Feel better and I'll see you in a few hours. Love you."

Mayah arrived at The Church of Faithfulness and was in the process of being ushered to her seat when a group of women from Thursday Night's Bible study gestured for her to come and sit with them. She really desired to sit by herself; however, she gave in and sat with them.

The singers lined up in formation, and the lady was back on the organ. All of a sudden, the singers took a breath in unison and a glorious sound came from the choir.

> "I can hear the sounds of worshippers praising and worshipping God. I can hear the sound of worshippers singing out to the Lord. They're saying, I love You, I love You. They are praising and worshiping almighty God."

Mayah eyes welled up. She glanced to her right, realizing Kyle wasn't there and let the tears flow. She wondered if Kyle's absence freed her emotions, but the song had really pricked her heart.

The church followed the same service pattern as it did the previous Sunday. After offering time, Pastor Earl took his stance in the pulpit.

"Church, it's flu season, and it seems we have quite a few people who are out ill this morning. We've had numerous calls this week from many who desired prayer. So, let me take a few minutes right now to pray for all of those who are out ill as well as those who have other challenges that they're facing." He prayed for the people and then continued.

"This morning, I will be taking my text from 2 Cor. 6:14. My subject is, *Yoked Up—Equally or Unequally?*"

Mayah's interest was piqued, and she now sat on the edge of her seat. She could hardly wait to hear Pastor Earl's message. She'd already heard Minister Samantha's interpretation of the subject and longed to hear his.

"Church, there's a lot of people running around preaching on how it doesn't matter if you're equally yoked or not. But I'm here to tell you today, it does. It matters in marriage. It matters in your selection of friends. It matters in your choice of business partners and so on. Those who preach anything contrary to this are in error. Many women are saying since there's such a shortage of men, that they're dating unsaved brothers. On the other hand, I have the brothers saying, churchwomen are so religious, they can hardly stand to date them. Therefore, they're going outside the church chasing worldly women. God does not stutter nor has He changed his mind. Even in the Old Testament, God gave the Israelites guidelines to follow, and this same principle is carried over into the New Testament."

Except for Pastor's Earl's voice, the sanctuary was void of sound. Not a congregant mouthed a word.

"I know some of you are feeling somewhat uneasy and very uncomfortable right now, and possibly even struggling with what I'm saying, but the truth is the truth. Let's talk about problems associated with being unequally yoked. Before I move on, let me say this too, because someone is saved and you're saved doesn't make you equally yoked either. Don't marry any ole person just because they're saved or say they're a Christian. You need to marry the person that God has for you. I have Christians that are being counseled every week because they assumed since they were both saved that was a green light for them to get married. They didn't receive any type of premarital counseling, just ran off, and got married, and now, they're facing some real issues and want a divorce.

"We have Christians who can't even sleep in the same bed or eat at the same table together because they literally can't stand their *Christian* spouse. They assumed Christianity would be their common bond, and now they can't even agree on what the Bible says. They're having disputes over the Word of God. They can't seem to agree on anything, other than they're both miserable in their marriage."

The pastor went on for quite some time. In fact, he spoke for about forty-five minutes on the subject. The message came to an end, and the worship team assumed their position up front.

"Have you ever searched for words to say to the One who gave up everything for you? Did you ever think that you would find pure love so divine for you? What a loving God we serve. What a loving God we serve. He knows our heart and sees our faults, yet He loves us still. What a loving God we serve."

Mayah listened intently to the words of the song. She looked up at the projection screen, and then reached down to grab pen and paper to jot down some of the lyrics. "He knows my heart and sees my faults, but He loves me still." While listening to the singers, she meditated on that portion of the song. The singers continued.

"Did you ever think that He would send a Comforter better than a friend to you? Did you ever think what He went through to prepare a place for me and you with Him? What a faithful God we serve. What a faithful God we serve. He knows my heart and sees my faults, yet He loves me still. What a faithful God we serve."

Losing control of her emotions, Mayah wept aloud. Some of the women from Thursday night's Bible study embraced her. She was so far gone and so caught up in the emotion of everything, she had literally forgotten about herself as well as her surroundings. She sobbed and wept uncontrollably. A few of the ushers came over to console her; they fanned her and rubbed her shoulders. At some point, Mayah came back to herself.

Oh, my Lord! What just happened to me? I've never lost it like this in public. I'm so embarrassed. She looked at the ushers, so mortified, and whispered, "I'm okay."

The ushers and the women from class all backed away, giving her adequate breathing room. The service concluded. She wanted to run somewhere and hide her face and never come back; however, as she attempted to make a hasty dash out of the church, someone grabbed her hand.

"Sweetie, are you alright?"

Mayah turned around to see who was impeding her hasty exit. It was Sylvia, the pastor's wife. "Yes, ma'am. I'm fine. I don't really know what happened, but that song just got under my skin in a good way, and all these emotions just began to surface."

From Church to Church

"Sweetie, God was just dealing with you, that's all that was," she said laughingly, but not mockingly. "Most likely you began realizing just how loving and faithful God has been to you, right?"

"Yes, ma'am."

"It's okay, sweetie. We all have moments like that and that's a good thing. Don't be embarrassed or feel uncomfortable. Don't ever quench your emotions here. It's good to know that your heart is so tender and responsive to God and the flow of His Spirit." Sylvia then hugged Mayah and said, "I'll see you at Bible study."

"Yes, ma'am. I can hardly wait to come back."

Mayah left church and rushed to her car. Just as she inserted her keys into the lock, she saw Minister Samantha heading toward her. *Oh, God, please don't let her say anything to me about what just happened in church. Nor, let her say anything about the pastor's message.*

"Hi, Sister Mayah. I hope I'll see you on Thursday night."

"Yes, Minister Samantha, I'll be there. I need to leave now because my brother is ill, and I have to go to the store for him."

"Okay. I'll see you Thursday night. You are aware that I'm teaching this Tuesday night at church too, right?" she said with a look of conceit on her face.

"Yes. I'll be there too. See ya!"

Mayah unlocked her car door, jumped swiftly into her vehicle, and let out a long sigh. "Whew! I have *never* experienced anything like that before in church or anywhere." She guessed she'd need to get over the embarrassment, since everyone else thought it was a normal reaction.

"What would Minister Samantha be teaching on Thursday night? The pastor sure refuted everything she'd taught last week. I have to see how she's going to clean up what she said or handle what Pastor Earl taught this morning." She so wanted to call Jan, but decided against it, as she didn't want it to appear that she was gossiping.

Mayah stopped at the store to pick up numerous items for Kyle. She glanced in the mirror at her makeup, making sure there were no streaks or smudges from all those tears. After a few quick touch-ups to her face, she entered the store and purchased everything she could think of for her brother. She paid for all of the items and as she walked toward her car, she remembered Kyle was oblivious to what occurred at church and she determined she'd leave it that way.

After finding a parking space close to Kyle's unit, Mayah grabbed both bags, took the elevator up to the tenth floor, and arrived at his two-bedroom penthouse apartment. Upon moving into his unit, he had hired a professional decorator who decked his place out. The elevator, stairwells, and hallways were either carpeted or marbled in his building. Kyle had expensive taste and surrounded himself with the like. Mayah loved the décor; it suited Kyle.

Mayah unlocked the apartment door, peaked through his slightly open bedroom door, and saw that he was fast asleep. Not wanting to awaken him, she put the food and herbal preparations away and tiptoed out, slowly closing the door to make sure she didn't disturb him.

As she heads home, her cell phone rang. She looked at the caller ID and saw it was Jan.

"Hi, Jan. What's up?"

"Hi, Mayah. I got your number off my caller ID. I hope that's okay. I just wanted to check on you. You really got blessed today in church."

"I'm glad you called. I've never had anything like that happen to me, at least not to that degree. I was mortified."

"Don't be embarrassed. When the Spirit of God moves upon people, they tend to say and do things out of the ordinary, at least out of the ordinary for them. There was absolutely nothing wrong with the way you responded. Just watching you blessed us. It's so refreshing to see someone who hasn't been tainted by religion."

"What do you mean by that?"

"Well, a lot of times as children we learn how to respond, act, or perform in certain situations in church by watching others. You haven't been influenced by any superficial acts or Christian stimulants, and it's so refreshing. You're like a school girl on her first date. When it comes to Christianity, there's no pretense with you. You're not trying to impress anyone or appear to be more than what you are. That's what I mean. You're just real. There's nothing fake about you and that's refreshing."

"Oh, but there's so much that I don't know or understand."

"That's a good thing. That's why it's such a joy talking to you and observing you in church. You're just real."

"Girl, as I was leaving church, I thought about calling you. I wanted to get your opinion on what the pastor taught this morning versus what Minister Samantha taught on Thursday night. But I didn't want it to appear like I was gossiping. Girl, I thought I was going to lose it in church. I wanted to locate where Minister Samantha was seated and just stare in her face, but I didn't."

"Mayah, I knew you'd probably feel conflicted in what you heard today. Pastor Earl is absolutely correct. Minister Samantha is wrong. What are you doing right now? Do you want to have tea or coffee?"

"That would be great. I'm near Larry's Coffee House. Do you know where that is?"

"Yes, I do. I'll meet you there in about five minutes."

Mayah parked in front of the Coffee House just as Jan pulled up alongside her car. They both walked in together and were seated.

Mayah was anxious to resume the conversation from where they left off. "Jan, if Minister Samantha is wrong, then why doesn't someone correct her? Does the pastor know what she teaches? I was confused on today because I really didn't know for sure who was right and who was wrong for a moment."

"Hmm. Minister Samantha teaches a lot of things contrary to what we're taught by the pastor, at least since I've been there."

"I don't understand. If you all know that, then why hasn't someone told the pastor? I don't understand how they continue to allow her to teach. Jan, excuse me. I've been told that I can be a little opinionated, and I guess that's true."

"That's okay. I don't know how to respond to you without making Pastor Earl appear derelict in his pastoral duties. I haven't been at this church very long. Perhaps he doesn't know or he doesn't know the full extent of what she's teaching."

"Well, if you don't know, then there must be someone in the church who does. What about the women who attend her class? That seems so strange to me."

Jan bowed her head in an apparent attempt to avoid making eye contact with Mayah.

"I really don't want to attend Thursday night's class," Mayah said, realizing this subject was difficult for both of them to understand. "I'm only going because I've already committed to doing so. However, if what she's teaching is incorrect, then I'll have to politely excuse myself. I don't want to be confused; I just want to be taught the truth."

"I understand, Mayah. At one point, Minister Samantha had tons of people in her class, so I've been told, but the attendance has started dwindling down for obvious reasons."

"Alright, I understand, I think. But she shouldn't be allowed to teach unless she's teaching the truth, right."

"I agree."

"And she's going to be teaching Bible class at the church on Tuesday night too. I don't understand that either."

"We just need to pray. The pastor's wife will be in the class on Tuesday, and perhaps she'll correct Minister Samantha."

The waiter came and took their orders.

After further sharing and having coffee and a bagel, Mayah stood up to leave. "Well, I need to get home. I'm a little drained. I'll see you at the church's Bible class."

"Okay. I truly enjoyed our conversation. We need to pray for Minister Samantha."

"I'll pray, although I don't really know what to pray about if people already know that she's not teaching the truth."

"Mayah, pray that her eyes and ears will be open to God and that she'll be able to see, hear, understand, deliver, and minister the truth."

"Okay. I'll pray just that. I'll see you at Bible study."

They embraced each other and both went to their respective cars.

Mayah remained a little confused over the fact that Jan and others were aware that Minster Samantha had been teaching false doctrine; however, no one was challenging her. After awhile, her mind drifted back to some of the words of the song. *He knows my heart, sees my faults, yet He loves me still.* After mulling over those words, she felt bad for a moment.

"God if You know my heart and see all my faults and still love me, then You know Minister Samantha's heart and see the faulty teaching that she's doing, and You still love her too?" Mayah scratched her head as she tried to gain more understanding concerning the situation.

As she walked into her apartment, her phone rang. She hurried across the room to answer it—it was Kyle.

"Hey, Kyle. Are you feeling better?"

"Yeah, I'm much better. Thanks for all the stuff you brought over. I just finished eating some of that soup and I'm much stronger. I didn't even hear you when you came in. How was church?"

"It was fine." She thought she'd better tell him what occurred that morning. "Okay, I had a moment where I just lost control of my emotions and began sobbing out loud," she said quickly.

"You're kidding."

"Nope. All these people came over to where I was. They were patting me on my back, fanning me, and wiping the tears from off my cheeks. I was so humiliated."

"What was up with all those tears? Did you miss me that much that you had to cry?" He laughed to himself.

"You wish. No, the singers were singing, and the words of the song just tore me up—it was as if the words ripped all the debris that was blocking this river of emotions inside of me. And all of a sudden, the dam broke, the debris was moved, and the water began to flow out of my eyes."

"Wow!"

"Okay. Let me change the subject for a minute. How did your date go?"

"Girl, Sharon almost fell out of her *seat* when I told her that I heard her singing in church on last Sunday. She's related to the pastor."

"Really?"

"Yep. She told me that she didn't see anything wrong with going to the club. However, she doesn't broadcast it. I then jammed her about the preacher who was at the club. She told me, he didn't see anything wrong with going to clubs either; they're young and the old folks want to put too many restrictions on them. She also said that what they're doing is nothing compared to some of the stuff that's happening in that church."

"What did she mean by that?"

"I didn't ask her. She just said there's a lot of 'things' happening there and people know it and don't say anything about it. Then she said, 'I dare any of them to say anything to me. I'll turn that place out.' After she said that, I just changed the subject."

"Man! What's up with all this stuff happening in a lot of these churches?"

"I don't know, sis. You may as well just select one of the churches that you've already visited, because it doesn't seem like it gets any better, only worse."

"I'm not going to do that. I made a commitment to myself and I *will* complete what I started."

From Church to Church

"Okay. But I told you that I didn't have a good feeling about that church, right?"

"Yes, you did."

"See, you need to listen to your brother sometimes." he said as he laughed.

"Well, I see you're doing much better and are back to your usual joking and judgmental self." She laughed too. "So I'm going to hang this phone up and lie across my bed. I took last Friday off as a vacation day, and I need to be energized and ready to face my workload on tomorrow. I have to get my clothes ready because I plan on going in a little earlier."

"Okay, sis. Thanks for bringing all this stuff over and I'll be talking to you mid-week."

"Kyle, one more thing, are you going to work tomorrow?"

"I'm not sure. I won't know until I awaken, but more than likely, I'll be there."

"I'll talk to you later then."

CHAPTER 17

Days passed by rapidly for Mayah. She was a little keyed up about attending Tuesday Bible class that evening. As she left work, her stomach started gurgling. She hoped she wasn't catching what Kyle had.

Instead of driving toward the direction of the church to find a restaurant, she decided to detour and stop home first. Upon her arrival home, she could barely make it inside the front door before running to the bathroom. The repeated gagging, coughing, and diarrhea wiped her out. She thought it best to excuse herself from attending Bible study.

She climbed the stairs as if headed toward the electric chair, and when she finally made it to her bedroom, she flopped down on her bed. It dawned on her to call Kyle and inquire about the symptoms he had experienced over the weekend. After he relayed his symptoms to her, she determined she had the beginning stages of that virus. Mayah spent a protracted amount of time running back and forth to the bathroom, and felt she had better leave a message on her manager's phone. She presumed she wouldn't be at work the following day, and just in case she overslept, she wanted to alert him.

She awakened Wednesday morning around ten o'clock and called her job again. She informed her manager that she'd probably be out the following day as well, as she was beginning to experience chills. She was advised to take the entire week off since things were rather slow and she needed to get well. Mayah thanked her boss and crawled right back into bed. Other than opening a can of soup and running to and from the bathroom, she remained in bed.

After lunch, Kyle telephoned her to see if she needed anything. He told her he'd been worried that she was coming down with the flu, and had called her job first. They informed him she'd called in sick. Being up and down all night running to the bathroom, the only thing Maya wanted to do was sleep, so she told Kyle not to bother coming over.

Although she felt somewhat better on Thursday morning, she was still feverish and decided not to go to the Women's Bible class.

Later that evening her phone rang. She looked over at the caller ID and saw Jan's name.

"Hello, Jan," she said as she attempted to clear her throat.

"Hey, Mayah. I thought you were coming to class tonight."

"I thought so too, but I got sick on Tuesday as I was leaving work. I've been in bed ever since."

"I was wondering what happened to you. Do you want me to bring you something?"

"No. I have everything that I need. How was study?"

"Well, let me say it this way, Minister Samantha was in rare form. One of the women challenged her teaching based upon the pastor's message."

"What did she do?" Mayah asked excitedly.

"Well, she became very defensive and almost made it seem like we were attacking her, which we weren't. She said, the pastor knew what she was teaching, and he had never had a problem with it, and she went on from there."

"Oh, my. What did she teach on tonight?"

"Girl, you do *not* want to know."

"Yes, I do. What did she teach on?"

"Premarital sex and other things that have to do with sex."

"Hmm. What did she have to say about premarital sex?"

"Well, let me put it this way, she said if and when we make mistakes, sexual mistakes, we just need to ask God to forgive us, and He will."

"What? I don't understand."

"She said that God knows our hearts and that we mean well, and if we have sex, just get up and repent."

"I'm not following you."

"Well, she made it sound as if it was okay to have sex as long as you repent afterward."

"I still don't understand. There's no logic behind what you're saying."

"Yes you do. She made it sound as if it was okay to have sex, just get up and repent. And if or when it happened again, just get up and repent again, so on and so forth."

"I'm glad I was sick tonight. Whew! What did the other ladies say when she was teaching that?"

"Some said, 'Well, alrighty then,' and others were stunned, at least that's the expression that was on their faces."

"Did anyone challenge her?"

"No. No one challenged her. I think we were all apprehensive since she was so defensive earlier."

"Jan, I don't think I can come back to her class. I've been studying on my lunch hour with a coworker who is a Christian, and she continues to warn me about sitting up under erroneous teaching and/or preaching. I don't think I can sit in her class anymore without saying something or challenging her. My only problem is, I don't know enough of the Bible to really challenge her. She would eat me alive. One good thing, this is my last week at the church."

"That's how I feel too Mayah. I've only been attending this church for a short time."

"I keep forgetting that you're relatively new like me."

"That's right."

"Well, Jan, I believe you need to pray or talk to someone, and stop going to that class so you won't get all confused thinking something is right and it's wrong."

"You're right. You know, you have a lot wisdom for someone just coming back to church."

"Thanks, Jan, that's so kind of you to say, but I have a long way to go."

"Me too."

"I need to make a run to the bathroom. I'll see you on Sunday."

"If it's okay, I'll call you possibly on Saturday just to see how you're doing."

"Thanks. I'll talk to you later."

Mayah couldn't believe what she'd just heard. However, there was a much more pressing issue at hand—the bathroom.

CHAPTER 18

Mayah remained in her apartment almost the entire week. Both Kyle and Jan had stopped in to check on her. She awakened Sunday morning feeling well, and decided to take a shower and go to church. She telephoned Kyle to tell him that she would be at his apartment shortly.

While they were on their way to church, Kyle decided to query Mayah about some things.

"Mayah, how were the Bible classes?"

"They were okay. I like Tuesday night class at church much better than the Women's Thursday night class."

"Why?"

"Well, it seems the teacher in the Thursday night class is confused about the Bible or something."

"Mayah, how can a Bible teacher be confused about the Bible, either they know their stuff or they don't."

"You're right. Can we just ride to church this morning and not have this conversation. I really don't feel like talking right now."

"Sure, that's no problem. I forgot that you've been sick. That stuff zaps your strength, huh?"

"Yep."

Mayah located a parking spot as they drove up. She parked the car and they make their approach to the walkway when Minister Samantha suddenly appeared.

"Hi, Mayah. We missed you. I thought you were coming to class?"

"Minister Samantha, I took ill Tuesday on my way home from work and today is the first day that I've been out my house since then," she said somewhat firmly.

From Church to Church

"Oh, I'm sorry to hear that. Will you be with us on this Thursday night?"

"No, I won't be with you on this Thursday. In fact, today is our last day here."

"Why is that?"

"Because I'm searching for a church, and I have a couple more to attend before making a decision as to which one to join."

"I didn't know that. I thought you were attending here because you wanted to be a member. You really need to join this church because you're not going to find too many churches like this one. I had plans for you also. I was going to see if you wanted to travel around with me and some of the other ladies, ministering at conferences and women breakfasts."

"*Ministering*? I don't know enough about the Bible to go around ministering. I'm new at this, and I have decided that I wouldn't join a church until I've visited all the churches on my list."

"That seems a little extreme. You're already here and you might as well join here."

Mayah tried not to show her agitation toward Minister Samantha. "Minister Samantha. I don't think you're really hearing me. I don't plan on joining this church or any church until I've visited the other churches that I've selected. I feel as if you're *bullying* me into joining this church, and that's not something I want to do."

"Oh, Mayah. I'm sorry you feel like that. I wasn't bullying you. I just wanted to know what was wrong with this church that you wouldn't want to join it."

Kyle stood there in the middle of this confusion, remaining solely a spectator. Mayah continued.

"Well, it seems you and the pastor have different point of views on certain things in the Bible, and that's confusing for me."

"Like what?"

"Well the first thing was whether Christians should marry non-Christians. But I don't have time to talk about this. We need to go. Church is about to start."

"Okay. If you like, here's my card. You can call me anytime, and we can discuss this issue as well as any other Bible issues you may have."

"Thank you."

Mayah took her card knowing there was no way she'd be calling her. She simply accepted it to silence Minister Samantha. She looked at the card and thought this was one card she'd be losing when she got home.

"Mayah, what's up?" Kyle asked.

"I'll talk to you on the way home."

"Fine." He held his hands up in a stop motion.

Normally, she would've slugged him or pointed her bony index finger in his face, but she wasn't in any kind of mood to be joking with her brother.

They entered the church and were seated. Mayah attempted to clear her head from the ridiculous conversation. The worship team was already in place and singing.

> "I want Your glory. I need Your glory. Show me
> Your glory. Fill me today. Fill me with Your
> glory. Fill me with Your glory. I need Your glory.
> Fill me today."

Pastor Earl took his place in the pulpit and greeted the congregation as well as the visitors. He taught once again on the *Fruit of the Spirit*. In the middle of his sermon, Mayah's ears perked up when she heard, "Church, right above the Fruit of the Spirit is the works of the flesh. Please take note as to what they are."

Subsequently, he recited them. However, he paused when he got to adultery, fornication, and lasciviousness. "Can I just park here for a moment to expound upon these three works of the flesh?"

He broke down the meaning of adultery and fornication from two perspectives, both spiritually and naturally. Following that, he talked about lasciviousness.

"Church, that word means *no restraint*. You know how you just can't help it. And that's a lie. You *can* help it. Don't let the devil deceive you. You just don't want to discipline your flesh! Many think it's okay to fornicate a little—whatever that is—and then pray a prayer of repentance, but they never really repent. If one repents of an act, that means they will *not* practice it any longer: It will *not* be a habitual act in their life. Have you ever read Hebrews 10:26-27? Let me read it from the Amplified Bible so you can get a real good understanding.

"'For if we go on deliberately and willingly sinning after once acquiring the knowledge of the Truth, there is no longer any sacrifice left to atone for [our] sins [no further offering to which to look forward]. [There is nothing left for us then] but a kind of awful and fearful prospect and expectation of divine judgment and the fury of burning wrath and indignation which will consume those who put themselves in opposition [to God].'

"Okay. So for those of you who think you can just keep on sinning, that is repeatedly doing or practicing any of the works of the flesh, and all you have to do is say 'I'm sorry'; you're *dead* wrong, and if you don't truly repent, when you die you just might open up your eyes in hell!"

Pastor Earl had everyone's attention, including Mayah's and Kyle's. He extended an invitation to anyone who desired prayer because they knew they were practicing sin, missing the mark, or struggling with some sin issues. After seeing the drove of people heading for the altar, he advised everyone to stand where they were, and he would pray a corporate prayer over the house. Again, all that could be heard were people crying out to God, sobbing, saying how sorry they were, and of those who were fortunate enough to make it to the altar, many were crying and on their knees, repenting.

At some point, Mayah glanced over at Kyle, and tears were streaming down his cheeks. She immediately closed her own moistened eyes.

Pastor Earl dismissed church; however, he advised he was leaving the altar open for anyone who desired to remain or come down to kneel and pray.

Mayah opened her eyes as did Kyle and they prepared to leave. She didn't mention to him that she saw him crying. As they walked toward the exit, Minister Samantha was heading in her direction. However, Jan stepped in front of her, placing her body between the two of them so as to keep Minister Samantha from interacting with Mayah.

"Oh, excuse me, Minister Samantha. I just want to walk with Mayah to her car."

"No problem, Sister Jan. Sister Mayah, give me a call when you can."

Mayah simply nodded her head.

"Thank you, Jan. I don't think I could've taken anymore of her today. Oh, this is my brother Kyle; Kyle, this is Jan."

"Hi, Kyle. It's nice to meet you."

"Likewise."

Jan conversed with Mayah as she walked with them to their car, and they exchanged farewells. Mayah advised her that she wouldn't be coming back as she had three other churches to visit.

Jan hugged her and said, "Please remember me, and let's stay in close contact with each other—I mean for real. Let's not say we will, but don't."

With eyes welling up with tears, Mayah responded. "Jan, I'll never forget you, and I'll make it my business to talk to you at least once a week. How about that?"

"That's great! I'll be talking to you. Nice meeting you, Kyle."

"The pleasure was mine," Kyle responded.

Mayah and Kyle drove off.

"Mayah, she's really a nice woman. How do you know her?"

Mayah explained about the Thursday night Bible class and how she met Jan. Then he began asking personal questions about Jan.

"Is she married? Does she have any kids?"

"No, she's not married nor does she have any kids. Why? You interested?"

"Maybe."

"Okay, brother. If she asks me something about you, I'll put in a word for you. But she's a Christian, and I'm not sure that she'll date you because you're not one."

"Okay. We'll see. Just mention me to her when you talk to her."

"Will do."

"So Mayah, this is our last Sunday here?"

"Yes. I've seen and heard enough. I really like Pastor Earl, but I don't like how he allows Minister/Prophetess/Teacher Samantha to teach contrary to what he preaches and contrary to the Bible. I don't understand that. But wasn't that a good service? It really made me focus on things that I've done and perhaps still doing that are considered 'works of my flesh.' What a penetrating and convicting message."

"Yeah, sis. It caused me to inventory some things in my life too. I got all choked up behind that. It was really good."

"Yes, it was."

Mayah and Kyle's conversation came to an abrupt halt as each reflected on the pastor's sermon. Within minutes, Mayah dropped off her brother and was on her way home.

She already knew the name of the next church they would be attending. It was called "He's Alive Church," and she prayed the church would live up to its name.

CHAPTER 19

Mayah continued to meet with Lesley weekly for their scheduled Bible study. She grew stronger and stronger in her faith. Her understanding had also increased in terms of many things in the Bible, especially regarding salvation.

Mayah telephoned Kyle on Wednesday evening to advise him of the next church they would be attending. No sooner did she get the church's name out of her mouth when Kyle asked, "Have you spoken with Jan yet?"

"No, not yet. I'll probably talk to her on Friday night. Why?"

"Don't forget to mention me."

"You're serious, huh?"

"Yep, there's something about that girl and it's not a lust thing. I have nothing on my mind but getting to know her better in a healthy way."

"Hello? Is this really my brother or has someone taken over his body?" Mayah laughed uncontrollably.

"Go ahead. Make fun of me if you like. But I'm serious. There's something about her that captivates me. I've been seeing her face every day, including what she was wearing that day. I even remember the color of her suit. Mayah, I know you think I'm playing, but there's something about her. I need to know her."

"Kyle, in all your dating years, I've never heard you say anything like that. You're really serious, huh?"

"Yes I am."

"Okay. I'll call her on Friday. I'd call her tomorrow, but she has Women's Bible study."

"Alright. Don't forget!"

"I won't. You don't have to shout," she said with a silly laugh.

From Church to Church

Mayah had never heard her brother this interested in a woman, especially one that he'd only seen once. She questioned his motives; he was a player. He usually dated several women at a time. He was happy with his single lifestyle. She couldn't understand why his interest in Jan, but she determined to make sure he didn't take advantage of Jan. She was now Mayah's friend.

Jan was a very stunning young woman. She stood five feet five, weighed approximately one hundred and forty pounds, and was very shapely. She was an exquisite dresser. In fact, there was nothing that wouldn't look great on her. She could sport a garbage bag and it would look like the latest fashion on her. Her hair was long, silky, and always in place. When the wind hit her hair, it flowed. She had a smile that would light up any room. She also had an inner beauty that would draw anyone to her. Mayah didn't want to jeopardize their friendship, but would mention Kyle's name and only his name to her.

* * * *

Mayah found herself sitting at home on Thursday night, wondering what Minister Samantha was teaching at the Women's Bible study, when suddenly her phone rang.

"Hello."

"Hey, Mayah, it's Jan."

"Jan, I thought you'd be at Minister Samantha's Bible study," she snickered.

"After you left, I thought about some of the things you said, and I can't attend that class anymore either."

"I was going to call you on Friday because I knew you'd be at study tonight. This is such a pleasant surprise."

"Hey. What church are you going to on Sunday?"

"Well, Kyle and I are going to He's Alive Church. Have you ever heard of it?"

"No, I haven't. Have you been to The Church of Glory?"

"It's funny that you should ask that Jan. That's the next church on my list following He's Alive. I have a coworker and a friend who attends The Church of Glory."

"When you get ready to go to that church, do you mind if I tag along with you?"

"Nah. We'd love to have you go with us. That'll be so good. Now, before we do all that, I have to tell you something. My brother has a serious crush on you. Not a lust crush, but a different type of crush. I can't explain it. I've never seen him like this before."

"Hmm…"

"What's wrong?"

"Nothing."

"Something must be wrong; why else would you say that?"

"Okay, I must confess. There's something about your brother. I can't explain it either. When our eyes made contact, it was as if I'd known him my entire life."

"Okay, this is starting to get a little spooky."

"I know. It's strange." Jan paused a moment. "I've heard some real good reports about The Church of Glory."

"It'll be fun to have another person go with us. Now, what do you want me to do about Kyle? I mean—is there something you want me to say to him?"

"No. Just tell him I said hello."

"That's it?"

"Yes, that's it."

"Okay. I'll tell him as soon as I hang up so he won't be pestering me tomorrow."

They both laughed about the whole thing and hung up the phone. However, Mayah quickly called Kyle.

"Hello."

"Hey, Kyle. I spoke with Jan."

"You did? What did you say and what did she say?"

"I just told her that you had a healthy crush on her."

From Church to Church

"What? What did she say?"

"She laughed."

"She laughed! Was that it?"

"No, she wants to go to the Church of Glory with us when we visit it."

"Is that the next church?"

"Nope. The next church is He's Alive."

"Can't you change it?"

"Nope. I need to keep it in the order that I have it in."

"Does she seem to be interested in me?"

"I don't know."

"What do you mean, you don't know? Yes, you do."

"I think when we go to the Church of Glory you'll find out everything you need to know about her. She'll be riding with us."

"For real?" He asked.

"Yes, for real."

Mayah had fun toying with Kyle. She could've told him what Jan said, but she chose not to because she wanted to make sure Kyle wouldn't try to take advantage of Jan, although he said he didn't have feelings like that for her. Mayah hung up the phone while yet laughing at him. She thought it strange that the two of them felt something drawing them to each other. She questioned what it was but determined she'd find out in a few weeks when they traveled to church together.

CHAPTER 20

Mayah found herself running late and rushing to get ready for church on Sunday morning. She called Kyle to advise him of her potential late status. When she arrived to pick him up, he looked extremely happy about something; he had this rather huge smile on his face.

"What are you so happy about?"

"I don't know. I just have some good vibes going on around me."

"Is this about Jan?"

"Yep. You know, my phone rang all weekend, but I chose not to go out or have dealings with anyone. I'm cleaning up my life, getting all these women out of it."

"Excuse me?"

"You heard me. I also heard what the preacher said on Sunday about my flesh. I'm turning over a new leaf."

"Excuse me again?"

"You heard right. It's time for me to handle my business in a different way."

"You mean in a Christian way?"

"Yep. I really heard the preacher. Mayah, I don't want to die and open my eyes up in hell! That was more than enough to scare me straight."

"Kyle, I'm at a loss for words—you?"

"Me. And besides, when I marry Jan I want to be right, with all those other women out of my life."

Mayah shook her head. "When you do what?" she giggled. "You don't even know her," she said, continuing to laugh. She'd never heard anything so preposterous in all her life.

"That's okay. But I do know that she's my wife. There's something about that girl and I know she's my wife. Hey, I'm getting everyone else out my life. I don't want any other women calling me or nothing. In fact, I'm going to change my home and cell numbers, because when I start dating Jan, I don't want any women calling my phone. I want her to know that she's the *only* one."

"You're serious, huh?"

"You got that right. She's my wife. Don't ask me how I know it, I just know it."

"Okay. We'll see. Oh, this is the church."

"This is the church?" He asked as he visually took inventory of the property. It was a moderate-size, peach colored church trimmed in white, with dark, smoky windows. As he gazed up, he saw a steeple, which housed a rather large bell.

"Yes. Let's find a parking stall and get out."

They both approached the church and watched the people going in; however, many looked and acted lifeless. They didn't have smiles on their faces. This was already a much different atmosphere from some of the other churches visited, but Mayah vowed to reserve judgment until she actually attended the service.

They were greeted at the door by a man with a stoic face and ushered to their seats. About three hundred people or so sat quietly in this slumbered atmospheric service.

The choir began singing.

> "Here I am again, standing before You Lord. Telling You of my love, Father above. How I long to be, always close to thee. Here I am again, standing before You Lord."

That was kind of dry, Mayah thought. What type of a church was this? She looked over at Kyle and he was staring at the singers.

After the choir finished, a rather timid preacher, Pastor Josiah, arose. He talked about a lot of political things occurring globally. He then changed directions in his message three of four different times. Mayah couldn't follow where he was going. She turned to look at

Kyle and smiled. The pastor's teaching went on for about fifteen minutes, and then he was done and dismissed the service. The ushers stood at the rear of the sanctuary receiving the offering as people left.

As they reached the exit door, being the gentleman that he was, Kyle opened it for Mayah to walk out before him. "Wow, little sis, this is the shortest service I've ever been in. I'm sure people could get use to this. How long were we here, an hour?"

"Yes, maybe an hour," she answered as she stepped outside into the sunlight. "They say they have three morning services, and I can see how that can be."

"Did you learn anything today?"

"Not really. I see they have Bible study on Tuesday nights. I'll be here at that time. Kyle, I must be honest, if Bible study is like Sunday morning service, I can't do two weeks of this. We'll have to go straight to The Church of Glory."

"That's what I'm talking about. We can go there next week, if you like."

"You're just trying to see Jan. Confess up."

"You're right, but this church is dead. There's nothing going on here. Their name says, "He's Alive Church," but where is He alive at? They seem all dried up in here."

"I know Kyle. I'm somewhat disappointed and surprised by what we *didn't* experience today. But if someone is looking for a church where they can get in and out in a hurry, just to say that they attended church, this would probably be the ideal place for them. Well, I'll call you after I attend Bible study on Tuesday. At that time, I'll let you know if we'll be here next week or not."

"That's fine with me, sis. Take me home so I can finish cleaning out my apartment."

"You're really serious. I don't think I've ever seen you this serious about a girl before. Kyle, you don't even know her. You may start dating and not even like her, and you would've torn up all of your girls' numbers and changed all your phone numbers. Do you really feel comfortable about doing all of this so quickly when you haven't even really talked to Jan?"

"Sis, I feel fine doing this. What you need to know is this; even if Jan and I don't get together, I need to change my life. So it's not all about her, it's about me getting right so I won't go to hell. It's time I did the right thing."

"I'm so glad you said that. Now that you've voiced that, I must tell you something. I wanted to make sure you were making these changes for the right reasons and not because of a woman. Jan said when she saw you, she felt something too."

"I knew it! I knew it!" Kyle bounced on the seat of the car, doing a dance move. "I knew there was something. Mayah, it was like an electrical connection or something like that. I can't explain it, but I knew it!"

"Okay, you were right. You'll get a chance to talk to her while we're going to and from the next church. So just calm down and handle all your business so she won't be in the middle of some crazy, jacked-up, female drama."

"Don't worry. It's all taken care of. But I knew it!"

Mayah drove up to Kyle's home.

"Alright, sis. I'll be talking to you this week. If you talk to Jan again, tell her I said hello."

"Will do, brother. I'll give her a call after I attend Bible study on Tuesday night."

"Luv Ya."

"Likewise. Don't get your hopes up yet. You need to get to know her."

"I'm cool with it. I'll talk to you this week."

On the way home Mayah reflected on the rather terse service. She felt as if she hadn't even attended church that morning so she turned on the radio so she could hear some preaching and singing.

* * * *

Mayah headed to Bible class with hopes that it would be more fulfilling than the Sunday morning service. If it wasn't, she had already concluded that they would be attending the next church on her list.

Walking into the church, she saw about fifty people or so in the sanctuary. She supposed many of the members probably didn't attend class because of the messages on Sundays.

A young man played a song on his guitar, followed by another man, who stood and walked to the podium. He was somewhat overweight with a salt and pepper beard, but had a pleasant smile on his face.

"Hello. For those of you who don't know me, I'm Frank. I'm the Bible class instructor. Pastor Josiah does not teach this class unless I'm out of town. I pray that you'll receive something from tonight's lesson. Let me just pick up where Pastor Josiah left off on Sunday morning."

Oh no. He can't be teaching the same stuff, Mayah thought.

Frank asked the people to turn their Bibles to Matthew 24, and after praying, he began teaching.

"What Pastor Josiah was ministering on Sunday morning is found in this chapter. Let's just dissect this Word." He read the scriptures and then closed his Bible.

Frank commenced breaking down the signs of the last days. He tied it all into what Pastor Josiah preached on Sunday morning. Pastor Josiah's message now made sense to Mayah. She could see the correlation and understood what Pastor Josiah had said, or at least what he was referencing.

When class was over, Mayah sat in her seat momentarily as she focused on what she'd heard that night. She hadn't known all of that was in the Bible. "It's a good thing Frank broke it down like he did, but it's unfortunate that more people don't come out on Tuesday nights for study. If they did, they could understand what the pastor preached if they were confused," she thought.

Although it lasted for only one hour also, she gleaned a lot from Frank's teaching. She went home well pleased.

When she awakened the following morning, the phone rang before she could get out of bed.

"Hello."

"Hey, Mayah, how did it go last night?" her brother asked.

"It went quite well. The class lasted for only an hour. However, the instructor, Frank, expounded upon what Pastor Josiah spoke on Sunday, and it all made sense."

"So what does that mean?" His voice dropped.

"It means I'll be going back on Sunday morning and also attending Bible class again; after which, we'll be on our way to The Church of Glory. Because Sunday service is somewhat laid back and you don't attend Bible class, you can't get the fullness of the entire message. So, if you want to miss Sunday morning's service, you can, and I'll do the stint by myself."

"No, I'll come on Sunday morning. In fact, I'll even pick you up on Sunday morning and come with you to Bible class on Tuesday. I hate I didn't go tonight because I didn't really understand what the preacher was talking about on Sunday, and probably seventy-five percent of the people in there didn't either."

"What? You're coming and driving. Let me make sure I heard you correctly. You're coming to Bible class?"

"Yep. I told you that I'm changing. You don't believe me, but I'm changing. You'll see."

"Yes, I guess you *are* changing if you're talking about coming to Bible study and *driving* too. You got that right; you're changing. Well, I'll talk to you later. I have to get ready for work. And before you ask, no, I haven't spoken with Jan."

With a silly laugh, Kyle responded. "I wasn't even going to ask you that."

"Yes, you were. I'll talk to you later. I need to get ready for work." She hung up the phone, the excitement of her brother's apparent change boosted her spirit; she hoped it was for real.

* * * *

Mayah arrived home from work Friday afternoon and was in the process of changing clothes when her phone rang. She checked the caller ID and smiled to herself.

"Hi, Jan."

"Hey, Mayah, you saw my name on the caller ID, huh?"

"Sure did. What's up?"

"How was the new church?"

"Well, Sunday morning service lasted for about an hour. It was somewhat dry, but I attended Bible study last night and it only lasted an hour, but it was good, real good."

"That's great. What are you doing this evening?"

"Nothing, I was just getting out of my work clothes. What's up?"

"My family is having a little celebration for me; it's my birthday, and I was wondering if you want to attend."

"I'd love to. Do you want me to invite Kyle also?"

"No. I just want you to come."

"Oh," Mayah was surprised. "Give me the address and I'll be there."

Jan gave her the address. Mayah thought Jan was interested in Kyle and thought it would be great for him to join in the celebration too.

"Jan, I'll see you shortly. I have to make a stop. Is there something you'd like for me to bring?"

"No, just bring yourself. I've told my family all about you. The reason I'm calling you at the last minute is, they were trying to surprise me, but I found out. So I asked if I could invite you."

"No problem. I'll see you shortly."

Mayah promptly showered, changed her clothes, and headed to the mall to buy Jan a gift. She wanted to call Kyle, but decided against it. She didn't want to hurt his feelings, being that Jan didn't invite him.

Mayah arrived with present in hand. She had a great time with Jan's family. However, she was a little tired after the long day at work. An hour and a half later, she told Jan she'd be leaving. After saying goodbye to everyone, she headed home. While driving home, she turned on her cell phone, and noticed three missed calls; one was from Kyle, so she returned his call.

"Hello."

"Hey, Kyle. What's up?"

"Nothing, I was bored and wanted to know if you wanted to go out to dinner."

"Oh, I'm sorry. I had another engagement that popped up suddenly."

"With Tia?"

"No," she said, abruptly offering no more information than that.

"Well, why are you being so secretive? Who did you go with? You're not hiding anyone are you?"

"No. When I arrived home I received a call from a friend whose family was having a birthday dinner for her, and she invited me over."

"That was nice. Was the food good?"

"Yes, it was great. Listen, let me talk to you about this later, I'm a little tired and I want to focus on my driving."

"Alright. Do you want to go to dinner tomorrow around six o'clock?"

"That'll be great. Why don't you call Mama and we can all have dinner together?"

"Okay. I'll call her right now. I'll pick you up at a quarter to six."

Mayah hung up the phone and released a sigh of relief. Because of Kyle's usual persistence, she thought at one point that she'd have to disclose where she'd gone that night. She couldn't understand why Jan wouldn't invite him, but purposed in her heart to find out at a later time.

CHAPTER 21

It was a quarter to six Saturday night, and Kyle called Mayah from his cell phone. He had already picked up their mother and they were outside her apartment. She raced down to his car.

"Hi, Mama," she said as she kissed and embraced her.

"Hey, Baby. How are you?" She patted Mayah's cheek.

"Great. Hi, Kyle."

"Hey, Mayah. We haven't done this in a long time. This should be fun."

"Where are we going?" Their mother, Alberta, asked.

"Just wait and see," Kyle replied.

Within a few minutes, they arrived at a wonderful seafood restaurant.

"This is nice," remarked Alberta.

"There's no place too good for the two most important ladies in my life," Kyle said with a huge grin.

They were seated and Alberta wanted to catch up on her kids' lives, especially over the last several months. Mayah spoke first.

"Mom, I've been having a lot of fun visiting churches with Kyle. It's so good to be in his company. You did an excellent job raising him." She laughed as she patted his hand. "Work is crazy. I don't put in all those hours like I used to. I'm up for a major promotion and haven't decided whether or not I want it."

"Why wouldn't you want it?" Her mother asked.

"I don't want to be tied down to a job where they believe they own me. With promotions come greater responsibilities, and I don't want to work late nights during the week anymore because I attend Bible class, nor do I want to work on weekends, because I go to church on Sundays. I'm doing just fine with the money I'm making now. I have more than enough because I budget my money correctly."

"Baby, if they want to pay you more money for what you do, why don't you accept it? You're a paralegal and didn't earn your degree only to reach a certain level and then stop."

"Mama, I have this job because of my education. I've had four major promotions and I'm content. Only two people in the company posses higher positions than me, and I'm fine with that." Mayah hoped her mother was actually hearing her words. She took a deep breath and continued. "I like my life the way it is. If and when I meet my future husband and have babies, I don't want to be bogged down with weighty responsibilities of a job. I want to go home like someone with good sense. I don't want to sacrifice my family for a career."

"Baby, I understand. But—"

"That's it Mama. Let's change the subject," she said firmly, but politely. "Kyle why don't you tell Mama what you're doing?"

"What are you doing, son? You sister doesn't want me in her business."

"Mama, I'm cleaning up my life. I've met a woman who I believe is my wife."

"Where did you meet her?"

"At church."

"Church?"

"Yes Mama—church. At first I was real reluctant to hang out with Mayah while she was doing her church thing, but I really look forward to going with her every week."

"That's good. I'm sure your grandmother would've been proud of you two. But tell me about this girl. When am I going to meet her?"

Mayah smiled at Kyle and she responded for him. "Soon, Mama. Just hold on; you'll get to meet her soon."

At that juncture, the waiter came to take their orders. They all enjoyed their meal immensely. Kyle paid the bill and took his mother home first.

"Thanks for bailing me out, sis." he said after dropping their mother off.

"Well, Mama will meet her soon. I didn't lie. Either she'll meet Jan as my friend or she'll meet her as your girlfriend."

"I like the sound of that," he said nodding his head.

"I'll pick you up in the morning so we can go to the one-hour service."

"That's okay, sis. I told you that I'll pick you up."

"What's up with you? Why are you being so accommodating?"

"Girl, when that preacher talked about the works of our flesh, all that fornicating and everything, and when he said, 'You can keep on dipping and dabbing in sin, but one day after you die, you just might wake up in *hell*' that was enough for me. It was as if I could feel the intense sweltering heat of hell." He paused and exhaled. "Something changed on the inside of me. Perhaps I always knew what he said to be true, but I failed to accept it as truth for me.

"I started reminiscing and flashing back on so many things in my life that I'm not too proud of. When I looked back, I felt so dirty and ashamed. I also realized that the view I had on life, you know, all those women, was not right either. I felt embarrassed, and inwardly I was crying, and before I knew it, I was literally crying in church just like you did. I teased you about the tears running down your face and I'm sorry. I now understand what those tears mean. Mayah, I always thought I was a 'good person' but I was wrong in so many ways. That's what's going on with me. I'm just trying to be a better person."

Wiping tears from her eyes, Mayah reached over and rubbed Kyle's hand. "I knew something was up when you started talking about changing your phone numbers and getting the women out of your life. And when you said you wanted to take me to dinner and drive me to church, I knew something was *really* up. I saw the tears running down your face in that last church, but I chose not to comment. I didn't want to tease you, because I knew what you were experiencing was real and not a joking matter. One of those times when I was crying, I felt like someone was scrubbing the filth and crud out of my life—but it was my inside life, not anything external. So brother, I can relate to what you're experiencing. I'm so happy for you. Now we just need to work on Mama."

Kyle smiled at her and she smiled back. "That's a hard nut to crack," Kyle said. "Perhaps when she sees how we're changing, she'll come around."

"Maybe so. I need to tell you something. I celebrated Jan's birthday with her family on yesterday. That's where I was."

"Why didn't you tell me? I would've gone."

"Because she told me not to."

"Mayah, do you think she likes me?"

"Yes, I do."

"Then why wouldn't she invite me over?"

"I don't know, Kyle. One day I'll ask her, okay?"

"Alright. Girl, now you have me feeling all down. Did she have someone else there?"

"Nope, just her family. But don't worry about it. I know she likes you. I'm sorry I told you. I didn't think it would affect you like this."

"I'm cool. I just wonder why she didn't invite me."

"It was a last minute invitation. She called me on yesterday literally minutes before it transpired. Perhaps she could only invite one person. It started out as a surprise event and at the last minute they told her about it, and she invited me, her friend, to come."

"I'm cool. I'm cool."

They arrived at Mayah's apartment, as she got out of the car, Kyle told her that he'd call her when he pulled up in front of her apartment, and they both broke out in laughter over the irony of the situation.

CHAPTER 22

Mayah awakened and prepared something to eat prior to going to church. While cooking, she meditated on the things Kyle spoke on Friday night. She realized her brother really had changed and was on his way to becoming a Christian. She was so excited. She could hardly wait until she got to work to tell Lesley what has happened to Kyle.

"Oh, Nan. I wish you were here to see this day where both Kyle and I would be going to church and actually liking it. You'd be so proud of us. Thank you for your love and your uncompromised lifestyle you lived before us. I love you, and I miss you."

Mayah ate quickly, showered, and got dressed. Kyle called to advise he was outside. She hurried downstairs to meet him.

"Hey, brother, so good to have you picking me up," she chuckled.

"Yeah, yeah, yeah. I know."

"Did you sleep good last night?"

"Like a baby. I turned my phones off and went to sleep. I'm calling to get my numbers changed on tomorrow."

"You're really serious, huh?"

"Absolutely!"

Within minutes, they pulled up in front of He's Alive Church. They both let out a gentle sigh and made their approach to the building. As they walked inside, they heard the sound of music. The choir sung a hymn, sat down, and Pastor Josiah mounted the pulpit.

Mayah gazed at Kyle and said quietly, "I wonder what his sermon is about today?"

He shrugged his shoulders in response.

From Church to Church

"Church," Pastor Josiah said. "Let's talk about *love* this morning. I'm talking about unconditional love, that is, *agape* love. This type of love says, 'I don't care what you say to me; I'm still going to love you.' This love says, 'no matter what you do to me, I'm still going to love you.' This love says, 'no matter what trials you take me through, I'm still going to love you.' This love says, 'even when you use me and treat me wrong, I'm still going to love you.' This love says, 'through it all I choose to love you.'

"This is the type of love that God has for all of us. In spite of everything we've done, God yet loves and cares for us. Some of you can't relate to this type of love because you want to get even with folks. You can't relate to this type of love because you feel you have to *right* all wrongs. You see, you can't relate to this type of love unless the love of God is in you."

Pastor Josiah had a captive audience in Mayah. No one in the church said a solitary word. There were no verbal comments. The pastor concluded his message and asked a young lady by the name of Dana to sing a certain song. Dana approached the podium and a music track began.

"I want to raise my hands to You. I want to lift my voice to You. I want to serenade my King, as I worship You. I want to pour my love on You. I want to sing my song to You. Lord, I'll testify of Your love, as I worship You."

Both Kyle and Mayah's eyes were welling up with tears that were ready to fall at any moment. The singer continued.

"I worship You. I worship You. I want to pour my love on You. I want to pour my love on You, as I worship You."

Kyle and Mayah both wiped tears from their eyes, along with most of the church. The entire church was still silent. The not-so-timid pastor stood once again.

"Church, we do great things in the community and that's love. We have all types of clothing and feeding programs, and that's love too. However, as a church, we've forgotten how to demonstrate our love to God. We've become cold and lifeless in our worship and in service. Too often, we run in and run out of church with total disregard for the love that He has shown toward us all. He didn't have to die on the cross—but for our sakes, and for love's sake, He did; otherwise our souls would be lost. The fire seems to have gone out in many of our lives, and I plead with you this morning; no, rather, I challenge you to rekindle that fire again in your lives. God loves you. He is love.

"For some of you, it's going to require you forgiving some people before you can move on. You can't say that you love God and hate you brothers and sisters. Our church is named He's Alive Church, and this needs to be demonstrated in each of our lives. I implore you to rekindle the fire that once blazed and allow the love of God to overtake you once again."

Pastor Josiah concluded with an altar call for all who desired to reignite the fire of love in their lives. He also called forward those who wanted Godly passion back in their lives. Additionally, he called forth those who knew they were not in the place where they should be in their relationship with God. The altar soon was full, and standing close to the front of the altar was a sobbing Kyle Johnson. Mayah stood in the group too, but Kyle had pressed his way all the way to the front of the altar. The pastor prayed a tremendous prayer over the people and then dismissed church.

Numerous members greeted Mayah and Kyle as they exited the building. Neither one mumbled a sound as they walked to the car, until they got in and closed the doors.

"Mayah, that was really good. I thought this church was lifeless, just dead at first, and it was. But something happened to Pastor Josiah between last Sunday and this Sunday. The fire of love infused him, and he infused the church with it this morning. I feel so good."

Mayah nodded her head. "I feel good too. I just want to go home and lie down. Wasn't that song powerful that the young lady song?"

"Oh, Mayah. When that girl started singing, my eyes just started welling up with water. Pour my love on You. What a concept."

Mayah tried to contain herself, but she couldn't. She burst out in laughter. "Kyle, that's usually what I do. Listen to the lyrics and talk about them and study their meaning. This is too funny. Now you're doing it. Isn't it something how a little phrase in a song can make such a vast difference in your heart and in your life? Isn't it amazing how lyrics of a song can have such a profound impact on your life? That song was rich!"

"Yes it was. Now, what time do you want me to pick you up for Bible study?"

"Uh, a quarter to seven. You still want to come?"

"More than ever."

"Okay. I'll be waiting. You're really going to enjoy the study."

* * * *

Kyle dropped Mayah off and drove toward his apartment. When he arrived home, the tears returned and he bawled. "Man, I don't want anyone thinking that I'm weak for crying," he said while inside his apartment, "but I can't seem to help it. I got to stop this 'cause my boys will think I've gotten soft."

Kyle knew something was happening to him, however, he didn't quite know what to call it. He grabbed a trash bag and walked around his apartment, removing items given him by various women down through the years. "Man, I have to get all this junk out of here. I don't want any reminders of my sin days."

He spent all afternoon cleaning house and reorganizing things. Then he dropped to his knees with his hands over his face, and started praying. "God, I know you're real and you're doing something to me. I don't know how to pray, but I just feel like I need to say something. I'm trying to get my life right. I don't want to die and open up my eyes and find myself in hell. I'm thankful that You love me unconditionally. Thank you, sir." He wept again. "Oh, Nan. Thank you for showing up in Mayah's dream. Thank you, Nan." This church thing was messing him up in a good way.

* * * *

Kyle called Mayah on the phone at exactly a quarter to seven to say he was at her place, and she went right down.

"Wow!" she exclaimed as she hopped into his car. "It sure feels good having you pick me up and also having you attend Bible class with me. Thanks so much. I can get use to this."

"No problem. I'm starting to kind of enjoy this," he said, laughing.

Upon their arrival at church Mayah was amazed to find three times the amount of people at Bible class than had been there the previous week. They took a seat in the sanctuary.

A happy, smiling, Minister Frank stood and began teaching. "Wasn't that a wonderful message on Sunday?" he asked.

All the people responded with either an "Amen" or a "Yes."

"Let me just continue from where the pastor left off."

Mayah was overjoyed about Minister Frank continuing the message on love. He taught for about an hour and then dismissed everyone.

Mayah and Kyle stopped for a cup of coffee after Bible class.

"Mayah, what church will we be going to next week? What's the name? I forgot it." One of the workers placed their coffee order at the pick-up window, so they took their cups and found a small table where they could sit and talk.

"It's The Church of Glory."

"Hey, and my girl is coming too, right?"

"Yes."

"Okay. Is she going to meet us at your house or are we supposed to pick her up?"

"I think she's going to drive to my house."

"Good. I'll drive and pick the two of you up if you like."

"No, I think I'll drive, and that way Jan can sit in the front with me and you can ride in the back—all by yourself." She laughed.

"That's okay with me. What time do you want me ready?"

"I'm not sure. Let me call you tomorrow like I usually do and give you the time."

"That's fine with me, sis."

They left the coffee shop and he drove Mayah home. Before getting out of the car she said, "I'll call you tomorrow with the time, alright? Thanks for driving and for coming."

"Okay, Mayah."

They kissed each other on the cheek, and Mayah ran inside, changed into her pajamas, and got her clothes ready for work the next day. Then she went to bed with a warm feeling surging through her veins. She thanked God for getting hold of her brother, and she hoped Kyle's newfound zeal was for real.

CHAPTER 23

Mayah couldn't get Jan off her mind all week, so on Wednesday she finally called her.

"Hello."

"Hey, Jan, it's Mayah."

"I was just thinking about you. How did church go this week?"

"It was great! The pastor preached a message on unconditional love, and the Bible class teacher expounded on the same topic. I wish you could've been there. It was profound. Jan, this lady sang a song about pouring her love on God. It tore us up."

"I'm glad everything turned around for you there. I know you were struggling at first, huh?"

"Yes, that first Sunday I thought I wouldn't be back. However, when I attended Bible class, the teaching changed my mind, and I'm so glad."

"That's wonderful, Mayah. Well, I'm ready to go to church with you on Sunday morning. I don't want to talk bad about The Church of Faithfulness, but I have had it with Minister Samantha. She's out of control and needs to find a seat somewhere. And that's all I'm going to say about that subject. I just don't feel like I'm supposed to be there."

"Jan, you can surely go with us. We have two churches that we'll be visiting, and you're more than welcome to come along."

"Thanks, Mayah. I'll need to think about that. I know I want to go to The Church of Glory, as I've heard many wonderful things about *that* church. So let me commit to going there with you, okay?"

"That's fine. I have a confession to make."

"A confession?"

From Church to Church

"Yes, I told Kyle that I went to your birthday celebration dinner, and he felt a little left out. He was wondering why you didn't invite him."

"Well," she paused. "I didn't invite him for numerous reasons. First of all, you're my friend. Not that Kyle isn't, but because I know there's some type of a connection between him and me, I didn't want to send the wrong message to him or to my family."

"What do you mean?"

"I've been saved for approximately three years, but I've been in church all my life. I've seen many Christians move too fast when dating so I'm very guarded or cautious about what I do and its appearance to others. I don't want my good spoken evil of. Kyle would've been more than welcome to come over. However, that would've led to many of my family members assuming that he and I are dating, and we're not. So those are a few of my reasons. I have others reasons that I'll share with you at a later date."

"I understand. He was just hurt for a moment and then he perked back up."

"That's good. My intention was not to hurt his feelings; rather, it was to avoid subjecting either of us to any assumptions by any of my family members. You know how family can be."

"Sure do. Well, they have two services at The Church of Glory. We prefer going to the first service. Is that alright with you?"

"That's fine. What time do I need to be at your house?"

"You know what? You pass right by Kyle's apartment on your way here. Do you want to pick him up and then come here?"

"No, I can't do that." Jan responded without hesitation.

"Oh, it'll be okay."

"No, it won't," she paused. "That's not something that I do. I'll drive to your house, and we can all go together or I can meet you guys in front of the church."

"I didn't mean to offend you. I'm sorry." Mayah said.

- 163 -

"You didn't offend me. I'm sorry that I responded so abruptly. I know you're just starting to go to church, and so is Kyle, but there are some things I don't do as a single woman. For instance, I don't pick up men from anywhere unless there's another couple or party in the car or it's an emergency. Also, I don't date without there being another party or couple with us. If a man wants me to meet him somewhere, you best believe a friend is with me. I try not to put myself in compromising positions. Additionally, I had a bad experience where I gave a Christian man my phone number, and he later harassed me so bad that I had to change my numbers; therefore, until I have known a man for some time, I won't give him my telephone numbers either."

"Wow! That's interesting. I never would've thought about doing any of that."

"That's how a lot of singles get caught up in sexual immorality; they don't take the necessary precautions prior to an event or date. They just go and some find themselves in positions that could've been avoided if they'd only preplanned their date."

"Jan, this is a subject that you and I really need to talk about. Keep talking."

"For me Christian dating is totally different from worldly dating. One has to always be concerned about the appearance of evil and/or placing themselves in compromising positions where anything can happen. I don't ever go to a man's apartment alone. I guess if an emergency occurred, I would if I couldn't find anyone to go with me, and that would probably be the only exception. Oh, I'd go if he was having a dinner event and numerous people were present. However, I'd leave with the group and not linger behind."

"You're serious, huh?" Mayah hadn't heard anything like this before, but she respected her friend's perspective.

"Yes, I am. I don't want my witness tainted. I've seen this happen to too many singles and nothing was even going on, but they got labeled as being loose or fornicators. So, I'm extremely careful.

"My grandfather is a pastor in another state, and he and my grandmother taught my sister and me how to act and how not to. They taught us how a person's good name can be ruined in a few seconds just by them letting down their guard."

"Well, do you date?"

"I have dated, but again, another couple or a friend was there. I learned how to date God's way—the hard way. I once found myself in a position that I shouldn't have been in with a so-called Christian man, and he tried to force himself on me. I managed to push him away. But I vowed I would *never* do that again."

"Okay, Jan." Mayah thought about how Kyle was going to have it rough trying to date Jan.

"So, if you don't mind, I'll meet you at your house or at the church. Either way is fine with me."

"Just arrive at my house at seven-thirty and I'll be ready. Thanks for sharing all that information with me. I never really thought about dating that way, but I can see how that would really work."

"No problem, Mayah. I need to do a few things around my condo. I'll see you Sunday morning."

"Okay, Bye Jan."

Mayah hung up the phone and reflected on some of the things that Jan said. She was a virgin just like her and thought that was wonderful. She knew Tia and most of the gang wouldn't concur. Mayah loved Jan's method of Christian dating and vowed to get more information about it later. She felt a closeness with Jan that she hadn't experienced with any other friend, including Tia. She was ecstatic about having two Christian friends in her life: Lesley and Jan.

Mayah telephoned Kyle.

"Hey, Mayah."

"Hi, Kyle. Okay, Jan will be at my house at seven-thirty; that means we'll be at your house by seven-forty."

"Where does Jan live?"

"About two minutes from you."

"Do you want me to pick her up?"

"No, no, no. She's going to drive to my house and then we'll pick you up."

"That's silly. She lives right by me."

"Kyle, this is the way it has to be. She'll drive over here and then we'll pick *you* up."

"Okay. You don't have to get all testy about it," he said as he laughed.

"I'm sorry. I didn't mean to be testy. But we'll see you about seven-forty. Got to go. Luv ya." Mayah quickly hung up the phone.

"Whew," she said aloud. "I don't know how this thing is going to pan out. But Kyle is in for major adjustments if he's going to date Jan. This is going to be real interesting and challenging. She's definitely a different type of woman. Surely one that Mr. Kyle will appreciate, if he can stand all the rules." She laughed so hard her stomach ached.

CHAPTER 24

Jan arrived at Mayah's house on Sunday morning right on time, and they were on their way to pick up Kyle.

"Mayah, thanks for letting me come with you."

"You mean with us, right?"

"No, I mean with you. If you weren't going, I wouldn't be in your car."

"Alright, I get it." Mayah chuckled.

"I'm so excited about going to this church. I've heard so much about it. I hear they have excellent praise and worship, and preaching. Are you excited?"

"Yes, I'm excited too, but I've heard some really good singing and preaching at quite a few churches here lately." Mayah reflected on some of the churches. "It seems as if each church has its own identity."

"You mean 'flavor.'"

"Yes, that's it—flavor. Hmm. I like that Jan."

"You'll discover that all churches have their own identity or flavor, and they all have their strong points and faults as well."

"It's funny that you'd say that. I've noticed that to some degree."

"Please Mayah, don't let that discourage you. It's not the church that's imperfect; it's the members, and you'll have imperfect members no matter where you go. We all have issues that God is dealing with. For some it could be talking too much. For others, it could be a lack of trust or obedience to God. It doesn't have to be the major issues that everyone preaches about."

"I never thought about that before. You seem to know a lot about God and church, just like my coworker, Lesley, who attends this church."

"Mayah, I, like every other Christian, am striving to know God more and more each day. We all make mistakes; however, we repent and don't do it again, receiving the never-ending mercy and forgiveness of God. That's one of the guarantees that come with salvation."

"That's good. I need to call Kyle so he'll be outside. So, just hold that thought."

As Mayah approached Kyle's apartment, she rounded the corner, phone in hand ready to call him.

"Wow! He's already outside," she said, then decided to not make a big deal out of it. "Good. We'll be on time today."

Mayah pulled up in front of Kyle and he slid into the back seat.

"Hey, sis. Hey, Jan. How are you two doing this morning?"

"I'm fine brother."

"I'm doing great too, Kyle."

"Mayah, I know you've wanted to go to this church since the beginning of your search, huh?" Kyle said.

"Yes, but I'm glad I'm visiting it in the sequence of things. I only have two churches left to see: this one, and Blazing Tabernacle."

Jan quickly turned her head toward Mayah. "Blazing Tabernacle Church?"

"Yes. That's the last church on my list."

"Whoa. You probably should've gone to that church prior to this one."

"Why?"

"It's a little different. That's all I'm going to say because you need to see it for yourself."

"Thanks, I appreciate you not speaking positive or negative in regard to that church. I'd like to go in and make up my own mind. So often people will make negative comments about something or someone, and when a person encounters them or it, they've already formulated an opinion, and that's not good."

From Church to Church

"I know. That's why I didn't say anything," Jan said.

* * * *

Kyle relaxed in the back seat, staring at Jan's profile. He couldn't control his thoughts; there was something about her. There was some type of chemistry going on that Jan had his full attention and didn't even know it. There she sat totally oblivious to his thoughts. He hoped she'd soon pay attention to him. He sensed she could be the one that he could fall in love with and marry. Yes, she could be the mother of his children. After realizing what he had just thought, he shook himself out of his reverie, turned his head, and stared out the car window.

* * * *

"Alright. Here we are," Mayah said as she turned into the parking lot. "Man, look at the size of this church, it's as large as a high school. Oh, they even have parking lot attendants. I like this. Kyle, we haven't seen anything like this, huh?"

"No, sis. This is a new experience."

Mayah followed the directions of the parking lot attendant, parked her car, and they all exited the vehicle. As they were walking toward the church building, many people in the parking lot greeted them.

"Is this your first time here?" asked one of the attendants.

"Yes it is," Mayah nervously responded.

"Just follow me and I'll show you where to go."

"Thank you, sir," Jan replied.

The attendant escorted them to the entrance where they approached a group of greeters.

"Hello. Is this your first time here?"

They all responded yes.

"We're so happy to have you here. We know there are many other churches you could be attending this morning, but you chose to come and visit us. Let me give you some literature. If you could fill this card out sometime during the service and just drop it into one of the boxes at the exit doors, we'll be contacting you, if that's alright."

They all agreed it would be fine.

Ushers with smiles as large as the state of Texas stood at the main sanctuary doors.

"Is this your first time here?" inquired one of the ushers.

"Yes it is," Mayah responded. She stifled a laugh. They could have avoided hearing this question numerous times if they would've worn a badge that said, *Yes, this is my first time here.*

"The bathrooms are to the right, and there's a visitor's reception room to the right of the restrooms, should you desire to pick up your complimentary sermon CD or other literature," one of the ushers told them.

"Thank you, ma'am. We'll surely stop by after service." Mayah smiled.

They were ushered to seats on the main floor of the sanctuary. Seated first was Jan, followed by Mayah and then Kyle.

"Jan, this sanctuary is breathtaking. They seem to be very organized. I have never seen so many greeters prior to even entering a church."

"I know. This is so different from my church or any that I've been in." Jan eyed the beauty of the sanctuary.

Not too long after being seated, a large, multiage, multicultural, robed choir walked up on the enormous stage-like platform. It also held the orchestra, and there was still room for hundreds of people to occupy it. The purple curtains flowed from floor to ceiling. There were sculptured lions at each corner of the stage as well as numerous flags of various nations throughout the church. Centered at the back wall of the platform was a large, wooden cross, draped with purple, white, and gold satin fabric. The enormity of the building held a power of its own. Mayah guessed the sanctuary had to seat at least fifteen thousand people, if not more.

The choir walked in along with the musicians. As they moved to their appropriate stations on the stage, five important looking people walked in from a side door and took seats on the main floor, front row, and center.

Jan leaned over and whispered to Mayah. "The two in front are Sr. Pastors Shelly and Jon and the other three are associate pastors. A friend has told me a lot about this church."

The musicians began playing, and the worship team entered from another side door and uniformly took their positions in front of seven evenly-spaced microphone stands. After that, one of the singers stepped to the front of the stage and began singing and humming. The congregation followed her lead, and their hands immediately elevated as they began worshipping God.

Mayah recognized Teria as the Worship Leader. She remembered her saying that she attended the Church of Glory; however, she didn't know that Teria was a worship leader there. She was both joyful and astonished that her friend was the worship leader at this distinguished church.

Mayah was completely captivated by what was occurring on the platform as well as in the atmosphere. With closed eyes, and uplifted hands, she became absolutely lost in the moment. This seemed to go on for several minutes, and then the worship leader spoke.

"Good Morning. My name is Teria. We're the ones God has chosen this morning to lead you into His glorious presence. I want you to shake off all distractions that can take your focus away from God. Forget about what you have at home. Forget about what's happening at work. Let's just set our minds on Him and worship Him without any personal distractions this morning. Can we all do that?"

The congregants responded with "Yes" and "Amen."

"Well, that's a blessing. Let's just give God the glory and honor due His name. Let's direct all our attention on ministering to Him this morning. It's not about us. It's all about Him. He's a wonderful God! A mighty deliverer! He's a faithful God! He is above all things!" She then commenced singing and at some point, the choir joined in.

> "Oh Lord my God, my King, we welcome You. My God, My King, we welcome You. Oh Lord my God, my King, we welcome You. Lifting holy hands and songs of praise to You. Oh Lord, we welcome You. Oh Lord my God, my King, we give You praise. My God, my King, we give you praise. Oh Lord my God, my King, we give You praise. Lifting holy hands and songs of praise to You. Oh Lord, we give You praise. We welcome You. Lift holy hands to You. We welcome You. Oh Lord, we welcome You."

Mayah scanned the church and observed the faces of thousands of people totally captivated in worshipping God. Suddenly, dancers and others with banners and streamers took the massive stage as well as the center of the main floor, dancing and waving banners.

"Oh, my! This is awesome," she whispered to Kyle as she continued clapping to the beat of the music.

She continued focusing on all that was happening. Making eye contact with Jan, she whispered, "Wow."

Jan responded with an affirmative nod.

The choir and worship team sang several other songs. Then, Teria began singing the last song.

> "Oh, Lord. I want to be like You. Oh, Lord. I want to be like You. Wash me, cleanse me, touch my life anew. Mold me as it pleases You. Oh Lord, I want to be like You."

At this juncture, all three of their eyes welled up. Yes, even Kyle. He bowed his head and Mayah closed her eyes. She wanted to shut everything and everyone out of what she was experiencing at that moment. "Yes, I do want to be like you God," she said under her breath. "But I need a lot of help."

Mayah watched as the congregation did something that she'd never seen. People headed down each aisle, unbidden, kneeling at the altar.

She promptly got Jan's attention and asked, "What are they doing?"

Jan scooted over so she could speak softly. "They're convicted and moved by the words of the song and are responding to what they're experiencing. Therefore, they're walking down to the altar, laying their lives down before God. They want Him to wash and cleanse them just like the lyrics say."

"Oh," Mayah whispered.

At that moment, Teria, spoke gently. "There's yet plenty of room at the altar. For those of you whose heart-cry is *Lord make me more like You*, I want you to come down to this altar. There's plenty of space for the rest of you. Also, for those of you who know you need the Lord and you're not saved, or you're unsure of your salvation, I want all of you to come to this side of the altar," she pointed to the right side, "to be ministered to."

Kyle and Mayah made their way to the altar; however, as they approached it, Mayah veered to the left and Kyle to the right.

Oh! I can't believe it. Kyle is going to get saved. I wonder if he knows that's the side for salvation?

Kyle made eye contact with Mayah and nodded his head in the affirmative, letting her know he was officially accepting Christ that morning. Her heart leapt within her. When she first began this journey, she'd only concerned herself with her own spirituality. It never occurred to her that this might also be life-changing for Kyle. Nan would be so proud of him.

At some point, Jan joined Mayah at the altar and both were in tears.

* * * *

An altar worker approached Kyle, verified that he was there for salvation, and ushered him out of the main sanctuary through a side door into another room. His heart pounded, but he was never more sure of anything in all his life. While in that room, a minister explained the plan of salvation to him.

At the conclusion, he prayed a prayer of repentance as tears flowed unattended down his face. He then accepted Jesus Christ as his Lord and Savior and asked Him to come live inside him.

Suddenly, he felt clean, as if his insides had been scrubbed; just like what Mayah had told him happened to her. He truly felt like a new creature. The minister smiled along with him and hugged him. Kyle had never been one for hugging other guys, but this was different. As the minister embraced Kyle, it was as if Jesus had wrapped His arms of love around him.

The minister handed him a packet explaining the benefits of salvation and exactly what occurred that day.

He turned and left the room and was back at the altar. There were still hundreds of people at the altar weeping, kneeling, and some lying on the floor. He looked for his sister and Jan, and when he saw their radiant faces, he smiled. He headed back to his seat, but he couldn't make himself sit yet, as he was charged up from his experience.

CHAPTER 25

While others were still making their way to the altar, Pastor Shelly grasped the microphone. "This is what it's all about. It's not about what you have on, where you live, or what type of car you drive. It's about, do you know Him! And if you don't, you need to make your way to the altar today. Don't let this time pass you by. God said the day you hear His voice not to harden your hearts. So if you're feeling a gentle nudge in your spirit, come on down and receive ministry. There's still plenty of room. For those of you whose hearts are already right with Him, I just want you to pray or join in with the team, singing how you want to be like Him.

"I know a lot of you are waiting for other things to occur, but this is what church is all about. It doesn't matter if anyone preaches today. God is moving by His Spirit, and we don't want to move in another direction away or apart from Him and what He's doing. Therefore, you need to just enter into worship and ask Him to change your hearts, your minds, your lives, and your focus. Ask Him to purify your hearts because your desire is to be like Him. Ask Him to take away the filth or the stench of sin from you. Surrender to Him today."

The choir and worship team kept singing, further charging the atmosphere; it was electrified by all the happenings. Jan and Mayah returned to their seats along with many others. They both resembled wet mops. Tears adorned their faces. They reached their seats and Mayah hugged her brother. Jan also embraced him and patted him on his back, as she whispered, "You just made the best and most important decision you'll ever make in your entire life. I'm so happy for you."

Kyle thanked her and let her pass in front of him as she headed to her seat.

Pastor Shelly continued. "I know some of you are still waiting on a message. Let me say this to those of you who haven't gotten the message yet for this service. I'm going to quote a scripture so you'll feel like we're in order," she laughed quietly, "and this is the message for today and for the remainder of your lives." She read Romans 12:1-2.

"Today, many of you have come to this altar to present your bodies as a living sacrifice to Him. Others have remained in their seats; however, they too, are presenting their bodies as a living sacrifice. You see, it doesn't matter if you do it at the altar, in the pews, in your house or in your car. The important thing is that you *do it*! I'm not going to spend too much time speaking about this because there are countless people at the altar and many are still coming. Let me say this; it's time for us to be changed by the renewing of our minds. We want the mind of Christ. We should no longer want to pattern our life-standards based upon this decaying world and its corroding system. We need to be changed into His image—the 'What Would Jesus Do' image."

Pastor Shelly spoke for several additional minutes, and then a gentleman got up from the first row, walked up to the pulpit, and gracefully took the microphone from her.

"Hi, I'm Pastor Jon. Like my wife just said, don't let this time pass you by. If you need to come to the altar, make your way down here so the altar workers can pray with you; and those in need of salvation, you need to come to the altar. We want to give you all as much time as you need." He paused for a moment.

"Right now, we're going to dismiss those who have already been ministered to. You can drop your tithes and offering in the depositories along the inside foyer walls; you'll see the signs and slots. Check your bulletins for upcoming events. There will be no

From Church to Church

announcements on today. May you all have a blessed week, and we'll see you all for Thursday night Bible study. Be blessed!"

Mayah, Kyle, and Jan all proceeded out of the sanctuary. They located the depositories in the foyer, placed their tithes and offerings in the slots, picked up their visitor's packet, and headed towards the exit.

"Man, it's raining. I don't have an umbrella," Mayah said when she looked through the glass double-doors.

Immediately following her statement, one of the parking attendants walked up to them with umbrella in hand and said, "Let me walk you ladies to your car."

"Thanks," Mayah and Jan replied in unison.

After getting into the car, both Mayah and Jan begin to speak at the same time. Mayah stopped and let Jan go first.

"What a service! I know there wasn't a long preached word, but God had already begun touching everyone's heart in worship. All we had to do was respond to that which He was doing. I just love these types of services. The pastors are very sensitive to the Holy Spirit too. They didn't try to get up and do what they had initially planned. They didn't even try to get up and preach the message that they possibly had been studying and working on all week. They simply yielded to the Holy Spirit, and everyone was touched and blessed as a result."

"I know, Jan. I feel so wonderful! I can't explain it, but I feel real good. How about you Kyle? I'm so proud of you. You accepted Christ today. Nan would be so happy."

"Yes, Kyle," Jan said. "That was the most important decision you'll make in this lifetime. I'm so glad you accepted Him too."

"Thanks."

Mayah looked in the rear view mirror. Was that all Kyle had to say? "Are you alright brother?"

"Yes. I'm fine, Mayah."

"I don't remember the last time I've seen you speechless. You sure you're okay?"

"Yes. I'm fine."

Kyle then glanced down at all the literature he received at church and began reading the material. He never said another word until he arrived at his apartment and that was only "goodbye."

As Mayah pulled from the curb after dropping Kyle off, Jan questioned her. "Is he usually this quiet?"

"No. That's why I asked if everything was alright."

"Maybe it's just the excitement of the day. There was a lot to experience at this church."

"There sure was. From the time we drove into the parking lot until the time we left, there was a lot of good stuff going on. Jan, I felt special in this church, even among the multitude of people there."

"This is what church is all about, huh?"

"I guess so. Jan, are you going to Bible study on Thursday Night?"

"I'm planning on attending. Why?"

"I was going to ask if you wanted to have a snack somewhere close to the church so we wouldn't be late."

"I'd love to."

"Good. Let's check and see what's near the church. I'll meet you at five-thirty. Park in the lot and we can leave from there."

"What about Kyle?" Jan inquired.

"Kyle doesn't attend Bible class during the week. I mean, he attended two Bible classes with me and that's it."

"Then that's perfect. I'll meet you at five-thirty. I'll drive to the restaurant since you drove tonight."

"Okay. Well, here's your car."

"Thanks for everything, Mayah. I'll see you on Thursday."

"Toodles." Mayah snickered.

"Likewise."

From Church to Church

Mayah opened her door, hurried upstairs, and kicked off her shoes. After getting comfortable on the bed, she immediately called Kyle.

"Hello."

"Hey, big brother. Are you alright? You were so quiet."

"Yeah, I'm fine. When I went in the back room, the things that they shared about Jesus nearly knocked me off my feet. I mean it rocked my world. I knew Jesus died on the cross for my sins, but the way they broke it down, well, they had my full attention. I realized that I had let God down or disappointed Him on so many occasions and in so many different ways with my faulty lifestyle. I'm not saying that I can change overnight like you, but I'm really going to continue making drastic changes in my life."

"I didn't change overnight. It's a process and I'm still changing. I pray that I'll continue to change until I'm more like Him, just like the song said. So, how did you enjoy Jan?"

"When I see that girl, she puts a smile on my face. I really like her. She can be a good and positive friend for you too."

"I know it. I feel such a connection with her. It's as if she's my sister, I mean, blood sister. Unfortunately, Tia may have some issues with this, but it is what it is. Oh, before I forget, Jan and I are going to have a light snack before Bible class on Thursday."

"Ah, Mayah, I thought we could go to church together on Thursday."

"What? You're really going to Bible study?"

"Yep. Like the brother said in the back room, I have to get rid of all unhealthy and bad habits and in their stead, fill that space with good, healthy, righteous habits. Going to Bible class is a healthy thing. Since I have cut the unhealthy extracurricular things out of my life, you know, the ladies, I have more free time on my hands, and I want to stay focused on the right things. Changing my numbers really helped. Except there were a few that called me on my job, but I got rid of their calls quickly."

"That's great, Kyle. Why don't you meet us at church? If you arrive before we do, just wait in the lobby and we'll do likewise."

"Okay."

"Are you upset that you can't come and eat with us?"

"Nope. In due time."

"Alright. I'm going to prepare something to eat and I'll talk to you later this week. Luv Ya!"

"I love you too, baby girl."

As she prepared lunch, Mayah reflected on everything that occurred at church. She couldn't believe that her brother, the player, got saved. She also decided that she'd go out and buy him a Bible that following day on her lunch hour. For some reason, she just couldn't part with Nan's Bible. It had become that precious to her.

CHAPTER 26

Mayah ran out to the bookstore on her lunch hour and found the perfect Bible for Kyle. She would present it to him that night at Bible class. Following work, Mayah and Jan met up at the church parking lot.

"Thanks for driving to the restaurant," Mayah said when she got into Jan's car.

"No problem. There's a Salad Bar right around the corner."

"Great. Oh, Kyle is going to meet us in the lobby at church tonight. He's coming to Bible study."

"That's good."

"I know. I didn't think he'd ever come with me again, but I guess Sunday really changed his life."

"I guess so."

"Jan, you do like Kyle don't you?"

"Yes. He's a good person."

"No, I mean *like* him?"

"Like I told you, there's something about him, but all things happen in the timing of God. I'll allow God to do whatever He wants in terms to Kyle and me, should there be a Kyle and me."

"I admire you, Jan. I know plenty of women who would, and have thrown themselves at Kyle. In fact, we went to one church, and the women acted like he was the last piece of candy in a candy store."

Jan burst out laughing. "Well, your brother is very handsome, but more importantly, he has a warm, kind, tender heart. I saw that on Sunday when he teared up, and then later when he went to the altar. I also watch how he treats you with the utmost of respect. I believe he'll be a great man of God and God will really use him."

"Yes, he's a great man, friend, and brother. He has one of the kindest hearts that I know. He wasn't thinking about attending church; he did that for me."

"He may have thought he was doing it for you, but God had a greater plan than yours, Mayah. He used your desire to find a church to draw Kyle back to Him. That's so wonderful."

"I never thought about it that way, but it sure makes sense."

They arrived at the Salad Bar, ate their meal, and headed back to church. As they walked toward the sanctuary, amid the greeters and ushers was Kyle grinning from ear to ear. There were, however, a couple of women talking to him. After catching a glimpse of Mayah and Jan, he swiftly dismissed himself and walked over to them.

"Hey, brother." Mayah kissed his cheek.

"Hi, Kyle" Jan acted standoffish as she greeted him with a handshake.

"Hi, Jan. It's so good to see you again."

"Likewise."

"I have a surprise for you, Kyle," Mayah said as she handed him a plastic decorative bag with a flat box in it.

He opened the box to see a Bible with his name engraved on it as well as the date that he accepted Christ. "Sis, this is wonderful. I was thinking about buying a Bible this weekend. Thanks. You're the greatest."

He then turned toward Jan. "Jan, I have the best sister in the world. I don't know what I'd do without her."

"I know. She's a great friend too."

They made their way into the sanctuary, and this time Mayah positioned everyone so that Kyle sat between Jan and her. He looked like he was more than happy with these seating arrangements. He couldn't stop grinning.

The musicians were already in place and were playing very softly when a group of singers made their way onto the stage. A

From Church to Church

giant of man stood and read a scripture, followed by prayer. Then the singers sang, "I Want To Be Like You."

Pastor Jon stood up while they were yet singing and said, "I asked them to sing this song from Sunday again. Not that I'm trying to duplicate or mimic what occurred on Sunday morning; rather, because tonight the teaching is centered around being like Him."

Pastor Jon taught for about forty-five minutes or so. After the conclusion of the lesson, the singers did an encore performance. He advised the congregation that he was attempting to etch the lyrics of the song onto their hearts so that they'd be able to carry that message in their spirits for the remainder of their lives.

"Don't you want to be like Him?" he asked loudly.

Everyone said, "Yes" or nodded their head.

He wrapped up his teaching with prayer, and Bible class ended with him telling everyone that he'd see them all on Sunday morning.

Kyle escorted both Mayah and Jan to their automobiles. Of course, he and Mayah walked Jan first. They all said their goodbyes and headed home, all in separate vehicles.

* * * *

Mayah awakened Friday morning and decided to get dressed and go in to work early. Later that day, she finally got a chance to speak with Lesley, who had been on vacation.

"Lesley, I went to your church this past Sunday."

"I heard service was off the hook, simply unbelievable!"

"It was more than that. My brother accepted Jesus on Sunday."

"That's *terrific*, Mayah."

"We went to Bible class on last night, and we'll be back on Sunday morning. Oh, a girlfriend of mine is also coming with us."

"That's wonderful. I know I've been out of town for a few weeks; however, whenever you want to resume our studies let me know."

"What about next week?"

"Next week is fine; same time and same table," Lesley said, laughing.

"No problem, see you then. Perhaps we might see each other at church, too."

CHAPTER 27

Mayah and Jan drove to Kyle's apartment to pick him up. Once again, he was standing at the curb, neatly dressed, and ready for Sunday morning's service.

"Hello again, ladies," he said, grinning from ear to ear.

"Hi, Kyle" they both responded.

"I'm a little excited about this church, are you?" Kyle asked both of them, but he looked toward Jan.

"Yes, I am," Jan responded first. "I've done nothing but think about this church since last week. What about you, Mayah?"

"I could hardly sleep last night thinking about it. Oh, I spoke to my coworker Lesley. Since she's back from vacation, we're going to resume our Bible studies on our lunch break. I really enjoy the way she breaks down the Bible. She makes it real clear."

"That's good," Jan said.

They fell into a comfortable silence in the automobile. Mayah was meditating on what could possibly happen this Sunday in service, and figured the other two were also.

Mayah entered the parking lot. The attendants once again directed her where to park. After parking, Kyle quickly jumped out of the car so he could open the doors for them.

"Thank you, Kyle," Jan and Mayah both said.

"You're welcome, ladies. Just doing my job," he said as he laughed to himself. "The two of you look real nice."

They both smiled.

Once inside the church, they were greeted and ushered to their seats. However, this time, Jan was not seated next to Kyle. Mayah saw Lesley and waved and she returned the wave.

As church began a dancer named Tylee had already positioned himself on the huge stage, all decked out in a mime costume. The music began and the young man danced as a soloist sang.

> "No form or comeliness was about You. When they saw You, no beauty they desired. You were despised and rejected by men. Acquainted with grief were You. They hid their faces from You Jesus. No, they esteemed You not. Because they saw no value in You. No, they saw no value in You. Surely You have borne all our griefs. The weight of our sorrows You carried. You were smitten, wounded, afflicted, and beaten because of me. Yes, every lash they laid on You Jesus. It was all because of me. Yes, it was all because of me. So I'll declare my love forever. I'll declare my love for You. Yes, I'll declare my love forever. I'll declare my love for You."

"He's really phenomenal," Jan said.

"Yes, he is," Mayah replied. "And so is the singer."

Kyle didn't say a word. His eyes remained fixed on the young man, and he intently listened to the words of the song.

> "Now I long to see Your face, Jesus. Your true beauty I'll behold. The beatings You took in my stead. The spit on your face was because of me. You were wounded for my transgressions, bruised for all my iniquities. So I'll declare my love forever. I'll declare my love for You. Yes, I'll declare my love forever. I'll declare my love for You."

When the young man concluded his dance, and the singing had ceased, Mayah wept as she reflected on all that Jesus had done for her. Out of the corner of her eyes, she saw Kyle sitting with his face resting in his hands, and on the other side of her, Jan whimpered as she held a tissue against her eyes. Finding God again had been wondrous, and being able to share her joy with others who understood what she was going through gave Mayah the feeling she was a little lost lamb finding her way home again. Mayah wept even more.

Pastor Shelly arose from her seat and approached the podium. "Hallelujah! I'm about to be messed up this Sunday too. Thank you, musicians, and my niece, Jasmine for that solo. Thank you so much Minister Tylee. Isn't he anointed? This is his second time dancing.

"Saints, yes, Jesus did it for you and me. He didn't have to, but he did. Just like the scripture says, they did all those things to Jesus because they saw no value in Him. Who is He to you? Do you value Him? Do you give worth to Him—that is, do you worship Him? Okay. I'm just going to roll with this again. I'm going to stay right here and talk. Do you value the One who suffered, died, and arose for you? Do you value the One who laid His life down for you? Do you value the One who provides all things? Do you value the One who made a way so that we can have full access to the Father without a go-between person as it was in the Old Testament? Are you hiding your face from Him? Can you declare your love to Him today? Can you declare your love for Him outside these four walls? Can you just forget about yourself and just love on Him this morning—the giver of life—can't you just focus on Him this morning?"

Pastor Shelly subsequently preached an unparalleled message about the cross and all the benefits we have because of Christ. When she concluded her message, the altar was packed out once again with people repenting and crying out to the Lord, as well as those accepting Him as their Lord and Savior.

Pastor Shelly advised everyone that they would need to use the depositories again for their offerings. She also spoke to those who were new in attendance. "For those of you who are wondering why we use the depositories, which are located in the foyer, let me tell you why. When the service is high or the Holy Spirit is moving, and God is really doing a work in His people, we don't want to stop the service to take up the offering or read the announcements. We understand that giving our tithes and offering is worship too, and you'll see many walking to the front of the altar, placing their tithes and offering in these four containers during service. They do this during worship time as an act of worship." She paused and exhaled.

"However, when the Spirit of God is high, we have everyone put their offerings in the depositories in the lobby so as not to disturb anyone who's on the verge of a breakthrough or being ministered to at the altar. We do this as a courtesy to the Holy Spirit as well as those needing additional ministry time. We desire to remain sensitive to the Holy Spirit and forego any program when He starts moving so He can have *His* way."

Mayah glanced at Kyle, shook her head, and whispered; "Now I understand."

"I have one more thing to say," Pastor Shelly continued. "I don't know what God is doing in this place, but it's glorious. We don't want to quench the Spirit; we want to follow Him. So let's stay in a worship frame of mind. However, I'm sorry. I do need to make one announcement; there will be no Bible study this Thursday. Instead, we'll have our annual business meeting. I hope to see you all there. Go in peace and stay with God."

The three of them made their way to the foyer, placed their offering in the depository, and walked to the car.

* * * *

"Hey, you guys want to go get some breakfast? My treat," Kyle offered.

"That would be great. Jan, would you like to go with us?"

"Sure, I'll go with you."

Kyle's heart started racing. He would finally be spending some time with Jan outside a church setting, and he could hardly wait.

They arrived at the restaurant, and the seating hostess directed them to a booth and handed each of them a menu. Mayah sat next to

From Church to Church

Jan, and Kyle sat across from them. Perhaps this would be a great opportunity to find out some additional information about Jan.

The waiter arrived and jotted down their orders. As soon as he left, Kyle spoke. "Jan, could I ask you a few questions about yourself? Do you—"

"Hold up, Kyle," Mayah interjected. "There will be plenty of time later to get to know Jan. Let's just have breakfast and talk about service and that young man who danced in church today. He brought the house down. That singer was pretty tight too."

"That young man is so anointed and gifted. He appeared to be what—thirteen?" Jan asked.

"Yes," Mayah said. "Are you guys coming to the business meeting on this Thursday?"

"I think I'll pass on that, Mayah." Jan told her.

"I think I will also," Kyle said.

"Okay. That's fine. I'm going. I'm curious to see how they conduct business in this church. Since I'm not sure which church I'll be joining, I need to see as much as I can."

"You're so right, Mayah," Jan said.

They finished their meal and Mayah dropped Kyle off at his apartment.

"Well ladies, I'll see the two of you real soon."

"No you won't, Kyle. Today is the last Sunday at this church. The next stop will be Blazing Tabernacle." Mayah said.

"Oh, I forgot about that. I'm having such a good time at this church; I forgot this is the second week, sis."

"That's okay Kyle. You'll see me, but Jan's not going with us to the last church. She's going back to her old church."

"Hold on, Mayah. I won't be attending the last church with you, but I think I'm going to continue attending this church. I love how the Spirit moves and they have such a rich word," Jan replied.

"Okay, Jan," Mayah said. "I'll still call you. I've grown very close to you. You're like a sister to me."

"I know, but this isn't the end. We'll still do things together, and who knows, we just might end up in the same church."

Feeling somewhat saddened about Jan not attending the last church with them, Kyle spoke. "Well Jan. I'm not sure when I'll see you again. But it has truly been an honor meeting you as well as going to church with you. I'd like to see you some time. Perhaps we can all go out to dinner or something."

"That would be nice, Kyle. I'd love to go out with Mayah and you. No problem. Just let me know when, so we can coordinate our schedules."

"What about next Saturday? Is that too soon?" He hoped he wasn't taking advantage of the moment, but if what Mayah had told him was true, then she'd like to get to know him too.

"I'm not sure. Can I check my calendar and then let Mayah know?"

"I can give you my number and you can call me if you like. You can just call and tell me if it's okay."

"Let me call Mayah and she can relay that information to—"

"Yeah, just call me Jan because I want to talk to you anyway," Mayah said.

"No problem. I'll give you a call as soon as I check my schedule. Kyle, thank you so much for breakfast." She extended her hand out to him and shook his hand.

"You're more than welcome, Jan. Hopefully we can all hang out on Saturday."

Kyle got out of the car and waved bye. He wished he could've asked Jan some questions about herself. Why wouldn't she take his number? She must not like him as much as Mayah had let on. He headed into his apartment with the thought that if he'd missed the mark about her, then he'd take it like a man and continue to grow in the knowledge of the Lord.

* * * *

From Church to Church

Mayah drove to her home where Jan had left her car.

"Jan, I'm sorry if Kyle put you in an awkward position."

"There was nothing wrong with Kyle wanting to give me his number or asking me to dinner. I thought it was funny in a good way. And perhaps I'm making too much out of this, and if I am, please forgive me. I don't want to seem paranoid. I just want to do things differently. With Kyle, it has to be that way due to the connection he and I have in the spirit."

"Okay."

They arrived at Jan's car and said their farewells.

As Mayah was getting out of her car, her cell phone rang. She already sensed that it was Kyle, and it was.

"Hello."

"Hey, Mayah. What was up with that? Why did you cut me off?"

"I did it to protect your little feelings, I think. Let me share some things with you and I'm sure Jan won't mind. She doesn't date unless there's another person or couple with her. Nor does she go over to a man's house either unless there's a group of people there. She doesn't give a man her phone number unless she's known him for a little while and is comfortable with him. Jan has some rules that she follows to make sure she doesn't end up in trouble or in a compromised position. You understand?"

"I was just going to give her my number, and you jumped in like I said something nasty to her!"

"I'm sorry. I guess I should've explained how some Christians date. I'm just learning this from Jan so I hope I recite it right. They don't do like we've done in the past. The women try to make sure they're not in a position where they can be taken advantage of or where they'll compromise and sin. That's it. I think it's a good thing. She's saving herself for her husband, just like me, and she doesn't want to be tempted if she doesn't have to." Mayah took a deep breath.

"She has boundaries in place, and I rather like that. They make sense to me. If a man honors the boundaries she has set, then she knows he'll respect her wishes. If he has issues with her boundaries, then she has issues with him and won't date him. I just didn't want you to say something out of line or something that could be misconstrued. Personally, I think she's just not ready to give you her number yet. Just be patient. It'll happen."

"Thanks, sis. Hmm. That's different. But I already know that she's a different caliber of woman so I'll have to go along with the program. I'll wait until she calls you. She's really a respectable and intelligent person, and I like that."

"I know, and she's not running after you either. I like that. The girl's got class. She's not like all those other women who go *goo-goo-gaga* after you." Mayah burst out in laughter. "You'll have to work hard to get a date with this one, and more than likely, I'll be on those dates with you." She laughed even more.

"Yes, she does have class and so do you, and I don't mind waiting. From what I'm sensing, she's truly worth the wait. She has good Christian values and a good head on her shoulders and I like that. You never thought you'd hear me say that, huh? I hope she's going to come on Saturday. Watch…I bet she'll be there."

"No, I never thought I'd hear that coming out of your mouth. Anyway, if she doesn't have anything to do, I'm sure she'll come. Oh, before we hang up, I'll talk to you about the next church on Saturday at dinner—that is, if you and I are still on if Jan can't come."

"Girl, you know I'm not like that. If she doesn't come, you and I will go. Bye, I'll talk to you after she calls."

* * * *

Mayah arrived at the Church of Glory's annual business meeting with a few minutes to spare. She was greeted as she entered the foyer and was instructed to take a seat as close to the front of the sanctuary as possible so when others came later, they could take a seat without disrupting the meeting.

Pastors Shelly and Jon conducted the meeting along with nine others who were all seated at a long table on the stage. The worship team sang a song, someone prayed, and the meeting commenced.

The ushers passed out a booklet that outlined all the departments in the church and the heads of the departments. It contained financial spreadsheets showing all finances received, including tithes, offerings, and expenditures. It listed all the church's assets, how many people were on payroll, and the total amount paid for salaries. It didn't show the dollar amount for each individual salary; however, it did show who was on payroll. There were accounting sheets and balance sheets. Everything about the finances of this church was out in the open for all members to see.

This impressed Mayah that they're above board when it came to accounting for all money coming in and going out of The Church of Glory. Having a degree in accounting, she was amazed at how detailed the statements were.

After their orderly meeting concluded, she went home satisfied that this was a great church to be a member of. However, she was still uncertain if this was the church that *God* wanted her to join.

* * * *

Jan phoned Mayah at work on Friday to advise her that she'd be going to dinner with them. She told Mayah that she'd meet up at her house. Mayah immediately telephoned Kyle and gave him the good news. He's to pick them up on Saturday, at six-thirty, at Mayah's apartment.

CHAPTER 28

Mayah's doorbell rang. She looked over at her glass wall clock; it was six-fifteen. Could it be Jan already?

"Hey, Jan," she said as she opened the door.

"Hi, Mayah, I thought I'd arrive a little early." They embraced each other.

"Girl, that's fine. Come on in."

"You need to know that my brother is so excited about us all going out again."

"So am I," Jan smiled.

"You sure don't seem like it. You're as cool as a cucumber."

"That's on the outside. On the inside, I'm very excited, but I'd never let Kyle know that. So please don't tell him."

"I got you. I won't say a word."

Just then, the doorbell rang. It was Kyle, dressed to the max. Mr. G. Q. himself, wearing a fragrance that could take any woman's breath away.

"Hey, ladies, don't you both look nice."

"Kyle, you're early. Uh, what's behind your back?" Mayah asked.

"Oh, I thought I'd bring the two of you some flowers."

"Thanks, brother." Mayah gave Kyle a kiss.

"Thanks, Kyle. That's very nice of you." Jan released a big smile.

"You two are so welcome."

Mayah placed the flowers in separate vases.

"Are you guys ready?" Kyle asked. "We have reservations for seven o'clock."

Mayah looked at her watch. "We're ready. Let's go."

From Church to Church

Kyle first opened the apartment door for both of them, and then the car doors. Mayah sat in the front seat and Jan in the rear. While driving, Kyle often looked in the rear view mirror. Upon their arrival, he drove to the front of the restaurant, jumped out, opened the doors for the two of them to get out, and said he'd be right back after parking the car.

He found a parking spot and met up with them in the restaurant lobby. The seating hostess came and seated them promptly. He didn't have to pull the chairs out for them, as the seating hostess pulled the chairs out for all of them and unfolded each individual napkin placing it in their lap.

While waiting on their food, Kyle thought he'd take a few minutes to glean some additional information about Jan. "So Jan, were you born and raised in Georgia?"

"Yes I was, and how about you, Kyle?"

"Yes, Mayah and I were born and raised here. Did you attend college in this area?"

"Yes, and I graduated from the University of Georgia."

"UGA? So did I." He paused. "I got my Master's in 1984."

"Kyle, I got mine in 1985."

"You mean to tell me we were both at the same school at the same time and never bumped into each other? That's amazing. I can't believe we were there at approximately the same time."

"I know. Did you play ball Kyle?"

"Yep, basketball."

"I attended a few games, but I never really learned the names of the players."

"That's too bad. We could've met much sooner, and who knows," Kyle raised his eyebrows.

"Yeah, who knows," Jan smiled.

At this time, their food arrived and their conversation ended as they all now focused on their meal.

After eating, he took them both back to Mayah's apartment, walked them to the door, kissed Mayah goodbye on the cheek, and shook Jan's hand.

"Hey Mayah, I'll be ready for church tomorrow at eight-thirty," he said. Then he turned to Jan. "Thanks for coming with us and I'll see you again, soon."

"Thank you Kyle. I look forward to seeing you again. Oh, and thanks for the flowers."

After Mayah shut the door, she looked at Jan and said, "You're about to drive me crazy with all this laid back stuff." She laughed. "If I didn't know better, I'd think you were playing hard to get. I don't know how you do it, but it sure seems to work."

"Let me explain why I'm so guarded. Let's sit down." Mayah led them to the living room. They both sat on the sofa, kicked off their shoes, and curled their legs underneath them. "I've been hurt a few times and this is the way I protect myself. If someone is interested in me, that's wonderful, but I'm not going to turn into some type of stalker nor will I make them the center of my life. You have to work at relationships and it takes time to really know someone.

"I can see that Kyle is a polite and kind man, and I know it has a lot to do with his upbringing. However, I will *not* throw myself at *any* man. I'm more than sure he and I will be dating, and you'll be on all, if not most, of those dates—that is, if you're free. But I'm okay where I am in my life right now. I don't have anyone stressing me out or putting me through any unnecessary changes, and I hope to stay that way—stress-free."

"I really admire your ethics when it comes to men and dating. Yes, I had a few challenges in a couple of relationships too. One time I came close to giving up my virginity. I'm so glad that I didn't because he proved not to be worthy of it. As you can see, we're not together now. I would've just given it up and he would've moved on. Whew! I'm so glad I didn't do anything. Since you seem to have this dating thing down, what about the women who have had sex and now they're Christians? What happens to them?"

"When one accepts Christ as their Lord and Savior, they're *born-again*; they're a new creation in Christ. They're made new in Him. To *me* that means if they had fornicated, or whatever, and have repented and accepted Christ, all their past deeds are wiped away as if they'd never sinned. They start out fresh and anew. Therefore, they could be considered a *born-again virgin*, right?" She laughed.

Mayah also laughed. "God is really something else, huh? So they just clean up their act and go on as if they hadn't had sex?"

"Pretty much. However, the key is that they have repented and are no longer indulging in sexual sins or habitually sinning. However, if their fiancé asks if they're a virgin or if they ever had sex previously, although Christ has forgiven them, they would need to tell their fiancé the truth. Yes, they had premarital sex; however, since being saved, they've been living a life of abstinence."

"So there's always hope, huh?"

"Yes Mayah, there's always hope. Sisters just need to really repent and then keep their legs closed. I don't care how fine he is." She laughed. "Listen, I need to get home. Let me get my flowers and call me after you attend Blazing on tomorrow. I want to know how it goes."

Mayah embraced Jan and handed her the flowers. "You can keep the vase and I'll call you sometime tomorrow after service."

Shortly after Jan left, Mayah's phone rang. She walked across the room to answer it. It was Tia. Mayah told Tia about the dinner date that she, Jan, and Kyle had just returned from.

"So why wasn't I invited?" Tia asked.

"We planned this after we left church the other day."

"So you're saying since I don't go to church with you and Kyle that I can't be invited to go anywhere with the two of you?"

"No, Tia, that's not what I'm saying. We all were coming home from church and Kyle invited us out. In fact, this is the second time that we've been out together for a meal."

"The *second* time? I guess you've put me down for this *Jan* person, huh? We go way back, Mayah, and you *just* met her and you're hanging out already. What about *us* and *our* friendship? I can barely get you to do anything with me and you've gone out *twice* with her?" Tia paused and let out a loud sigh.

Mayah rubbed her face, and hesitated prior to responding. She and Tia had been the best of friends for years. Mayah knew from the tone of Tia's voice how upset and hurt she was over her newfound friendship with Jan.

"Are you *still* there?" Tia shouted.

"Tia, you're still my closest friend. But I enjoy being with Jan too. We talk a lot about Church, God, Christian dating, and etcetera. And you're not into any of these."

"Christian dating—what's up with that?"

"I'll explain it to you this week. You want to go to dinner on Friday after work?" She attempted to appease Tia.

"I can't, Mayah, I have a date. What about Thursday?"

"That'll work. Let's go to the Chinese restaurant."

"Alright. I'll meet you right after work around five-thirty."

"Take care, Tia."

Mayah hung up the phone and flopped down on the couch. "This girl is trippin', but I guess we really don't have that many things in common anymore. She doesn't want to talk about church, God, or the Bible so what's left? Work and men? I don't think so."

CHAPTER 29

Mayah called Kyle to tell him she was rounding the corner to his house. He advised her he would be right down. However, he took more time that Sunday than she'd expected. She kept looking at the clock in the dashboard. He finally appeared and Mayah wanted to chasten him, but she didn't.

"Kyle, you're something else. When Jan was coming with us, you were already outside and standing at attention, waiting for us. But now that she's not here, I have to call you again?" Mayah broke out in laughter. "Umm hum."

"You know a man's got to do what a man's got to do. I didn't want to miss one second of seeing her."

"Alright."

"So, what did she say? I know you guys talked about me."

"We had a brief conversation about you. However, we mostly talked about Christian dating."

"Yeah, yeah, yeah. What did she say about me?"

"She said you were very polite and mannerly, something like that."

"What else?"

"Nothing really."

"Girl, I know you're holding back. I can see it on your face. She said something else. I know she did."

"Kyle, let it go, because if there was something else, I wouldn't tell you. Look at you. I've never seen you like this before. This girl's got you going, huh? You can't sweet talk her and wine and dine her like you did the others, huh? She has rather high standards, unlike those others girls you've previously dated. She's not easy either. I love it!"

"Yeah, the girl's got me going and I don't even know her like that."

"And you won't know her like that either." Mayah said.

They arrived at Blazing Tabernacle; there were many people standing out in front of the church. Some were robed and others in regular clothing. Mayah and Kyle made their way up the walkway. Many of the people greeted them; however, most of the greetings seem to have worldly or street flavors to them.

"How you doin'? You sure looking mighty nice this morning," one brother said to Mayah as his eyes inspected every part of her curvy anatomy.

"Hey, how are you doing? Yeah, how are you?" said a couple of the women to Kyle.

Mayah and Kyle slowly walked up the stairs, wondering what was up with all of these strange, suggestive greetings. They entered the door of the sanctuary and were seated toward the middle. Another usher walked over and inquired if they were visitors and handed them both a card to fill out, which they did.

Although service was supposed to start at nine o'clock, it was five minutes to nine and the church was nearly empty. There were more people outside than inside the church.

She looked around at how the people were dressed. "Kyle, the women dress different in this church. Looks like some of them are on their way to a party, with those tight, low-cut dresses on."

"Yeah, you right about that," he said and then looked to his left. "This is different."

"Maybe this is what Jan was alluding to?" Mayah said.

Fifteen minutes passed, and it was now nine-ten and church still hadn't begun. The platform and pulpit remained empty.

Kyle glanced at Mayah. "Girl, I wonder when they're going to start?"

"Your guess is as good as mine, but I sure hope it's soon. If they say their service starts at nine o'clock, then they should be ready at nine o'clock and not ten or fifteen minutes after nine. I detest waiting on events or things to begin, especially when there's a specific start time posted."

"Girl, you're right. I think this is the first church that we've had to wait for church to start, huh?"

"Yep."

The musicians finally graced the platform with their presence at around nine twenty-five. Quite a few people had also entered the sanctuary. The musicians started playing; however, people were still conversing loudly with one another inside the sanctuary.

"I don't understand this," Mayah said quietly to her brother. "The musicians are playing, and the people are just talking as if they're outside at a park or somewhere."

"Girl, I don't know what kind of a church this is—Blazing Tabernacle, huh? It doesn't seem too hot to me." He laughed to himself. "Although the clothes those sisters have on are blazing."

The musicians played for about three additional minutes when the ushers asked everyone to please stand. As the congregation stood, the choir, who had been standing outside in the front of the church in their robes, marched in. As they made their grand entrance, they swayed from side to side. They all stopped and paused for a moment, then proceeded forward a little before stopping and pausing again.

"I'm getting dizzy just watching them," Mayah whispered.

Mayah and Kyle both looked at each other at the same time and smiled.

The last choir member finally stepped onto the platform and they began singing.

"Jesus, You've been mighty good to me. Paid my debt way back on Calvary. All I want to do is praise and worship You and thank You for all You've done. So I stand here, worshipping You. I stand here, worshipping You. Here I am. Here I stand. Lifting up holy hands. Here I am, here I stand. Lifting up holy hands."

Mayah scanned the congregation. She observed a few people really getting into the song. Others were merely doing dance moves in their seats, and some kept on talking to each other. The children were also playing with one another, distracting the adults around them.

As the song wound down, the ministers strolled into the pulpit. An elderly man walked up to the microphone and read a scripture, and then he prayed. After that, the choir sang again. Following the song, it was time for the tithe offering.

There was a lot of talk going on about the needs of the church; the tithe offering took care of those needs. In fact, the elderly man said the church needed regular tithers in order to stay afloat.

Following the offering, a dance team darted to the front of the church, positioned themselves, and the music commenced playing. As the dancers danced, Mayah and Kyle both glanced at each other with strange looks on their faces.

"Girl," Kyle whispered, "they're doing club moves up in this church."

Mayah simply nodded her head in agreement.

During the dance, the ministers and the choir stood, and they began doing some of the moves with the dancers.

"Girl, I can get on this floor and bust a move too—right with them," Kyle said, a churlish grin on his face.

"You *better not*," she said, gritting her teeth.

The music track ended, and the musicians continued playing the same song on their instruments. The ministers in the pulpit were bouncing all around as were many of the congregants. The dance team exited the church through a side door. At that juncture, another dance troop appeared—about ten of them. They too bounced all over the place. The pulpit ministers along with some of the congregants joined in with them also. Even Kyle stood up for a moment and did a

From Church to Church

few moves and then suddenly sat down, especially since Mayah was jerking and pulling his coattail.

"Have you lost your ever-loving mind? You better sit down!" She was not playing.

"I was just going with the flow, you know," he said as he laughed softly.

After the dance troop finished their number, a young woman walked up to the microphone and began singing to the beat and melody of what the dance troop had just danced to, but she didn't sing the same words; she made up new words.

A gentleman in flashy clothes got up and started speaking. Neither Mayah nor Kyle could remember what he said. However, the congregation knew exactly what he said as they all jumped to their feet. After preaching, or whatever one would call what he was doing, for about fifteen minutes, he conveyed that he got up to do the announcements, and that he'd better "get busy announcing them."

"My brothers and sisters, the choir will be hosting their annual bash at Sammy's Lounge. The bash is going to be in the Lounge's Banquet Room. Although you have to walk through the bar, you don't have to stop and have a drink, just keep on walking to the back. Wine will be served with our dinner, cause you know, even Jesus drank wine," he said with a smirk, "and so did His disciples, so we can too. Uh hm."

Mayah and Kyle look intently at each other again, saying nothing, just looking at each other in utter amazement.

After the announcement clerk ended his lengthy proclamation, he handed the microphone to the pastor.

"For those of you who don't know me, I'm Pastor Ricky." He then started doing some sort of a dance move to the music the musicians were playing and the congregation burst out in laughter.

Mayah couldn't understand what the pastor was doing. Was it comedy hour or what?

"Hey, ya'll didn't know I could bust a move like that, huh? Oh yeah, I can dance." He proceeded to do a few other moves, and then looked at a lady who was seated on the front row of the church.

"Stand up, baby. Doesn't my wife look good? You know, David was the apple of God's eye. Well, my wife is the apple, orange, banana, and all those fruits of my eye. I just love her to death, you know. She's been a good wife to me. I just can't stop saying enough about her." He then made a growling sound.

Subsequently, the pastor began preaching a message about his wife. "When I'm down, she picks me up. When I'm hungry, she feeds me. Yeah… She's better than water when I'm thirsty. Hmm… When I'm lonely, she satisfies me. Well…I better stop at that!"

"What kind of church is this?" Mayah softly asked Kyle.

"I don't know. You picked this church, remember?" He covered his mouth and laughed.

"Do you honestly believe Jesus or His disciples would've said something like that?" Mayah whispered. "Do you think Jesus' disciples would've used ministry time or the pulpit to elevate their wives or their personal agenda instead of the gospel? This is crazy. I need to stop talking so much myself, but I can't help it. This is ludicrous."

Kyle merely nodded in agreement.

Following the pastor's performance and sermon on his love for his wife, three ladies walked to the front of the church wearing skin-tight dresses, hair all the way down their backs, faces well made up, and their lips adorned with flaming red lipstick.

"Well, we just rose to tell you guys that we'll be having our annual Homecoming Celebration. We need money donations as well as food items. This event will be held in the park directly across the street. This year we're asking that no liquor be brought to the picnic. No drugs and *no* liquor. Last year, we had a little trouble because some of ya'll got drunk or high. Now you know that ain't right. This is a Christian event. What you do in your homes is between you and the Lord, but what you do in the open is between you and everybody else. So, please no *liquor* or *drugs* this year. For those of you who have to smoke, we have a designated area in the park for you. We would ask that you don't smoke at the picnic tables or at the barbeque pits. The signup sheets will be on the tables in the foyer. Remember, this is one of our family events that we have each year."

Mayah sat in total shock. She couldn't even look at her brother; she was too busy staring at the lady who spoke. She couldn't believe what the women were wearing, and if what they were saying and doing was really a joke. It didn't take her long to realize it was *not* a joke.

The pastor stood up once again. "Now you guys respect what was just said. You don't need to bring all that stuff to a family church gathering." After saying that, he sat down.

Following him, two more dancers come forth to dance as the choir sang.

"Open the eyes of my heart Lord, I want to see, Your mysteries. Open the eyes of my heart Lord, I want to see, Your majesty. I want to know You Jesus and see Your glory, learn Your ways, and worship You. I want to touch You Lord, like I never have before, sit at Your feet and worship You. I want to worship You. I want to sit at Your feet and worship You."

Their dance was much more contemporary than the first few, and both Mayah and Kyle thoroughly enjoyed it. However, there was still a lot of talking and laughter going on in the sanctuary even while they danced.

"That dance was really awesome," Mayah whispered to Kyle.

"I know and these people are just downright rude and disrespectful."

After the dance ended, two gentlemen walked up front holding two trays. "It's offering time," they said, pointing to the trays. "This one is for our regular offering and the other is for benevolence. In case you arrived late and didn't pay your tithes, you can put your tithes in an envelope, and place it in the regular offering tray."

The congregants eagerly marched to the front of the church and deposited their offering in the appropriate tray.

Subsequent to the offering, the pastor raced up to the microphone. "Alright. I want to take my text from. . . well, before I give you the scripture, let me just say this. Today, I will be speaking on, *Devil, You Have Gone Too Far Now.* Tell your neighbor, *Devil, You Have Gone Too Far Now.*" He waited a moment while the people looked at one another and repeated his words, most getting a good laugh out of it.

"Looking at the economy and various situations all around the world, I've come to the conclusion that the devil has gone too far now. Yes, he's taking people's jobs and their livelihood. He's taking the lives of many of our young people. He has people hooked on crack cocaine, and I say, *Devil, You Have Gone Too Far Now.* Our babies are having babies and I say, *Devil, You Have Gone Too Far Now.*"

The pastor went on for about thirty minutes, his voice rising and falling in an almost animated fashion. He never cited a scripture. In fact, he never opened his Bible. He got caught up with what he was saying, which was *that the devil had gone too far.* Every time he would make that statement, his voice would elevate up to a higher pitch, and the congregation would yell and holler, "Amen!" or "Preach it, brother!"

Mayah and Kyle sat quietly in their seat, numb, as neither could believe all that was transpiring in this church.

The pastor finally finished, and the ushers walked to the front of the church with the offering trays in hand for a third time, saying they wanted to take a pastoral offering. So once again, everyone had to march around the church and place their offering in the tray.

Following the final offering, one of the ministers stood to his feet. "We have some visitors today." He read their names off the visitor cards. "Could I please have Mayah Johnson and Kyle Johnson stand? I see you both have the same last name, but you stay at different addresses. Are you related?"

"She's my sister," Kyle said.

"I hope that's the truth, brother, and not you trying to pull one of those Old Testament Abraham moves on us, saying she's your sister," he laughed as did everybody else, except Kyle and Mayah.

Kyle didn't comprehend what the gentleman was referencing, but he assumed it implied that Mayah wasn't his real sister. He paused for a moment. "No, sir. She's my blood sister."

"I'm just kidding. Is there anything you'd like say this morning, son?"

"No, sir," Kyle said and Mayah shook her head no.

"Well, if you guys are ever in the area again, please come back and see us. We're a church that loves God. Thank you for coming to Blazing."

Mayah and Kyle took their seats. Everyone was asked to stand for the benediction and church was dismissed.

As she walked toward the door, she whispered. "Kyle, don't say anything to me until we get inside the car. And you *better* not laugh on your way to the car either."

"I won't," he said as he bit his lip in an attempt to keep from laughing.

"I mean it, Kyle," Mayah said under her breath.

"I know you do," he replied with a huge smile on his face. He looked like he was close to losing the battle. A little chuckle slipped out.

Many of the members greeted them as they approached their car. However, when they got inside Mayah yelled, "Not yet! Don't say a thing. Wait until we are further down the street." Fumbling with her keys, she finally managed to get them in the ignition switch, and pulled off the lot. All of a sudden, both she and Kyle started laughing uncontrollably.

"Wait, Kyle. I got to pull over. I can't laugh that hard and drive." She got out the car and laughed, hitting the car as she attempted to catch her breath. Kyle exited the car and joined in.

"What was all that about, girl? Are they for real?" He kept laughing.

"I believe so. Whew! I can't go back there. Whew! I already know this is not the church for me," she chortled.

"Blazing Tabernacle, huh? Yeah, they're blazing alright— blazing with those tight dresses on. Blazing with that nightclub dancing up in there. Blazing with the parties at the park with drugs and liquor. Yeah, they're Blazing alright," Kyle said as he snorted out another laugh. "It ain't no fire, no blaze up in that church. Mayah, they were doing club dances; not that last couple, but the other dancers were. I didn't even know churches did that. But wait, at the last picnic folks was drunk and high; what kind of mess is that?"

Mayah realized it probably wasn't right or proper for her to be laughing, but she couldn't stop. "Kyle, I'm through with my search, unless you want to join Blazing." She continued snickering.

"Nah," he replied. "I got to pass on Blazing. Blazing will turn me back into a sinner, you know. I'll eventually go back to my old ways. I know there's a lot of activity going on in *that* church. I can tell just by the way some of the men and women were posturing themselves. Girl, this made my day. This church was hilarious."

"I know, hilarious in a funny way." She stopped laughing and they both got back in the car. "But also sad in many other ways." Her demeanor toned-down as she reflected on all the happenings at Blazing Tabernacle. She also felt somewhat disappointed in not just the church, but also in the fact that she was laughing about it. However, she said nothing to Kyle about what she'd been thinking.

"Well, I'm going to review everything I like and dislike or didn't understand about all the churches we visited. I really liked a few. Some of them had a few issues, but I still enjoyed the preaching and

From Church to Church

singing. So what I'm going to do is spend some time really studying these churches."

"Good luck."

"Kyle, luck has nothing to do with this. I'm going to pray, and hopefully I'll be able to make up my mind. I like a couple of the large churches, but I really like that one where the ladies were chasing you too. I especially like the warm feeling I had when I was there. I felt like I could approach Pastor Jack if I had an issue. At some of the others, I'd have to go through their bodyguards or entourage. I don't like that feeling. Not that I'd ever call my pastor or anything, but I'd like to believe he or she is accessible. Perhaps the others are too; how else could they have such a large congregation?"

Mayah pulled up in front of Kyle's apartment and she parked to let him out. As he swung one leg out of the car, Kyle started laughing again. "Blazing." He then composed himself. "Mayah, I know you'll select the best church for you. You have a lot to choose from and sift through. I'll talk to you later. Call me when you make up your mind. I really want to know which one you choose."

"I sure will. Please pray that I make the right decision."

"I will. Love ya, sis."

"Likewise."

Mayah arrived home, went straight upstairs, and put on pajamas. She planned on staying inside the remainder of the day. After changing her clothes, she decided to call Jan; however, she was certain she was still at church. "I'll just call her and leave a message on her phone."

"Hello."

"Jan, what are you doing home?"

"Oh, I woke up late this morning and decided to stay home. Also, I'm thinking about changing churches, so I've been praying all morning."

"I know how you feel."

"Enough of that, Mayah, tell me how was church?"

- 209 -

"Well, hmm. How can I say this? Let me just come right out and say it; I didn't like it at all, and neither did Kyle."

"Why not?"

"You know I'm a novice at a lot of things, but I think I'm learning how to sense God's presence in some of the places that I go. Well, I didn't sense His presence at this church. They seem to be kind of 'worldly' as you would say. They dance like the world. They sing like the world. They dress like the world. I think the preacher even preached differently. However, there were a couple of dancers who were really anointed. You should have seen them. But anyway, Kyle and I left and I don't have to return this week or *any* week. I know it's not the church I'd want to be a member of."

"I figured you wouldn't want to join there. There's a lot of compromise in that church. It seems they were once on fire for God and then turned totally cold to the things of God. They subsequently decided to just straddle the fence from that point on, which left them neither hot nor cold. Additionally, it's not a good place for new coverts, as they can possibly pick up some bad, unchristian-like habits, if there's such a word. Believe it or not, many say the pastor has a good message when he lets the Holy Spirit use him. But anyway, I'm extremely happy that you made up your own mind absent the influence of anyone."

"Me too. Now comes the rather complex segment of my journey—the final decision. I've attended some really wonderful churches, both large and small, great preachers and great singers, some with issues and some without."

"Let me stop you right there, Mayah. Every church has issues, visible or hidden. You need to know what church God has called you to attend. Once you find out the will of God for your life, then it's your job to advance quickly without vacillating. No one can help you with your decision. You have to go to God in prayer and ask Him. Let me know if you have any questions or if you need to bounce

From Church to Church

something off me. I'm here for you, just like a sister. But the final decision rests in God's hands. Just ask Him and He'll direct you."

"Thanks, Jan. I truly appreciate you. If people saw the way we interact with each other, they would swear we've been friends for years. Thanks for your friendship. I must say, it's one that I'm most comfortable with. I'm sure down the road we'll clash on some things, but we'll be able to get through those times because we don't mind working things out together."

"So true, girl. Well, I'm going to get off this telephone because you have a lot of thinking, praying, and soul-searching to do."

"I'll call you as soon as I make up my mind. Talk to you later."

"Bye, Mayah. Be encouraged. I know you'll select the right church."

At the conclusion of her conversation with Jan, Mayah took off the pajamas she had just put on and took a long, relaxing soak in the bathtub. She later climbed out of the water and put pajamas back on. Walking into the kitchen, she started opening up cabinets to see what she had to munch on. She decided to call the Chinese restaurant and have them deliver something.

Forty-five minutes later, her food arrived. After eating, she went upstairs and climbed into bed with the heavy question on her heart of which church she'd be joining.

Deciding her brain needed a rest, she turned on the TV, hoping one of the preachers would say something that would help her make the right decision. After watching TV for two hours without getting a revelation, she fell asleep.

Mayah tossed and turned all night, pondering that question in her spirit. Each time she rolled over, she would awaken to find herself asking which church was the right one. She finally fell into a deep sleep and had another dream.

In this dream, Nan appeared once again, not sitting in a rocking chair, but standing up. Mayah reached her hands out to Nan; this time she was able to touch her. "Nan, I love you so much." Mayah felt the gentle touch of Nan's warm hands as her grandmother caressed her cheeks and smiled. At that juncture, Mayah abruptly awakened. *Oh, Nan. Where did you go? I wish I could've had just a few more moments with you.*

She hated awakening at the point she did. She was still left with a dilemma. Perhaps she'd be able to go back to sleep and resume the dream. Mayah fell back to sleep, but she did not dream nor see Nan again.

CHAPTER 30

The alarm clock sounded and Mayah reached over and gently shut it off. Once again, she realized she had a decision to make. Kyle did exactly what he promised. He went to church with her and missed a football game, even though he said he wouldn't. She wished he or Jan could make the decision for her, but they couldn't.

Mayah decided to call in to work and take two vacation days. They permitted her to take time off, as business was still somewhat slow. They had been encouraging her to take some time off anyway, because she had accumulated so much vacation time carried over from multiple years.

She turned on her radio, found some Christian music, and relaxed on the couch to think and pray. Mayah had come to a crossroad in her life. *I'm so happy they've allowed me to take these two days off. I just want to be able to assimilate all that I've seen and heard these last fourteen weeks. There's good in all of them. But who do I want to be my Pastor? Just where do I fit?* This decision shouldn't be taken lightly or made abruptly without careful consideration on her part. She'd gone from church to church trying to find the perfect house of worship for her.

As she meditated on the churches, she decided to get dressed and go for a light run, as jogging always brought a higher level of focus and revelation to her. She left her apartment, stretched, and started out with a vigorous walk.

With each step, she spoke to God. "Help me make the right choice." However, she felt somewhat abandoned, as if it were a personal, individual decision to be made solely by her.

She picked up speed and started to jog. The various songs from most of the churches echoed through her spirit. She again picked up her pace, and as she rounded a corner, she started hearing some of the sermons and teachings resonate in her head, playing over and over again.

Finally, she stopped, bent over, and caught her breath. "I wish someone else could make this decision for me. Oh well, I'll figure it out."

Mayah returned home and jumped into the shower. After stepping into a comfy set of lounging pajamas, she telephoned Kyle at work.

"Good morning. This is Kyle Johnson, may I help you?"

"Hello, my favorite brother."

"Mayah, I'm your only brother. What's up? I know you want something by the way you've started this conversation."

"Not really. I've taken two vacation days, and I want to know if you can meet me for lunch or dinner today."

"I already have plans for today; what about tomorrow?"

"That'll be fine. I'll meet you at Rafferty's around a quarter to twelve. Is that alright with you?"

"That's good. Hey, did you make up your mind yet?"

"Nope. Pray for me, okay?"

"Sure will. I'll see you tomorrow."

"See ya."

Mayah met with Kyle on Tuesday for lunch. She still hadn't made up her mind as to which church to join. Therefore, she called her job to see if work had picked up or if there was anything pressing that needed her immediate attention. Being advised that things were still slow, her manager asked if she'd like to take the entire week off for vacation, reminding her they had been asking her to take some time off for months. Therefore, she agreed to take the entire week off.

"Whew, this should make my task a lot easier," she said as she breathed a huge sigh.

From Church to Church

    Tuesday and Wednesday passed and Mayah still hadn't made up her mind. She had even driven by all of the churches, absent Blazing Tabernacle. She had hoped something supernatural would transpire—that is, some sort of a sign from God when she arrived at one of the churches. However, nothing occurred.

    On Thursday, she called Kyle again at work.

    "This is Kyle Johnson, may I help you."

    "It's just me, Kyle."

    "Hey there. Been missing you. You must have made up your mind."

    "Not really. I've been off all week and I still haven't decided. Do you want to go to lunch today?"

    "I already have plans for today. I have a departmental luncheon. What about tomorrow night or Saturday evening."

    "You do know that tomorrow is Friday?"

    "Yes, I know it. And?"

    "I thought since your fourteen-week sentence was up, you'd really be out there partying."

    "No, I haven't thought about partying. But what I *have* thought about was the promise that I made to you with regard to your birthday, which has long passed. Remember, I told you I'd take you out and we'd celebrate it real big?"

    "You sure did."

    "Well, let me take you out tomorrow night. Where do you want to go?"

    "I really don't feel like partying or anything like that. However, we can go to the Marina and grab some clam chowder."

    "I'm shocked. I thought you'd be ready to celebrate your twenty-first birthday. You've really changed during your church search."

    "You can say that again. Some weeks ago, I probably would've been partying hard. But I'm not that person anymore. I don't long for something I've never done and possibly never will do. Wow! I can't believe that came out of my mouth."

"Me either. What's up with you?"

"I don't know, but it's all good. What time do you want me to be ready?"

"How about seven o'clock?"

"That's fine. I'll see you then. I love you, Kyle."

"I love you, too. Now get off the phone with all this mushy stuff. Hey, if you want to invite Jan, I'd love to take you both out. Give her a call and ask her."

"I'll call her and see if she's free. Bye."

All that day Mayah watched a little TV, read her Bible, and prayed. She desperately wanted to make a decision prior to Sunday, and perhaps even before she had dinner with Kyle on Friday night. However, she was no closer now than she was when she first set out to find the perfect church. She decided to call Jan, and just as she reached for her phone, it rang.

"Hello."

"Hi, Mayah, what's up? I called your job and they said you were off work this week. Are you alright?"

"Oh, Jan, I just needed some time to decide which church I want to join. I'm great."

"Well, I thought there was one in particular that you liked."

"There was, but I'm not sure it's the right church for me or the one that I'm supposed to be at."

"I really enjoyed The Church of Glory."

"Me too, Jan. But I'm still not sure. Hey, I was just picking up the phone to call you. Do you want to have dinner with Kyle and me on tomorrow? He's taking me out for a belated birthday dinner."

"I'd love to join you. What time do you want me to be ready?"

"Why don't you come over 'round six o'clock? I'm not going to tell Kyle that you're coming. We'll surprise him."

"You may want to tell him because he just might be bringing someone else."

"Nah, I don't think so. He's not seeing anyone and hasn't since he met you."

"Hmm, that's interesting."

"You just don't know how interesting it really is." Mayah laughed. "I'll see you tomorrow."

"Okay, Mayah. I'll see you then."

As Mayah hung up the phone, her other line rang.

"Hey, Tia."

"Hi, Mayah. What's up? I called your job and they said you're on vacation." Mayah shook her head and rolled her eyes. She had no idea taking a week off work would cause so many people so much consternation.

"Well, I'm trying to decide which church I want to join."

"I just thought people went to a church and just joined. I never saw anyone put this much time and effort or do this much research when finding a church; however, because you're so analytical, I should've known," Tia said.

"Yeah, you're probably right. Hey, Kyle is taking me out for dinner at the Marina tomorrow for my birthday. Would you like to go? Jan will be coming too. I know we were supposed to meet up and have Chinese food today, but this is so much better. You want to wait until Friday night?"

Tia snickered. "Sure. Let me change some plans. I can put up with Kyle for a meal, with his fine self; especially when he's paying."

"Just be at my house around a quarter to seven and we can all ride together."

"Okay, Mayah. I'll see you tomorrow. Enjoy your day off."

After hanging up the phone, Mayah felt she'd better call Kyle and tell him that she'd invited Tia to come along with them.

"Hello. This is Kyle. Can I help you?"

"Yes you can, brother," she said as she giggled. "I just want you to know that Tia will be joining us for dinner tomorrow."

"You're kidding, right?"

"No, I invited Tia to come along with us. That's okay, isn't it?"

"I guess so. You know who I really want to be there. But Tia is your friend and that's fine with me. I just don't want her going 'ghetto' in the restaurant."

"Kyle, she wouldn't do that."

"If you say so, but I think the girl's got it in her. I've seen her out at the clubs."

"Alright. I'll see you around seven on tomorrow. You don't have to bring flowers either," she teased.

"Don't worry. I wouldn't dream of bringing flowers for Tia or for any of your friends, with the exception of Jan. I'll see you tomorrow."

"Alright." Mayah hung up the phone "I can't wait to see his face when he sees Jan at my house. He's going to be so surprised."

Mayah sat down on the over-stuffed chair in her bedroom and reflected on the seven churches. She even pulled out a tablet and drew columns, writing positive and negative traits about each church. To her amazement, they all had some type of flaw. Some of the flaws had nothing to do with the church per se, rather, with some of the people in attendance and perhaps a pastor or two.

Glancing down at the columns, she blurted out, "I'm shocked! I thought for sure there was a church without some type of drama or flaw. I guess I was wrong. Looks like there was *one* with hardly any visible issues, a couple with fewer issues, and the others, hmm…I wonder if I should seek out a few more churches." She shook her head in disbelief. She then remembered what Lesley and Jan had told her, that there was no perfect church.

Mayah lounged around her apartment all day and ordered pizza. She spoke to no one else on the phone, which had become her main mode of communication these last fourteen weeks.

CHAPTER 31

It's Friday and Mayah got up and immediately ran bath water. She poured her favorite rose fragrance into the water. She climbed into the bubbled-filled tub and laid her head on the bath pillow. At the forefront of her thoughts was the question of which church to join. After thirty minutes of soaking, she grabbed the fluffy, yellow towel and walked upstairs to her bedroom. As she dressed, she experienced a sudden epiphany.

"Oh my!" she said aloud. "I got it! I know which one! I can't wait to tell everyone."

The doorbell rang at exactly six o'clock and Mayah ran downstairs to answer it.

"Hey, Jan." They embraced each other. "You're right on time. I also invited my friend Tia. You've heard me mention her name quite a few times. She and I have been friends forever."

"That's great, Mayah. I think this is the first time that I'll be actually meeting one of your friends."

"I know. She's not in church right now. But I believe she's on her way and just doesn't know it. Funny thing, Jan, a few months ago, I was in the same unchurched state that Tia's in. Who would've thought?"

"God would've thought. He knows all things. I know you're a good example for her. She'll be able to see the positive changes in your life and eventually be drawn in."

"You think so?" Hope for her friend grew in her heart.

"Yes I do."

"Jan, have a seat. I'm going to run upstairs and get my purse and jacket. You really look nice."

"So do you. Happy belated birthday. Why didn't you tell me that you had a birthday when I invited you over to my parent's house?"

"Because it was no big deal."

"Alright. I'll let you slide on that one, but next year, I'll remember it."

Mayah made her way upstairs. Right about then the doorbell rang again. "Can you answer that for me Jan?" she called downstairs. "It's just Tia."

"I sure will," Jan called up to her.

Mayah heard muffled voices coming from downstairs. "Hey, Tia," she hollered. "Have a seat and I'll be right down."

Mayah gathered her things and headed downstairs, but she didn't see Tia anywhere.

"Where is she?" she asked Jan, and Jan looked toward the kitchen. As Mayah rounded the corner, Kyle jumped out, "Gotcha! Now who's surprised?"

She jumped. "Kyle, what are you doing here so early? I thought you were Tia."

"I thought I'd come early and I'm glad I did."

The doorbell rang again. "Let me answer that. It has to be Tia."

"You think?" Kyle said, laughing.

Mayah answered the door and it was Tia. She embraced her.

"Hey Tia, seems like I haven't seen you for quite some time."

"Yeah, I know. You've been a busy girl."

She introduced Tia and Jan to each other.

"Tia, it's so good to meet you," Jan said. "Mayah has spoken of you quite often."

"Thanks, Jan. I've heard good things about you too. I'm glad to finally meet you. Hey, Kyle."

"Hi, Tia," he responded.

Mayah knew Kyle didn't think much of Tia; however, he put up with her because she was her friend.

Tia then glanced at Mayah and asked the million-dollar question, "Well, have you decided?"

"Yes, I have!" Mayah shouted, unable to conceal her excitement any longer.

Tia laughed quietly. "Wow, aren't we a little wound up. Okay, tell us."

"Nope. I'll tell you guys at dinner."

"Girl, you're going to make me wait until then?"

"Yep, all of you."

Kyle helped all the ladies on with their coats, opened the front door, and they headed out to his car. Tia and Jan hopped in the back seat and Mayah joined Kyle in the front.

"Girl," Tia said, leaning toward the front seat. "Are you really going to make us wait until we arrive at the restaurant?"

"Yep, if not longer."

"What?" Tia shouted.

"Just calm down. I can't believe you're so eager to find out which church I've chosen. It's not as though you attended them with me. Why are you so impatient?"

"I've just missed you while you were window shopping for a church," Tia said softly.

"Tia, she's not going to tell you," Kyle said over his shoulder. "I don't know why you keep asking. You might as well wait until we get to the restaurant like Jan and me. If you haven't noticed, neither one of us are asking anything. I know my sister, and she's not going to divulge anything until she's ready."

"Yeah, I guess you're right." Tia sat back in her seat, but Mayah saw her out the corner of her eye as she made a quick face at the back of Kyle's head.

They arrived at the restaurant and Kyle headed toward valet parking.

"Aren't we uppity tonight?" Tia said sarcastically.

"Girl, I'm always like this. You just haven't had the pleasure of going anywhere with me," he said comically; however, with a stern tone.

After leaving the car with the valet, they walked toward the hostess desk. Kyle came alongside Mayah, and took hold of her elbow to slow her down a bit. He leaned toward her and whispered, "I'm sorry I sounded snippety toward Tia. I was just thinking about our prior conversation where I said I didn't want Tia to go 'ghetto' on us. At the same time, I didn't want Jan to think I was phony or cheap, but I guess I'm just trying too hard. Forgive me?"

"Of course," she said, smiling up at her brother—her ever-changing brother.

They stepped up to the front podium, and the hostess asked, "May I have your name, please?"

"Johnson, Kyle Johnson. I have reservations for seven-fifteen."

"Oh yes, Mr. Johnson. Your table is ready. However, I have you down for a party of three. Can you just give us a moment while we make that adjustment? We need to place one more setting on the table. If you like, you may head to the bar and have a drink."

"No, ma'am. We don't drink."

"You mean *you* don't drink, Kyle?" Tia commented as her mouth dropped open.

Mayah stared at Tia, disappointment stabbing her heart. "No, *we* don't drink."

"My bad," Tia said.

"Mr. Johnson, your table is ready. Please follow Skylar as she takes you to your table."

"Thank you," Kyle said.

At their table, Kyle hurried to assist each of them as they took their seat.

"Um, aren't you the gentleman," Tia said.

Kyle looked over at Mayah and rolled his eyes, and slowly shook his head.

From Church to Church

Mayah mouthed, "I'm sorry."

Kyle mouthed back, "No problem."

The waiter took their orders. Mayah thought this would be the perfect time to talk to some of the people whom she loved very much. "Before revealing which church I've decided to join, Kyle, I want to thank you for doing something you really weren't excited about doing; but out of love and concern for me, you put a portion of your life on hold. I don't know too many people who would do that for anyone, let alone for their sister. I love and appreciate you very much. I have a gift for you. But don't open it until you arrive home."

She handed him a colored envelope, which he took and placed inside his jacket pocket. Inside were ten crisp, one-hundred-dollar bills, which she had promised to him back when she first started this quest, and a note of thanks to him for taking fourteen weeks out of his life to attend church with her. She also wrote on his card that if he decided to stay around town, he could use that money to finance his dates with Jan.

"Sis, it was an honor to be a part of your little venture. But I must confess something to you. While I thought I was doing you a favor, it turns out you were really doing me a favor. I hadn't been in church since Nan died, some years ago, and I hadn't given church a thought since then. I was just going about my life, living it the way I wanted to with no regard for God or man. However, since attending these churches, my life has radically changed. You know. I can't even begin to list all the ways church has benefited me. I know initially I gave you a hard time. That was because my heart wasn't in what I was doing. But now, I'm ready to go to church too with or without you. I realize that I'm nothing without Christ in my life. In fact, I'm a better man because He's in my life. I owe that to you, Mayah Johnson. Oh, and you owe me a trip and don't you forget that," he laughed and then hugged her.

"Kyle, when you get home look inside the envelope. Debt paid in full."

He took the envelope out of his pocket and patted it a few times, smiled and said, "Well alrighty, sis. Yeah, debt paid in full," he continued smiling.

Jan and Mayah were both grinning and wiping tears from their eyes. However, Tia just looked around as if she felt uncomfortable or something.

"What's up with all this crying? Did I miss something?" Tia asked.

Turning to Tia, Mayah slowly took a deep breath and then spoke. "Tia, I know it appeared our friendship was a little strained as I pursued something I deemed vitally important to me. I know we haven't spent a lot of time together these last few months, but I want to thank you for being patient with me. I hope one day you'll come to church with me."

"We'll see, Mayah," Tia said.

Kyle gestured for Mayah to hurry up. "Can you just tell us and drop all this suspense?"

"Hold on one more minute, Kyle."

"Jan," she said, turning to face her new friend sitting beside her. "From the moment we spoke at the Bible class, I knew there was something real special about you. I've learned so much from you— from Christian dating to the Word of God. You've been a good resource and friend to me. When I couldn't find what I needed, both you and Lesley were there with answers. You've played a very vital and major part in my salvation experience, and for that I'll always be grateful to you. You've become a good, Christian friend and I'm most grateful for that also." Mayah thought she saw Tia cringe, and she knew she needed to be sensitive to her. There was more that she wanted to say, but she didn't want to slight her long-time friend.

"Thank you, Mayah," Jan said, wiping tears from her face again. "You've been a sister and a friend to me. I thank you, as you're a very thoughtful and caring person. I'm so happy that we met also."

From Church to Church

Grinning from ear to ear, Mayah finally was ready to reveal her news. "I've learned a lot on this journey. What I now realize is this; God's physical church—that is, the church building, can and will be perfect in design and material. However, His people, the temple of God, will be flawed until Jesus returns. It's God's people who bring their issues, personalities, love, unloveliness, and drama to church, which dictates the tone of the church. It's the sins or the wrongs that we tolerate that change the atmosphere of God's church. But, what I've discovered is this; there's no perfect church, just people being perfected."

"What?" Tia said.

"Again, let me say this, I realize that there's both good and bad in every church that I visited. It's not that the church is either good or bad, but it's the people who attend the church who can make or break the reputation of that church. From attending these seven churches, I think I've seen enough to know how to conduct myself in church. I think I've learned how to draw others to the Christ in me and represent Him correctly. I've seen enough to know that the size of the building, the size of the congregation, the wealth of the church, the location of the church, or the ethnicity or gender of the pastor does not matter. What matters is that I'm in the will of God. I want to be where He wants me to be."

Kyle stared at Mayah with this blank look on his face. "Wow. Your summation is deep. I mean, it's right on the money. I never thought about it in those terms. What a profound observation. Girl, you're so right."

Mayah was so excited she could hardly sit still. "Yep, therefore, when Sunday comes, I'm going to join a church."

"Which church?" Tia blurted out, then slithered down in her seat as if to hide herself from the eyes of the other diners.

"Tia, have you not heard what I said? In some cases, it doesn't matter which one as long as they're striving for holiness, righteousness, and godly perfection. As long as they're serving Jesus

Christ and as long as the Holy Spirit can move in that church, sometimes it really doesn't matter. There's no perfect church. That's what I believe I was to come away with. I believe God has already set in my heart which one *He* wants me to join, and I'll be doing that on Sunday."

"If it doesn't matter, why did you have to go through all of this?" Tia asked.

"Because the Bible speaks about not forsaking the assembly of ourselves so I started going to church, and now I want to be in the church that God is planting or setting me in. Also, my friend Lesley from work showed me how I needed to be covered by a local church."

"That's true," Jan said. "I'm glad Lesley shared that with you. Girl, you're talking like a mature saint. You're making more sense than some who've been in church for years."

"Thanks. I feel that I've matured spiritually these last few months. The combination of all the ministry, teaching, and singing has really inspired me to read and study my Bible more and pray. There were times that I'd miss meals, because I was so into my Bible reading."

Mayah paused and sighed. "There's one more thing. I had another dream Thursday night. Nan was in my dream again. This time, she was so happy, not crying. She even gently caressed my cheek and kissed me. Kyle, she had that big grin on her face that we'd see all the time when we were children. And then I woke up. I knew it was a dream; but I wanted Nan to make the decision for me, but she couldn't. Kyle, I even thought about having you or Jan make the final decision for me, but you couldn't either. This was a decision that I had to make on my own, and I did it with the help of God."

"Sis, I don't know what church you'll be going to. But…I mean…uh…I never thought I'd be saying this, but me too. Yes, me too. Call me on Saturday night and let me know what time to be ready because I'm going to join church with you."

"Really, Kyle?"

"Really, baby girl. Now let's eat because I'm starving."

After she finished wiping lukewarm tears from her eyes and hugging Kyle, with a gigantic grin on her face Mayah proclaimed, "This is the best, belated, twenty-first birthday celebration anyone could ever have had! Yes, Kyle, you were so right, I did celebrate it *'real big.'*"

Original songs are from the following C.D.'s
Written and Produced by Jacqueline (Jackie) Jenkins:

Out of Shiloh Comes Bits of Praise
And
I Stand Here Worshipping You

SONGS

Make His Praise Glorious (p.11)
Father I Thirst For You (p. 12)
Let Him In (p. 20)
Shout It (pp. 28,69)
Draw Me Closer To You (p. 29)
Who Is Like Thee (p. 44)
Changing My Focus (p. 60)
In Your Presence (p. 71)
We Celebrate You Lord (p. 77)
La…I Love You (p. 77)
Give God What He Wants (p. 95)
The Sound Of Worshippers (p. 118)
Have You Ever (p. 119)
I Want Your Glory (p. 134)
Here I Am Again (p. 143)
Pour My Love On You (p. 157)
Oh Lord My God (p. 172)
I Want To Be Like You (p. 172)
Declare My Love For You (p. 186)
I Stand Here Worshipping You (p. 201)
Open My Eyes (p. 205)

About The Author

Jacqueline, "Jackie," is a woman of God who walks in humility and awe of the Holy God. She ministers the Word and worships under an open heaven, releasing a fresh revelation of the presence and power of the Lord and His call to the bride.

Jackie is a wife, mother, ordained minister, worship leader, teacher, songwriter/psalmist, conference speaker, and published author. Her first published book, *Cain, Ishmael, David* was released in September 2007. Published in 2008 was *Eve, Abigail, Sapphira*. Her first CD, *Bits of Praise*, is a clarion call to the body of Christ to worship. Her new CD, *I Stand Here Worshipping You*, will be released in 2010. The songs incorporated in this book along with many additional songs can be found on both CD's.

Jackie also moves in numerous spiritual gifts as the Lord uses her across denominational lines, teaching the Word and Worship at various churches, workshops, conferences, and seminars. Most importantly, she is a "worshipper," one whom the Father seeks. It thrills her heart and brings great joy to her soul as she ministers, leading others into the presence of God. Jackie also has a B.A. Degree in Theology.

For more information on the ministry of Jacqueline Jenkins, as well as other products, please contact:

Jacqueline Jenkins
P.O. Box 440903
Kennesaw, GA 30160
Jackiejenk@aol.com
www.jacquelinejenkins.com

Additional Books by Jacqueline Jenkins

It is my sincere belief that God's desire is that none of the negative characteristics, personality flaws, or blemishes uncovered in this book be resident in any of His servants. Although this book is covering several male characters in the Bible, these same traits can also be prevalent in women. If through self-examination one or more of these traits are resident within, it is God's desire that we, the readers of this book, surrender our will to the Lord, allowing the Holy Spirit to purge and cleanse these impurities out of our temples.
Jackie Jenkins

* * * *

There is a lot to be said about becoming unequally yoked and all of the trials and consequences that come in tow. "Cain, Ishmael, and David" gives the insight we wish we knew before dating, before that first bad relationship, and for some before the first, second, and third marriage. This is a necessary read for young teens, singles, and those who have tried, failed and now are seeking fulfillment in all the wrong places.

God knows what His purpose is for our lives and the course we should take. Instead, we help His will along by entering into distracting and defeating relationships taking us far off course. "Cain, Ishmael, and David," peels away the layers giving its reader a vantage point into non-gender specific character traits, both negative and positive, of themselves and the mate of whom they seek. "Cain, Ishmael, and David" allows its reader to make informed decisions before soul ties and marital ties are forged. It is about intangible faith, discernment, and patience to hearken our will to that of God's. **Pastor Merilee Parker, Church of the Sovereign God – Sacramento, CA**

In an American culture that is constantly drifting away from moral values and biblically defined gender roles, the voice of Jacqueline Jenkins cries in the wilderness, "make His paths straight!", in her timely new book, *Eve, Abigail, Sapphira...*, Jacqueline remixes the biographies of major women in the bible and presents them as character building learning models in a fresh new way. Each chapter is a journey into the feminine psyche of these leading ladies of scripture.

Eve, Abigail, Sapphira..., not only is a voice in the wilderness to women, but also helps men to understand their God given responsibilities. Jacqueline gives meaningful insight into helping men develop holistic relationships. This book is a must read for men and women looking for successful relationships. **Dr. Yaahn G. Hunter - Senior Pastor, Rescue Mission COGIC - Vallejo, CA, C. H. Mason Bible College, Associate Dean**

* * * *

Jackie has done an awesome job of analyzing personality traits in the lives of some very colorful women in the Bible. Jackie carefully isolates the positive traits of each character and encourages today's Christian woman (and man) to embrace these qualities. She also isolates negative character traits in a way that will enable women (and men) to isolate and eradicate negative traits in their own character.

We encourage everyone, male and female, to read this book. Accentuate your positive traits and eliminate the negative as you see parts of yourself revealed in each and every character study. You are going to love it! Sometimes you will laugh and cry! Sometimes you will be in pain. That pain though, will be a good pain; a Godly pain that will lead to repentance. You can be much more than you are today! Let *Eve, Abigail, Sapphira...* bring out the best in you! ***Joel and Kathy Davisson - "The Man of Her Dreams/The Woman of His!"***